Marked at Birth

Marked at Birth

Theresa A. Campbell

www.urbanbooks.net

Urban Books, LLC
300 Farmingdale Road, N.Y.-Route 109
Farmingdale, NY 11735

ISBN 13: 978-1-64556-465-2
ISBN 10: 1-64556-465-7

First Trade Paperback Printing March 2023
Printed in the United States of America

10 9 8 7 6 5 4 3 2 1

Distributed by Kensington Publishing Corp.
Submit Orders to:
Customer Service
400 Hahn Road
Westminster, MD 21157-4627
Phone: 1-800-733-3000
Fax: 1-800-659-2436

Marked at Birth

by

Theresa A. Campbell

Dedication

This book is dedicated to anyone who has ever been made to feel "different." It's your peculiarity that makes you who you are—a special child of God.

"So God created man in his own image, in the image of God created he him; male and female created he them."
—Genesis 1:27

Acknowledgments

My life has encompassed moments of being bruised but not broken, shaken but not defeated, wounded but not conquered, and through it all, Lord, you gave me the words to write this compelling story. I love you and thank you.

Many thanks to you, readers, for reading this book and thus supporting what I do. It's because of you that I write, and I hope that the message of this story uplifts you and has a lasting impact on you.

Prologue

Clarendon, Jamaica, West Indies, 2010

The warm, gentle breeze danced over the cluster of luscious green trees that fanned the quiet countryside, their leaves gently swaying and birds chirping in greeting. The usually roaring Rio Minho River seemed asleep, its water flowing softly over the rocks and green moss, its fish hugging the curves of the riverbed. On every side, hills and mountains stretched toward the heavens and humble houses nestled in the valleys.

Just then the tranquility that filled the air was shattered.

"Look at me with your ugly face when I talk to you, gal!" Burchell Pigmore roared, his big, rough, calloused hand coming down hard on the back of Bella's head, sending her flying. A second later she landed facedown on the concrete floor of the veranda.

Screaming out in agony, nineteen-year-old Bella rolled over and curled up in the fetal position, her scrawny legs pulled toward her chest. "I'm sorry, Papa," she mumbled, tasting blood in her mouth.

"Sorry? You are always sorry," her father yelled before he began kicking Bella with his dirty heavy-duty work boots. "You are too ugly." He kicked her in the back. "Too lazy." Another kick landed on her bottom. "You give me too much talking." A kick in her side. "You have the devil in you." Two more kicks in her back. "You are worthless, good-for-nothing trash." A few more kicks in her side.

Her body was vibrating with pain from the beating she was taking. Bella closed her eyes and transported herself to her hiding place deep in the crevices of her mind. She floated through a large, beautiful field filled with exotic flowers and tall, scented trees. The luscious green grass under her feet felt like cotton balls. The bright yellow sun kissed her beautiful face, while the cool breeze tickled her body all over. Bella smiled and raised her dainty hands in the air, happiness and joy swimming through every pore in her body.

I'm in paradise, Bella thought. *I don't ever—*

"Get your skinny behind up," Burchell shouted, bringing Bella back to reality. He reached down, grabbed his daughter by her slender neck, squeezed his fingers with all his might, and pulled her to her feet.

Bella squealed and kicked wildly, but she was no match for her beast of a father. "Let me go, Papa! Somebody help me! Jesus, help me!" But Bella's screams went unheard in the small community, and no one came to her aid.

"Jesus? You think Jesus wants anything to do with your ugly behind?" Burchell's fist rivaled that of the great Muhammad Ali when it connected with the girl's stomach.

Bella saw brightly colored lights dancing in front of her eyes as the ground began spinning around.

"I've had enough of you!" He landed another uppercut to her stomach, one that felt as if it went inside and twisted up her intestines like a pretzel.

Burchell released the hold on her neck, and Bella grabbed her stomach and bent over, tears streaming down her face. As she choked and coughed, she sucked much-needed air into her burning lungs. Her head pounding, her stomach cramping, and her body aching, Bella took a few baby steps away from her father.

But Burchell grabbed ahold of her blouse and brought Bella as close to him as possible. With heavy blows to her body, he proceeded to beat her within an inch of her life.

As the girl's eyes rolled to the back of her head, and blood poured down her face, she slumped toward her father, having lost the battle of consciousness. With a smirk on his face, Burchell stepped to the side and watched with satisfaction as Bella's body crumpled to the floor once again.

"That's what you get for not listening to me," he said before spitting a wad of chewed tobacco on Bella. "Worthless, just like your whoring mother. May her soul rest in the pit of hell." Burchell turned and walked into the three-bedroom house, then slammed the door shut on the sight of his daughter's unconscious body.

A few minutes later, groaning in agony, Bella tried to open her eyes, but they seemed to be locked shut. She gingerly rolled over onto her back, biting her lip to stop the scream trapped in her throat. Her body was throbbing from head to toe. Finally, Bella managed to get one eye half open and glanced around, confused. She realized she was lying on their veranda, and the memory of the beating she had taken minutes before came flooding back. Bella wasn't sure how long she had been passed out, but she resented the fact that she had awoken.

"Why didn't you just let me die?" Bella mumbled through bloody, swollen lips, looking up at the ceiling. "Lord, why do you continue to let me suffer like this?" Tears seeped down the sides of her face onto the floor. "Mama, can you hear me? I want to be with you, Mama," Bella said, talking to her mother, who had passed away a year ago. "I want to die too." But neither God nor her mother responded.

Part One

Chapter One

Isabella Pigmore (Bella)

Twenty years earlier . . .

"I'm pregnant!" forty-year-old Agatha announced as she entered the living room, her grin stretching from ear to ear. "Burchell, after all these years, we're having a baby." She threw her handbag down on the couch beside her husband and lifted her hands in the air. "Thank you, Lord."

"I thought you were a mule," Burchell replied and took a big gulp of the cold Red Stripe beer in his hand. "I hope it's a boy, because I don't want another slut in my house."

The grin fell from Agatha's face, and she looked down sadly at the man she had been married to for ten years.

"Agatha, you can't marry that nasty alcoholic man," her sister, Dorothy, had told her a decade ago. "He's going to make your life a living hell."

"That man is no good," a friend had warned her. "Don't do it."

"Oh, Burchell is a sweetheart," Agatha had responded. Ever since she'd met him, he had always been the perfect gentleman and had treated her with so much love and kindness. Yes, he would drink a little too much at times, but he had never been violent with her. "He may look a little rough around the edges, but he's as gentle as a new-born baby," she'd told them. Agatha had lived to eat her words when a week after their wedding Burchell beat her into unconsciousness.

"The chicken is too tough," Burchell had spat that day, using the fried chicken leg to slap Agatha in her face. "You can't even cook a little fowl?"

Agatha had been hurt physically and mentally by the beating she endured. What had gone wrong? Was what everyone had warned her about really true?

Instead of it getting better, it had only got worse. Burchell beat Agatha almost every day for a variety of reasons—the food wasn't cooked properly, the house was dirty, her clothes were too tight, she was flirting with the elderly man next door—or for no reason at all.

"Leave him," Agatha's friends had begged her countless times. "He is going to kill you." But their words had always gone through one ear and come out the other.

"I'm not leaving my husband," Agatha would tell them. "I'm the one who makes Burchell mad. I just need to do better."

So for ten agonizing years Agatha had stayed in her private hell. She had sometimes thought of running away after yet another beating, but she'd quickly change her mind when Burchell cried crocodile tears of apology or bought her a gift to say he was sorry.

Now she was pregnant with their first child.

"What are you staring at?" Burchell barked as he stood unsteadily to his feet, his face twisted up and one hand folded in a fist.

Agatha jumped back from fright. "Nothing, Burchell. Sorry." She quickly scurried away to their bedroom.

Nine months later, Agatha gave birth to a beautiful baby girl at Percy Junor Hospital in Spalding, Manches-ter. She named her Isabella after her deceased mother. Burchell was absent for the birth.

"That's woman's business, and I don't have time to waste on foolishness," he had informed Agatha when she went into labor that morning. "Just make sure you bring back a son, or don't come back in my house," he'd added before she was rushed to the hospital in their neighbor's car.

He was just talking, Agatha reasoned in her head as she entered the house three days later with her daughter. "Once Burchell takes a look at your pretty little face with this beauty mark, he's going to love you on sight," Agatha cooed to the baby in her arms.

"Burchell?" Agatha called out, but the house was empty. Burchell didn't think it was necessary to take off from work to welcome home his wife and baby. "Daddy is at work, but you'll see him later." Agatha placed the baby in the middle of their bed in the master bedroom and lay down beside her. Soon they were both fast asleep.

"Woieee!" Agatha cried out loudly when a fist slammed into her jaw. Jumping off the bed, she went right into another fist to her stomach. "Burchell, please stop," she pleaded.

Baby Bella woke up and began to wail.

"What's that ugly little thing you carry into my house?" Burchell asked, slapping Agatha hard across the face. "Didn't I tell you if it wasn't a boy to not come home?" He pushed Agatha against the wall and pounded her repeatedly. "The little creature was marked by the devil. You don't see that?"

"It's a beauty mark," Agatha managed to get out through bloody lips he continued to beat her.

"I'll show you a beauty mark." Burchell abruptly stop beating Agatha and walked over to the baby on the bed. He grabbed her up by one leg and dangled the screaming baby high in the air. "Now watch and see what I'm going to do with baby Shaka Zulu." With a nasty grin on his face, Burchell opened his hand and let the baby go.

"Nooo!" Agatha had anticipated what he was about to do and had found the strength to throw herself on Burchell, but it was too late. The baby was in midair. With the skill of a baseball catcher, she threw herself across the floor and swiftly stretched out her hands to catch three-day-old Baby Bella a few inches above the concrete floor.

Her heart slamming in her chest, Agatha bawled, her screaming baby held tightly in her arms. Burchell had almost killed their daughter.

"Get rid of it, or I will," Burchell warned before he exited the bedroom and headed to the kitchen, where his vodka was stashed.

It took a few minutes for Agatha to stop crying and then hush the baby. Her head was hurting as the scene of Baby Bella flying through the air kept replaying over and over again in her mind. "He was going to kill you." Agatha rocked her daughter from side to side.

Slowly, Agatha stumbled to her feet, the baby still safely tucked in her arms. She sat on the edge of the bed and breastfed Baby Bella, muttering words of praise. "Thank you, Lord, for saving my daughter."

As the baby hungrily sucked at her breast, Agatha stared down at her face. With Burchell being dark skinned and Agatha light skinned, Baby Bella had a rich chocolate complexion. Except for the left side of her face, which was so light, it looked almost white. But while Burchell saw the birthmark as the devil's mark, Agatha thought it was unique and was Baby Bella's beauty mark.

But in the superstitious small, rural town, some people reacted unkindly to Baby Bella's noticeable birthmark on her face.

"Mama, look. The baby has two faces," a little girl remarked loudly the first Sunday Agatha took Baby Bella to church.

"This must be a sign of some sort from the Lord," exclaimed the neighbor when she came to visit Agatha and the baby.

"That's a . . . uh . . . very interesting birthmark on the baby's face," said the teenaged cashier at the supermarket when Agatha stood in line with Baby Bella.

"It's her beauty mark," Agatha snapped protectively. Was she the only one who could see the birthmark for what it was?

With nowhere else to go, Agatha had no choice but to remain in Burchell's house. Her only ray of light was her daughter, Bella, whom she watched over like a hawk.

When Baby Bella was one year old, she was a challenge to keep up with, as she had recently learned to walk. Taking wobbly baby steps, she wandered excitedly all over the house, with her attentive mother always close behind, encouraging her.

One afternoon Bella wandered into her father's bedroom, and one of her chubby little legs knocked over an open bottle of beer that had been left on the floor.

"Get out of here!" Burchell screamed from where he sat on the edge of the bed, and the frightened baby began to cry. Angrily, he stood up and grabbed Bella by her arm just as Agatha burst through the door.

"Let her go!" Agatha yelled, punching Burchell on the arm that held Bella.

Surprised at his wife's action, Burchell quickly let go, his eyes wide. Almost in a daze, he watched as Agatha scooped up the distressed baby and hurried out of the room. "I'm going to kill her later," he muttered under his breath. "I'll show her I'm the boss around here." He paced the floor, mumbling about what he was going to do to Agatha. "When I'm through—"

A loud sound and then a burst of pain cut him off.

"Argh!" Burchell grabbed his head and quickly spun around, in shock. A large frying pan had connected with the side of his face, almost numbing it. "Woman, have you lost your mind!"

"Leave my baby alone!" Agatha was breathing hard, her long hair flying around her face, tears running out of her wild eyes. "Don't you ever put your hands on her again!" she screamed. She hit Burchell hard on the knee with the frying pan and was happy to see him buckle over.

Burchell was more stunned than in pain. He had been beating Agatha's behind for years, and she had never fought back. Now she was attacking him in his own house? Of all the nerve. He threw himself at Agatha, but she jumped out of the way, sending him crashing to the floor.

"I let you mistreat me for years." She hit Burchell hard on the back with the pan. "But I'd rather die than let you do the same to my sweet baby girl." She wacked him in the head. Agatha proceeded to beat Burchell with the frying pan as if Bella's life depended on it.

Burchell was in pain and was too weak and too drunk to go head-to-head with his furious wife. With his hands covering his head, he took his whupping with grunts, moans, and groans, swearing and calling Agatha every nasty name under the sun. "I'm going kill you one day for this, Agatha. I swear, as God is my witness."

Agatha, on the other hand, felt rejuvenated from giving Burchell a dose of his own medicine. After all these years it was a mother's love that had given her the courage to stand up to the beast who had been physically and men-tally abusing her. "If you ever go anywhere near my Bella again, I promise I will kill you," she hissed in Burchell's ear as he lay on the floor.

Despite his threats, Burchell heeded Agatha's warning for years to come. He had seen the fierce love she had for their daughter, and deep down inside he knew Agatha meant every word she'd said. So not only did he stay away from Bella, but he also left Agatha alone, at least physically. He still verbally insulted Bella and Agatha every chance he got. This bully wasn't going down so easily.

"Mama and baby she-devil," he'd sing, shaking his big head from side to side, as if he was performing onstage. "Miss horse and little kangaroo."

Agatha had taught Bella how to swim when she was a toddler, so they often went to the river to escape Burchell. They would spend hours on weekends swimming and playing and enjoying their time while they waited for the washed laundry to dry.

But the nasty remarks kept coming over the next few years. Bella was constantly teased at school by her peers, starting in primary school and continuing all the way through to high school. She grew up feeling like an ugly freak, and as such, she was very introverted.

One afternoon after school was dismissed for the day, Bella, now finishing up tenth grade, walked out of her last class with her head hanging down. She hurriedly weaved her way through the groups of animated students, hoping to make it out of the high school before someone picked on her.

Bella made it outside, and as she passed by the drama room's exterior, she heard loud music and laughter. She walked over to one of the open windows and peeked inside the room. There she saw a group of teenage girls trotting around in their swimsuits, wearing high-heeled shoes. The girls were contestants in the school's beauty pageant, which would be held in a few weeks, and now they were busy rehearsing.

Bella looked at the girls from head to toe, but then her attention returned to their pretty faces. They were light, brown, and dark skinned, but each of them had an even-toned, smooth complexion, unlike her. As her fingers slowly ran over the white left side of her face, Bella realized these girls were what she was not. They were exquisitely beautiful.

"Hey, Bella," said a male voice from behind her.

Bella guiltily looked away from the window and glanced over her shoulder to see three boys from her class standing behind her.

"Are you thinking of entering the beauty contest?" one boy asked, and the others chuckled. "I must admit your body doesn't look too bad."

"Maybe they'll let you wear a bag over your face to hide the mark of the devil," another one said, and they all roared with laughter.

Humiliated, Bella ran off and cried all the way home.

"Don't pay them any mind, baby," Agatha told Bella after she got home and related what had happened. "God made you special." She kissed her daughter on the milk-white birthmark on her pretty face before pulling her into a tight embrace.

As Bella hugged her mother she thought, *God made me special indeed. He made me into a monster.*

"You're beautiful, Bella," Agatha whispered in her ear, running her hand through Bella's long, curly hair.

Suddenly an image of the beauty contestants with their pretty faces flashed in Bella's mind. *No, Mama. I'm not beautiful. Those girls are.*

Agatha was Bella's best friend, and the two clung to each other. Only to be permanently separated months later by death.

Chapter Two

"Mama! Where are you?" Eighteen-year-old Bella entered the living room and threw her book bag on the long brown couch before she went in search of her mother. It was her first school day as a senior, and she was expected to graduate next June. "I'm home," she exclaimed dramatically upon entering the kitchen, her arms open wide, a big grin stretching from ear to ear.

But the grin quickly fell away. "Mama!" Bella dropped to her knees beside Agatha, who was lying on her back on the floor, a pool of dried blood around her head. "Mama, what's wrong?" She shook her mother's shoulder, but Agatha didn't move or speak.

Tears flowing down her face, Bella gently tapped Agatha's cheeks. "Wake up, Mama. Come on! Stop playing."

Agatha remained still, and it was then that Bella realized that her shoulder was cold and as stiff as a walking cane. As she stared down at her mother's face, she noted that it was a few shades paler. It didn't take long for her to realize her mother was dead. She had been to a few funerals in her lifetime, and she knew the pale, ashen look of death.

"Nooo." Bella's scream ricocheted around the kitchen, bouncing off the walls.

With snot and a small river of tears running down her face and dripping onto her mother's lifeless body, Bella's petite body shook from intense pain as she bawled.

Minutes later, as she sat on the kitchen floor, still wearing her light blue school uniform, Bella moved her mother's head onto her lap. She ran her fingers through the long strands of hair as she softly sang, "Amazing grace, how sweet the sound . . ."

Once the tears were all used up, Bella rocked her mother's body gently for hours, until the sunshine gave way to darkness as night fell. Although she was hoarse from singing, she sang over and over every song she had ever learned at church as she remained sitting on the kitchen floor in the dark, with Agatha in her arms.

Later that night Burchell pushed the front door open and staggered into the house. He fired off some curse words after bumping his leg against the couch in the living room. After flicking on the light, he slowly made his way toward the kitchen. There he turned on another light, flooding the room with brightness.

His bloodshot eyes ran over his daughter, who was sitting on the floor, with his wife's corpse in her arms. "So, the heifer is really dead, huh? Good riddance." He turned around and made his way into his bedroom, then slammed the door shut.

Bella flinched at the sound of the door being slammed. As if coming out of a trance, she slowly moved her mother's head from her lap, noticing how stiff her whole body was. She winced at the crick in her neck and the cramps in her legs and back as she pulled herself to her feet. Robotically, Bella walked into her mother's bedroom and took a pillow and sheet off the bed. She returned to the kitchen, tucked the pillow under Agatha's head, and covered her body with the sheet.

"I'll be right back, Mama." With that, Bella hurried out of the house and headed on foot toward the police station, which was approximately two miles away. She would have called, but the house didn't have a telephone.

The tears returned as Bella walked to the police station, wrapped up in a blanket of grief. Upon arriving at the station, between sobs, Bella informed the officer on duty of her mother's death.

"I'll call the coroner," the officer said to Bella. "Then another officer and I will return with you to the house."

On the ride back to her house, Bella sat quietly in the back seat of the police jeep. She gazed into the night, replaying over and over in her mind the sight of her mother's lifeless body on the kitchen floor. The only person who loved and protected her was no more. What was she going to do?

"Where's Burchell?" asked one of the officers, the one who was friendly with Burchell, after parking in front of the house. They all got out of the jeep.

Bella pointed at the house and then walked ahead of the officers, who followed her in silence. Once inside the house, Bella noticed that Burchell's bedroom door was still shut. She ignored this and led the officers into the kitchen, where Agatha's body lay.

"Please step outside the room," the other officer said to Bella as he pulled on the pair of white gloves he had taken out of his pocket. He pulled the sheet off Agatha and handed it to his partner. Leaning over, he pressed two fingers to Agatha's neck and then said, "There is no pulse. She's dead."

From the kitchen doorway, Bella watched as the police knelt down and removed the pillow she had placed under her mother's head. "Look at all this blood. She must have hit the back of her head. But the coroner will tell us more when he gets here," said the first officer, the one who was friendly with Burchell.

"Let's go and talk to Burchell while we wait," his colleague suggested. "I have a few questions for him." As he walked by Bella, he said, "We'll be keeping these as part of the investigation." He held up the sheet and the bloody pillow. "And please stay out of the kitchen."

Bella went and sat on the couch in the living room. She rocked from side to side as she waited.

It took almost two hours for the coroner to arrive. He and his assistant were led into the kitchen by the police officers. Bella remained in the living room, where Burchell now sat slumped on the couch across from her, his face void of emotion.

Ten minutes later the coroner and his assistant stepped into the living room with the officers and gave everyone a preliminary report. "There is a deep laceration at the back of her head. She may have fallen and hit her head, or she was hit with a heavy object. I'll know more once I do the autopsy."

"I don't want any autop . . . autopsy." Burchell burped loudly as he shakily stood to his feet. "That woman was as clumsy as a one-legged goat."

"Wait a minute, now. This is an unexpected death. I have to do an autopsy to find out exactly what happened in there." The coroner nodded toward the kitchen.

"You cut open my wife and there will be trouble." Burchell pointed his finger at the coroner, his bloodshot eyes filled with fury. "Agatha always said she didn't want anyone to cut on her when she died."

Bella sat and watched the exchange between the men, knowing she was powerless to do anything. She opened her mouth to speak but quickly closed it again out of fear. *Why doesn't Papa want them to do an autopsy on Mama?* Just then Bella remembered the words Burchell had spoken when he came home earlier that night. *So, the heifer is really dead, huh?* What had he meant by that?

The coroner persisted. "This is my jurisdiction," he informed Burchell. "I have the authority to perform an autopsy if I think there may be foul play."

Burchell's head snapped back and he sobered up instantly, as if he had been hit by a bucket of ice-cold water. "You think I killed my wife?"

"I'm not sure what happened to your wife, sir. My job is to find out how she died." He glanced over at the officers. "And it's their case to investigate."

"Well, hmmm, we did question Burchell earlier," one officer informed the coroner, "and the investigation continues. We look forward to receiving your report."

The coroner nodded, and he and his assistant walked back into the kitchen. The two men placed Agatha's body in a black body bag. With one of them at either end, they carried the body out to the van, Bella following close behind them. She watched them until the vehicle drove off with her mother, and she was still staring down the road fifteen minutes after the van had disappeared around a bend.

The homegoing service for Agatha was two weeks later. The service was held at the Frankfield Church of God. Bella didn't say a word that day. She bobbed or shook her head when spoken to, going through the motions with lifeless, grief-stricken eyes.

Burchell, on the other hand, put on a performance of a lifetime. He howled and wailed for his dead wife, with snot and tears running down his face. With the exception of his few pals, very few felt any sympathy for him.

"Look at that fool acting like he care," Ms. Gracie whispered to her husband. "I have a sneaky suspicion he's the one who killed sweet Agatha."

"I'm so tempted to go over there and give that wife beater something to cry about," hissed Mr. Dufus. "Poor Agatha suffered at his hands for so many years."

"He'll get his soon," the lady sitting beside him responded. "God is not dead."

Agatha was buried that cloudy, gloomy, rainy day at Commissary Cemetery. That night Bella cried herself to sleep in Agatha's bed.

"Get up!" Burchell poured the bucket of water all over Bella on the bed.

"Wha . . . what's wrong?" Bella quickly sat up, water running down her face, her nightgown drenched. "What's the matter, Papa?" she asked fearfully, wiping water from her eyes so she could see.

Instead of answering, Burchell reached down and grabbed Bella by the back of her neck and lifted her off the bed. "What's wrong? I'll show you what's wrong." He proceeded to drag the terrifying girl into the kitchen.

"That's what's wrong." Burchell pointed to the empty stove. "Where's my breakfast, huh?" He backhanded Bella across the face so hard, she flew across the room like Superman and landed on her back.

Sobbing loudly, Bella rolled herself into a ball as her father stomped her repeatedly. The intense pain she felt wrapped tightly around her like a life jacket. The beating seemed to last forever.

"Make sure my dinner is on the stove when I get home," Burchell finally spat, breathing heavily, his chest rising and falling from the exertion of beating his daughter.

Bella did as she was instructed that day and every day thereafter. She would get up early every morning and make her father's breakfast before she went to school. After school she prepared dinner, washed the laundry, and cleaned the house. However, she still took a whupping almost every day. With his wife now gone, Burchell could do whatever he wanted with his daughter without interference, and he took full advantage of it.

***

"Bella! Bella! Bella!"

Bella lay curled up on the bed, trying to ignore the sound of the familiar voice, hoping the person it belonged to would go away.

"Bella, it's me. Where are you?" Aunt Dorothy yelled.

The voice grew closer, and Bella knew her aunt was now on the veranda. "She's not going to leave," Bella mumbled to herself. She groaned loudly when she lifted herself up off the bed, as pain vibrated all over her body from the beating she had taken the night before. Gingerly she made her way down the hallway and out to the veranda.

"Mercy!" Aunt Dorothy's scream rang out in the early morning when she saw Bella. She fell to her knees and began to wail, pounding the ground with her fists. "Monster! Satan!"

Bella peered out of a black eye at her aunt. The other eye was swollen shut. Her face was puffy and bruised, and her lips were fat and busted. But Burchell always made sure the most damage was done to her upper body, which was hidden by her clothes. The long-sleeved blouse and long skirt that Bella often wore took care of it. "It's okay, Aunt Dorothy."

Aunt Dorothy raised her wet face to look at Bella. With one hand holding on to the wall, she slowly pulled herself to her feet. She walked over to Bella, the tears still trickling down her face, and pulled her into her arms.

Bella gasped loudly before biting her sore lips to keep in the scream that rose up inside.

Aunt Dorothy pulled back and stared at her. Without a word, she lifted a part of Bella's blouse and saw the angry, ugly bruises. "Enough," she spat, the anger rising up in her. "Let's go." She grabbed Bella's hand. "We're going to the police, and this time they are going to lock up that dirty old dog once and for all."

"Auntie, stop." Bella pulled back her hand. "Please, I'm begging you. He'll kill me if you report him again."

The last time, Aunt Dorothy had gone to Burchell's workplace and cursed him out like a dog in front of his boss and coworkers. After that, she'd marched next door to the police station and filed a complaint about him abusing Bella. That night Bella had paid dearly for her aunt's actions.

"You know they won't arrest him," Bella said to her aunt now.

"They have to, Bella," Aunt Dorothy yelled. "He's going to kill you, just like he did your mother." She turned pleading eyes to her niece. "He killed my sister and got away with it, and now he's trying to kill you too." Her voice went up a few decibels. "How could they say Agatha's death was an accident?"

The coroner's report had been sent to the police seven weeks after Agatha's death. It had noted that she died as a result of an injury sustained to the back of her head. And while the wound was deemed suspicious, it was not determined if it was a result of her falling and hitting her head on the concrete kitchen floor or of sustaining an intentional blow to the head from a blunt-force instrument. With no solid evidence of foul play and no murder weapon found at the scene, the police had closed the case on Agatha Pigmore's death, ruling it an accident.

"I have reported it to the police over and over that he's beating on you, but he's friends with them," Aunt Dorothy practically screamed.

Bella looked away. The police had come and spoken with her after they'd received from Aunt Dorothy and the neighbors' numerous reports of Burchell harming her. But Bella had denied everything. She, too, was aware her father was drinking buddies with some of these cops. They would probably just talk to him, and this would only infuriate Burchell and make things even worse for Bella at home.

"You know I don't have the space to keep you, baby." Aunt Dorothy's voice recaptured Bella's attention. She lived in Trout Hall, a few miles away, in an old, dilapidated one-bedroom board house with her crippled husband and his ailing elderly mother.

Bella, with her eyes fixed to the ground, nodded her head in understanding, and without another word, she walked back inside to her own private hell.

Bella became a mute at home, except for her screams when she was beaten. She rarely spoke at school and mostly nodded greetings to the neighbors. She cooked the meals but barely ate any. She wore long, oversized clothing to cover the welts, cuts, and bruises on her body. Her hair fell out in patches, her eyes were dull and lifeless, and her sharp cheekbones protruded out of her thin face. Bella was a shell of the young girl she had been before her mother's death. A girl slowly withering away at the hands of her abusive father.

Chapter Three

The scorching hot sun beat down on Bella's back as she stood in the shallow water of the Rio Minho River, doing laundry. She had her father's dirty khaki pants stretched out on a huge rock, and she pounded them over and over with a big stick. Unable so far to get Burchell's heavy-duty work clothes clean, she decided to use her special soap. Bella paused briefly and took a deep, tired breath as she used the end of her T-shirt to wipe off the sweat running down her face. She then grabbed the piece of blue soap, popularly called "dirty gal," and vigorously rubbed the stubborn stains in the clothes with it.

Even though they had running water at home, Burchell had forbidden her from using it for washing. "Do you know how much the water bill is every month? Don't let me ever catch you wasting this water to wash clothes," he had warned Bella. "The river water is free, so use it."

With the beautiful green body of water flowing around her, the tall bamboo trees gently swaying in the wind, and the miles of beautiful sand stretching along the river, Bella was oblivious to everything except the clothes she was washing. She needed to hurry up so she could get home to make dinner before her father got there.

Moments later, animated laughter and the splashing of water up ahead caught Bella's attention. She laid out a wet shirt on the rock to dry before looking up the river. It was one of her neighbors, Mrs. Burger, and her four children. The kids were swimming and playing in the water, while their mother sat on a rock, watching them.

"Bella," Mrs. Burger called loudly when she caught sight of her, waving her hands high in the air. "Come here, baby."

Bella stared at her indecisively. The children's laughter tickled her ears and created a longing in her heart. Would she ever laugh again?

"Bella, please come and talk to me."

But Bella slowly shook her head, wringing her hands together from uncertainty. She glanced around her at all the clothes spread out on the grass and rocks to dry.

"Your mommy would want you to have a little fun," Mrs. Burger called.

The mention of her mother got Bella's feet moving, and she took small, hesitant steps toward the family. She went and sat down a little way from Mrs. Burger and watched the kids play.

"God is going to deliver you soon, Bella." Mrs. Burger had tears in her eyes as she looked at the scared girl.

Bella dropped her head in shame. Everyone knew what she was going through, but no one could rescue her from her father, not even God.

"You know Burchell almost killed Mackie the other day?" Mrs. Burger asked. Mackie was one of Bella's neighbors.

Bella shook her head, her eyes fixed on the sand.

"Oh, yes, dear. Mackie confronted Burchell about his abuse of you, and Burchell didn't like it. I heard, before you know it, that man rushed Mackie, and the two began to fight in the middle of the street. Poor Mackie was no match for that big gorilla, and Burchell got the upper hand. He really put a beating on Mackie."

That's my daddy. No one takes him on and wins.

"Bella, I have been fasting and praying for you since your mother died," Mrs. Burger said. "Psalm fifty, fifteen, says, 'And call upon me in the day of trouble: I will deliver thee, and thou shalt glorify me.' That demon parading as your father is going to get his soon. As long as there is a God."

"Bella, come in and play shark with us," one of Mrs. Burger's daughters called out to her.

"Go on," Mrs. Burger remarked when Bella hesitated. "Go and play, sweetheart."

Bella hadn't taken a swim since her mother died. She gingerly stepped into the river in her shorts and T-shirt, and a big splash of water hit her in the face.

"You're it," one of the kids yelled before they all swam off in different directions.

Bella smiled before she ran and threw herself in the deeper water, landing on her belly and making a big splash. She dived underwater and paddled her arms and legs as she searched for the other kids. For the first time in a long time, Bella was enjoying herself.

One hour later, the exhausted kids went and lay on the sand on the riverbank. They talked and giggled while Mrs. Burger spread out her clothes to dry on the grass a few feet away.

"Run, Bella. Run," Mrs. Burger suddenly screamed, waving her hands wildly in the air.

Bella sat up and looked around in fright. Her mouth popped open before she jumped to her feet, ready to run, but it was too late. Rough hands grabbed the back of her neck and spun her around.

Burchell yelled, "Where you think you going?" He slapped Bella hard across the face, and blood gushed from her mouth.

"Leave her alone, you monster!" Mrs. Burger shouted as she ran closer to Burchell, tears pouring down her face. "I'm going to tell the police."

The kids all began to cry as they shouted at Burchell to leave Bella alone.

But Burchell ignored them, and swearing and cursing, he hauled Bella away by the throat and up the narrow dirt track that would take them to their house. After beating Bella and leaving her bruised on the floor, he went to get his clothes down by the river. He didn't bother to bring Bella's clothes, not caring if anyone took them.

After that day Bella retreated into herself even more. She tried to study but couldn't concentrate. Her grades went from As to Cs, but miraculously she didn't fail any of her classes. "I want you to study hard and become a big-shot lawyer or a doctor or a teacher, baby," Agatha had told Bella when she started high school. "You're a bright girl, and you can be anything you want to be. You hear me, Bella?"

Bella had nodded her head. So to keep that promise to her deceased mother, she decided to finish her last year in high school, even though she wanted to drop out.

Surprisingly, Burchell gave her the money to pay for her Caribbean Examinations Council examinations. The CXC exams were usually taken after five years of secondary school, by students who wished to continue their education at the tertiary level. So Bella sat for her maths, English, accounting, and biology exams, but during the exams she felt unenthusiastic and as if she was in another world as she sat at the back of the classroom, with her head mostly down on the desk.

"College?" Burchell laughed with scorn when Bella brought up the subject. "You better go and ask Mr. Sammy to give you a job packing boxes in the supermarket. I'm not wasting any more money on your ugly dunce behind."

Bella didn't attend her high school graduation. The one person she wanted to see her graduate high school wouldn't be there, anyway. Instead, she locked herself in her room, a broken eighteen-year-old young lady who was unsure of her future.

***

The next two years crept by, with no change for Bella.

"Papa?" She knocked softly on her father's bedroom door one morning. "Papa, your breakfast is getting cold." She knocked again but didn't get a response. Unsure of what to do, Bella stared at the door for a few seconds. She didn't want to disturb Burchell if he was sleeping in, because that would lead to a whupping. But if she let his breakfast get cold, she would also get a whupping. So, Bella gently turned the doorknob, pushed open the door, and timidly stepped into the room.

The windows were open over the bed, and the early morning sun was sneaking in through the thin white curtains. Bella, having noticed that the bed was empty and still made up, glanced around the room, a puzzled look on her face. It seemed as if Burchell had never come home last night.

Even though she was relieved that she wouldn't get a beating this morning, Bella felt on edge. Burchell had stayed out late before drinking with his buddies, but never all night. *Maybe he got drunk and is laid up somewhere*, she thought. But she shuddered at the thought, because she would no doubt pay the price when he got home.

But the day came and went without a word from or a sign of Burchell. And so did the night.

With a big grin on her face, Bella pulled the sheet over her head and comfortably adjusted her body on the bed. It was almost noon the next day, and Bella was still in bed. For the first time since her mother died over two years earlier, Bella hadn't been awoken by her father's fist, nor had she had to get up early and make his breakfast. Burchell was still missing in action, and Bella took full advantage of her freedom.

Later that afternoon, Bella finally left her bed, showered, and made lunch, for one—thick yellow slices of roasted breadfruit and golden chunks of ackee with saltfish. Sitting back on the couch, her feet on the ottoman, she ate contentedly while watching the small television, which Burchell had bought for his own viewing pleasure.

Bella spent the day in lazy bliss. The dirty plates and pots were left in the sink. There was no laundry done, no cleaning the house, sweeping the yard, or cooking dinner. She watched television for most of the day, giggling and laughing at some of the shows. That night she stayed up late in bed, reading one of the Nancy Drew novels that she had gotten from the public library, while munching on banana chips.

"I'll pay for this when he comes home, Mama," Bella said aloud, as if Agatha could hear her. "But it will be worth it. I just wish you were here with me." She angrily wiped away a tear that had leaked from the corner of her eye. Bella didn't know how long her freedom and new-found happiness would last, but she planned on enjoying it until the devil decided to come home.

But four days later, as she glanced at the partially empty fridge and the almost bare cupboards, Bella started to worry. Her father hadn't been home for five days now, and the novelty of being home alone was slowly wearing off. She had to contemplate the future.

What if he had left Clarendon and had decided not to come back? Bella pondered. *I don't have any money or a job.* Since graduating high school, Bella had rarely left the house except to go grocery shopping and to do the laundry by the river. *I need to find out what really happened to my father.*

The next morning, Bella walked to Burchell's job.

"Good morning, Mr. Latty," Bella called, greeting Burchell's boss, who was leaning against the gate outside, puffing on a cigarette. "I'm looking for Papa."

"I'm looking for your papa too, Bella." Mr. Latty had a big frown on his face. "He hasn't been to work for five days," he said. "For the first day or two, I was upset that he took unscheduled days off without notifying anyone, but now we are all worried. I sent someone by the house two days ago, but they said no one answered their call or the knock on the gate."

Bella guiltily looked away. She had heard the person calling for her father but had ignored the annoying voice, which was interrupting her TV show. "I was probably down by the river," she lied.

"So Burchell hasn't been home either, huh?" Mr. Latty asked. "Then something is wrong," he added after Bella shook her head. "He wouldn't stay away from his home for this long."

I agree, Bella thought to herself. *He wouldn't go a day without beating me unless something had happened to him.* "I'm going next door to report it to the police."

"Yes, you do that," Mr. Latty remarked. "I'll get a few men to drive around and look for him as well."

Bella walked away and made her way over to the police station. There were three police officers sitting on a bench and shooting the breeze under the big mango tree outside the station.

"Officer Williams, do you know where Papa is?" Bella asked one of Burchell's drinking buddies. "He hasn't come home for a few days now."

"Well, well, well. It looks like old Burchell is on lockdown with a sweet little honey." He roared with laughter, and the other two officers joined in.

Bella remained silent. *Why do I even care, when all he does is beat me every day? His own friends obviously aren't concern.*

"Your father will turn up soon, okay?" one of the officers said to Bella.

"Yeah, don't worry about Burchell," the third one added. "He's good."

With such assurance from the cops, Bella went back home.

Three days later Bella was sitting on the veranda, deep in thought. Burchell was still missing.

"Bella! Bella!" someone began yelling from the main road.

Bella jumped to her feet and looked down to the street to see one of her neighbors waving his hands frantically in the air. "What's the matter, Mr. Blake?"

"Come quickly, my dear. Come."

Without another word, Bella pushed her feet into the flip-flops at the top of the steps, hurried down into the yard, and made her way to the street, where Mr. Blake was standing, tight lipped. "What's wrong?" she asked, her voice trembling slightly when she saw the sullen look on the older man's face.

Mr. Blake looked away. "Follow me and I'll show you." He strode away, and Bella ran alongside him to keep up.

A few minutes later, they rounded a deep corner in the road where a waist-high wall ran for a few feet, protecting passersby from the deep ravine below. Mr. Blake stopped and pointed over the wall.

Standing on tiptoe, her hands on the wall to keep her balance, Bella peered over the wall. She gasped loudly when she caught a glimpse of the khaki pants that her father usually wore to work. Then she saw enough of him to recognize him, though he was partially hidden behind some bushes. Her hand covering her mouth, she stumbled back into Mr. Blake's arms.

"I have to see." Bella pushed away from Mr. Blake and hurried down to the end of the wall. She went around it and slid down the side of the dirt ravine on her bottom, her hands grasping at bushes and grass, before landing beside the figure.

Bile filled Bella's mouth as she stumbled to her feet and stared wide eyed at the body of her father. Due to the hot Jamaican weather, decomposition was setting in, and ants, wasps, beetles, maggots, and other insects were crawling all over his body. There was a deep hole where an eye should have been; it had probably been snatched and eaten by animals. Pieces of flesh were visibly missing from the face, hands, and neck, while the big, bloated gut looked like it was about to explode at any minute.

The stench was so strong, Bella used her thumb and index finger to squeeze her nose closed. Breathing heavily through her mouth, she tried not to vomit.

"I was running late to get to the field, so I decided to take a shortcut." Mr. Blake was now standing beside Bella. He had a small farm a few miles away. "First, I smelled the bad odor but thought it was a dead animal. I was walking away when I noticed the boots behind the bushes. I stepped closer, and that's when I saw the body. As you can see, the animals have gotten to him, but I knew instantly it was Burchell. The wife had also told me he's missing."

A flood of emotions ran through Bella's body—relief, then sadness, then pity—but she never shed a tear. For so many years she had hated her father for abusing and belittling her and her mother, and the feeling had only intensified when she suspected he had something to do with Agatha's death. The hatred had run even deeper after her mother passed and Burchell began physically abusing her. Many times she had wished him dead, but never like this. To die alone in the bushes and to have animals feed on your body was just horrible.

"It's karma," Mr. Blake said lightly at Bella's side as he looked down on Burchell's remains. He felt no sympathy for the man. "I hate to speak ill of the dead, but he was a wicked man. Until the day I die, I'll still believe he killed your poor mother. Almost every day I filed a report about him beating on you, but his police friends did nothing. But God stopped him, though." He turned slightly and locked eyes with Bella. "You're free now, Bella."

But free to do what? Bella thought. *What am I going to do now?*

Chapter Four

"So you're telling me you don't know what happened to your father?" Officer Williams stared pointedly at Bella and crossed his beefy arms across his big gut as he leaned back in his chair at the station.

"That's right, sir," Bella replied in a soft voice. Fear filled her eyes as she glanced around the small, semi-dark interrogation room, where she was trapped with the large detective.

"We know Burchell used to discipline you often," Detective Williams said. "I bet you didn't like him too much."

Bella recoiled in her chair at the word *discipline*. It was almost as if Burchell had just slapped her across the face.

Officer Williams stared at Bella, then barked, "I asked, did you kill your father, girl?"

"No, I didn't kill him," Bella replied. "And my father didn't *discipline* me." She said the word *discipline* with distaste. "He used to beat me, sometimes within an inch of my life. And none of you did anything to stop him."

Bella's eyes widened at the words that had just left her mouth. She didn't know where she got the courage, but now she was on a roll. "Morning, noon, and night, he beat on me since Mama died. Day after day, and even though my neighbors reported it, the police didn't help me. You left me there to suffer."

Officer Williams opened his mouth to speak, then closed it. He was one of Burchell's drinking buddies who had turned a blind eye to Bella's abuse. Yes, he had received numerous complaints from people about Burchell's mistreatment of Bella, but a child needed discipline every now and then.

"In fact, I reported to you that my father was missing," Bella reminded him. "You said he was probably with a girlfriend."

Officer Williams pursed his lips, the truth of Bella's words filling the room. What if the police had gone looking for Burchell? Maybe they would have found him injured but still alive. Maybe they could have gotten to him before he died.

"You could have reported it after killing him," Officer Williams muttered, but his words held no conviction. He still refused to take responsibility for the police's repeated lack of action when it was needed. "But we have no evidence that you did it . . . not yet."

"You know deep down inside it wasn't me." Bella's eyes met and held Officer Williams's, offering a glimpse through the window to her soul.

"We'll get to the bottom of it," Officer Williams said. "You can trust and believe that."

But Bella knew nothing else would be done about her father's death, whether it was accidental or intentional. That was just how the police in her community operated. In a few days Burchell would be old news and life would go on as usual.

"You can go for now." Officer Williams stood up. "And remember, we are watching you."

Bella didn't need to be told twice. She jumped to her feet, ran from the room, and collided with Mr. Latty in the hallway.

"Wow. Don't run me over, now." The smile fell from Mr. Latty's face as he looked at Bella. "Those fools were questioning you too, huh?"

Bella nodded and glanced back at the interrogation room, where Officer Williams was still standing.

"Yeah, I just finished with that one named Tate," Mr. Latty said in reference to Officer Tate. "Wasting hardworking people's time talking about interrogation." His voice got louder. "Nobody killed Burchell. His evil ways caught up with him, that's all."

Bella remained silent.

"Come on, Bella. Let's go home." Mr. Latty and Bella walked toward the exit. When they reached it, Mr. Latty stopped and shouted over his shoulder, "They need to start doing some real police work around here."

Bella hurried out of the police station with Mr. Latty.

Burchell's body was moved to the funeral home after being released by the police, and Bella agonized over what to do with it. Despite his abuse over the years, she still wanted to give her father a decent funeral. But she had no money. Walking aimlessly around the house one morning, a jackhammer hammering away inside her head, Bella pondered her situation. She went into the kitchen and lowered herself onto the big wooden box in the corner, which her father had often sat on as he looked out at the backyard. It was covered by a thick black tablecloth.

Suddenly, with her eyebrows knitted together and a frown on her face, Bella glanced down at the box. Her father had always warned her to stay away from it, because it contained his important documents. *But what documents?*

Her eyes now sparkling with curiosity, Bella ran to the back room, where Burchell kept his toolbox. She open the toolbox, removed a hammer, and rushed back into the kitchen. She lowered herself onto her knees in front of the wooden box, then pulled off the tablecloth, exposing a small metal lock. Excitement filled Bella as she hammered away at the lock. There was no Burchell to stop her now. It took a few minutes of hard banging before the lock gave way and split apart.

"Yes," Bella exclaimed, pulling open the big lid. Instantly, her smile fell away, and her mouth popped open. Her eyes dilated in amazement as they ran over the stacks of money in the box. "Oh, dear Lord."

Bella reached inside and took out a few bundles of hundred-dollar bills. "So, these are the important documents," she muttered, looking down at the money. After sitting down on the floor, Bella counted the money. Sixty thousand dollars. "Well, it seems as if I can now bury you, Papa."

Later that day, she shared the discovery of the money with her aunt.

"That little miser," Aunt Dorothy exclaimed. "He used to complaint to Agatha every day about her wasting water and running up the light bill when she watched a little TV. He even refused to get a telephone. And all that time he had been saving it all. I guess this was his little bank, huh?"

Bella nodded and said, "He always said bank people are crooks. They only want to rob poor people, take their money."

"I think you should take that money for yourself." Aunt Dorothy stared pointedly at Bella. "Just let someone dig a hole and put his body in it. As a matter of fact, just throw it away so the animals can finish it off."

"Aunt Dorothy!"

Aunt Dorothy rolled her eyes and sucked her teeth. "He doesn't deserve a decent funeral."

But Bella was adamant that Burchell would have a funeral. "It's his money, Auntie."

"No, it's *your* money now," Dorothy replied. "It's a good thing you opened that box."

Against her aunt's advice, Bella made arrangements for her father's funeral, and her aunt reluctantly helped her with it. The depreciation of the Jamaican dollar over the years had led to a drastic increase in the price of goods and services. This included the cost of funerals, with the casket being the most expensive item, with an average price of over fifty thousand dollars. Luckily, Aunt Dorothy knew the owners of a small funeral home, and they gave Bella an economical funeral package for forty-five thousand dollars, which included a simple wooden casket.

The funeral was small, with only a few people in attendance—Burchell's police friends, a few coworkers, Bella, and Aunt Dorothy, who let it be known she was there only to support her niece. Bella didn't shed a tear or show any emotion. She felt nothing. While her heart had been broken when her mother passed away, it seemed to have frozen with her father's death. Her mother was her earthly angel, and her father was her earthly devil.

That night, after her aunt had gone home to her ailing husband, Bella lay in the dark on her back on her bed, contemplating her future. After the cemetery fee and other miscellaneous expenses related to Burchell's burial, she had ten thousand dollars left. It wasn't much, and it wouldn't last a long time. "I'll have to get a job," she whispered in the quiet house. "It's just me now."

Soon exhaustion from the past few days crept up on her, and Bella dozed off. Her eyes were closed, and the house silent.

Bang, bang, bang.

Bella's eyes flew open, and her heart raced in her chest. Scared, she pulled the covers up to her chin and stared at the bedroom door. She had locked up before coming to bed and had even checked a few times to make sure all the doors and windows were closed. She now lived alone and knew she had to be careful. Had someone broken into the house?

Bella swallowed the lump in her throat as she listened keenly.

Tap, tap, tap. Three times, a fainted knock sounded on her bedroom door.

Bella screamed loudly. "Who . . . who . . . who is there?" Her voice quivered and her breathing was irregular as she peered through the dark toward the door.

"Bellaaa. Bellaaaa. Bellaaa." It sounded as if her name was floating on the wind.

Then silence.

Tears trickled down Bella's cheeks. It was the first time since her father had died that she felt afraid. While she was growing up, her mother had often told her stories about ghosts, but they had always seemed like creatures in fairy tales to her. Were they real, or was someone mortal in the house? Certainly, her mind was playing tricks on her because of the funeral earlier that day.

Almost robotically, Bella slowly forced herself to get out of bed. On tiptoe, she made her way over to the light switch and flicked it on. Shivering, as if she had the chills, she glanced around the room, but she saw no one. She was relieved that she was alone but still worried about who or what was outside the bedroom door.

After waiting a few minutes and not hearing anything, Bella began to relax, breathing in and breathing out. *I really need some rest.* She shook her head and walked back over to the bed. "Ahhh," Bella screamed when what sounded like one of the pots fell in the kitchen. She threw herself onto the bed and pulled the covers over her head. Trembling, and with her heart racing, Bella waited. She wanted to pray, but she knew God didn't hear her prayers.

So, she called on the one person who had been there for her in life.

"Mama, please protect me," she whispered. Her tears leaked out onto the pillow. "I think someone is in the house, and I don't know what to do." Bella continued to talk to her mother. When she finally paused and listened, the house was eerily silent again.

Suddenly out of nowhere a memory popped into Bella's mind.

"Listen to me," Agatha had told her as she knelt down and came face-to-face with her eight-year-old daughter. "You are a brave girl. I don't want you to be scared of anyone, especially those idiots who tease you. God has you covered, my beautiful Bella."

"I don't know about God covering me, Mama," Bella said now, a determined look on her face. She threw back the covers and slid off the bed. "But thank you for reminding me I'm not a coward." But she sounded braver than she felt as she grabbed a large white figurine off her dresser.

Biting her lip, Bella gradually opened the bedroom door and poked her head out. She glanced down the hallway but did not see or hear anything. Taking little baby steps, the figurine held tightly above her head, Bella moved toward the kitchen.

Bright light flooded the kitchen when Bella flicked on the light switch. On the floor was a big metal pot. Bella's eyes quickly scanned the empty room from the doorway, but nothing else seemed out of place. *I think I just left the pot too close to edge of the kitchen counter.* She breathed a sigh of relief and, leaving the light on in the kitchen, walked toward the living room.

Moonlight filtered into the living room through the windows. Feeling less afraid but still a little apprehensive, Bella entered the room and turned on a light. She glanced over to the couch and screamed. She was still screaming as she raced back to her bedroom and slammed the door shut.

Sliding on her heels like a cricketer, Bella slipped under the bed. She curled herself into a ball, and with her knees tucked under her chin, she closed her eyes tightly, as if to block out the image that was rooted in her mind—her father, Burchell Pigmore, sitting on the couch.

Bella knocked her head against the bottom of the bed. "Ouch." Wincing from the bump on her head and the crick she had in her neck, she wondered where she was. It took a few seconds for her to realize that she was under the bed. She must have fallen asleep and slept there. The events of the night came flooding back, and Bella couldn't stop the cold shiver that ran down her spine. She could have sworn that last night she saw her deceased father sitting in the living room.

Bella peeked out from under the bed. The morning sun was already kissing the room with rays of light. She crawled out and jumped to her feet. She now knew what she had to do.

As if the house was on fire, she reached into the closet and pulled out the old suitcase that her mother had acquired before Bella was born. She hurried around the bedroom, opening drawers and pulling out clothes and stuffing them into the suitcase. Next, she added a few pair of shoes. She grabbed her school backpack and stuffed other personal items into it.

In the daylight Bella wasn't as leery as she'd been in the darkness the previous night. She opened the bedroom door and rushed into the bathroom. There she grabbed her toothbrush, toothpaste, and a bath towel before hurrying back to the bedroom. Her suitcase and backpack now packed, Bella changed into jeans and a long-sleeved T-shirt. She was pulling the suitcase through her bedroom doorway when her eyes landed on the picture frame with a black-and-white picture of her mother on the opposite wall. It was the only one she had.

Bella swung the backpack off her back, took the framed picture off the wall, and stuffed it into the backpack. She turned back, and her eyes skittered over the bedroom one last time, and then she walked away.

Her head held straight, Bella didn't even glance at the couch in the living room as she tugged her suitcase through it. She had no idea what exactly had happened last night or if anything had happened at all. The whole thing had probably just been her imagination at work. But one thing she knew for sure was she wasn't staying in this house another night.

Bella walked out the front door, then locked up the house. She pulled the suitcase down the stairs into the yard. As luck would have it, a small minibus was just about to pass by when she reached the main road. Bella flagged it down, and the bus stopped to pick her up. While the driver stuffed the suitcase in the back, Bella squeezed into the bus and took a seat by the door, her head hanging low.

Fifteen minutes later she got off in Trout Hall, right in front of her aunt's little house. Bella paid the driver after he placed her suitcase at her feet, and then she watched until the bus drove off.

"Bella? What's going on?" Aunt Dorothy obviously had seen her get off the bus through the cracked front window. She had hurried out of the house and rushed to the street, where Bella stood. Her face was etched in concern. "What's with the suitcase?"

"Let's go sit under the tree." Bella pulled the suitcase through her aunt's lopsided boarded gate, which was hanging by one hinge, her aunt following behind her. She left the suitcase and her backpack on the gravel walkway and went and sat on the wooden bench under the big jackfruit tree in the front yard. Aunt Dorothy took a seat beside her.

"I'm leaving, Auntie," Bella blurted out, staring down at her lap.

"What do you mean, you're leaving?" Aunt Dorothy turned slightly so she was almost facing Bella.

Bella proceeded to tell her aunt the events that had occurred the previous night.

"Father God! That man is haunting you." Aunt Dorothy jumped to her feet and began pacing back and forth. "The no-good dirty dog went straight to hell. That's why his soul can't find any peace."

"Maybe I was just imagining it." Bella shrugged her shoulders, looking straight ahead. "We had just buried him, and the funeral was still on my mind."

"Did you ever experience anything like that when he killed my dear sister?"

"No," Bella replied. "I never felt afraid when Mama died. I know she's watching over me, despite everything I've been through. Mama loved me."

"See? Matthew ten, twenty-eight, says, 'And fear not them which kill the body, but are not able to kill the soul: but rather fear him which is able to destroy both soul and body in hell.' Your mother is at rest. But that rolling calf is getting his in the pit of hell for killing Agatha. Now he's trying to drive you stir crazy and out of your mind. He made you suffer when he was alive, and he still wants you to suffer now."

"I can't stay here. It's just too much." Bella's eyes flickered all over the yard, but she never made eye contact with her aunt.

"But where will you go? You know no one out there." Aunt Dorothy waved her hand toward the road. "There's a lot of evil out in the world, Bella."

Bella gave a sad smile. "Evil, huh? I've been living with evil all my life. I'm not scared to go off on my own. As a matter of fact, I'm looking forward to the change. Most of these people here only laugh at me and call me nasty names. I'm tired of them." She jumped to her feet. "I'm tired of being reminded that I'm ugly. I'm tired of them looking at me like I'm an alien. I'm tired of . . . of . . ." She burst into tears.

Aunt Dorothy walked over to Bella and rested her hand on Bella's trembling shoulder as Bella cried. "I know you have had it real rough, my dear. I wish I could have helped you more. But you see . . ." She pointed to the little board house, which leaned so far to one side, it seemed about to topple over. "I'm sorry, Bella."

Bella sniffed as her crying tapered off. She swiped the back of her hand across her face, and then her wet eyes shifted to her aunt before looking away. "I'll be all right away from here. I'm going to Port Antonio. I'll get a job and try to save some money for college."

"You know no one in Port Antonio," Aunt Dorothy exclaimed. "You can't just go off like that."

"Do you remember Sister Esther? Mama's friend who used to live in Port Antonio before she migrated to Miami?"

Aunt Dorothy nodded.

"Before Mama died, she came to visit, and she told us how nice it was in Port Antonio. I always told myself I wanted to go there one day, and today is that day."

"Bella—"

"Here." Bella stretched out her hand toward her aunt. In it were the house keys. "This is for you."

"What's this? For me?"

"I want you to move into the house and live there. I know you won't be scared like I am. Plus, you'll have your family with you."

It was now Aunt Dorothy's turn to cry. With the tears seeping out of her eyes, she glanced over her shoulder at her little dilapidated house, which looked as if it were about to flip over any minute. Bella offering them the nice three-bedroom house was a blessing she had never expected, nor did she feel she deserved it. "God bless you for such a kind heart, Bella. But I can't live there."

"You're afraid of him?" Bella asked, referring to her deceased father.

Aunt Dorothy sucked her teeth. "Afraid? Me? I dare that demon to try to mess with me. I plea the blood of Jesus against him. He knew we didn't like each other, so he best stay in that roaring fire and leave me alone."

"So why don't you want to live there? The house is just going to be locked up."

Aunt Dorothy looked away before glancing back at Bella. "I feel bad for not standing up to Burchell after Agatha died. I did nothing while that man beat on you every day, Bella. I went to the police so often, and yet they did nothing."

"I doubt anyone could have done anything more, Aunt Dorothy. It's over now, and I'm ready to try to start over somewhere else. So, are you going to take these?" She dangled the keys in the air, still not looking at her aunt.

Aunt Dorothy reached up and took the keys out of Bella's hand, then pulled her into a tight embrace. "You have the heart of your mother—loving and generous. Thank you, Bella."

Bella slowly pulled away, happy that she had done something to help her aunt and her family. "You're welcome. I'll write, so you'll know that I'm okay."

Aunt Dorothy nodded. "You have money?"

"I have about ten thousand dollars left over from the funeral. This will have to do until I get a job."

"Okay. Go with God, Isabella Pigmore." Aunt Dorothy patted Bella's cheek affectionately. "May He cover you under His wings and keep you safe from all harm. I'll be praying for you every day, my dear."

Bella nodded, feeling a little choked up over the possibility that she may never see her aunt again. She had no intention of coming back to Frankfield. "Take care, Aunt Dorothy."

She took a few steps over to the gravel walkway to get her suitcase and backpack. After hoisting the backpack on her shoulder, she went through the gate. Bella stopped and turned to wave one last time at her aunt. Then she took a few more steps and, with her suitcase by her side, anxiously awaited the arrival of the bus to Port Antonio.

"Goodbye, Mama. I'm going to start living the life you always wanted for me," she whispered.

Chapter Five

The bus rolled into Port Antonio's bus terminal two hours later. Bella was one of the last passengers to get off, her hand tightly gripping the suitcase's handle. She was excited to leave Frankfield but very nervous about what lay ahead. Her community had gotten used to her face, well, somewhat, but would strangers? What would the people of Port Antonio make of her? She guessed she was about to find out.

It was a busy town in comparison to Frankfield—more buses, taxis, businesses, and people. Standing still, scoping out her surroundings, Bella tried to figure out her next move now that she had reached her destination. She received a few weird looks from some passersby, but no one said anything rude or insulting to her.

"Well, the first thing is to get somewhere to sleep tonight," Bella said aloud.

"You said something, dear?" asked an elderly lady who was standing beside Bella and holding on to a shopping cart.

"I was just wondering where I can get a room to rent." Bella turned her face slightly to the right—the birthmark wasn't that visible from that angle—and avoided making eye contact. "I just came to town, and I need somewhere to stay for a while."

"Port Antonio is a very nice place," the lady replied in a friendly voice. "I've lived here all my life. By the way, I'm Sister Ruby."

"I'm Bella." Bella smiled politely, her eyes flittering all over the place as she avoided eye contact with the stranger.

"You look like a nice young lady, Bella." Sister Ruby peered at Bella as if she were x-raying her body and soul for anything contrary to her perception. "But what are you doing here by yourself?"

Bella hesitated. "Uh . . . both my parents have passed away, my father just recently. I just want to make a fresh start for myself, ma'am."

Sister Ruby's face was instantly filled with sympathy. "I'm so sorry, Bella. It must be hard on you. But remember, God is your ever-present help in your time of grief. Okay, dear?"

Bella nodded politely.

"My church sister, Mrs. Moon, occasionally rents a room in her house. It's mostly to visitors who come to our church that are recommended by someone she knows," Sister Ruby said. "It's about a mile down that road." She pointed in one direction. "It's a nice blue and white house, so you can't miss it. Tell her Sister Ruby sent you."

Relief flooded Bella. "Thank you, Sister Ruby. I'll head down there right now."

"You probably need to take a taxi, with that suitcase." Sister Ruby glanced down at Bella's suitcase. "It's not far, but the sun is out today with a vengeance." She used her hand to fan her face, emphasizing her point.

Bella looked at the suitcase, then down the street, where Sister Ruby had pointed. Her money was limited, and every cent counted until she could get a job. "I think I'll take my time and walk down there," she replied. "It will give me a chance to look around."

"All right. My friend Mertella owns that there grocery shop across the street, and I visit her often. So come and let me know how things are going with you. You hear me, dear?"

"Yes, ma'am," Bella replied, looking over Sister Ruby's head instead of at her face. "Thanks again."

Bella walked away, rolling the suitcase beside her. She made her way through the crowd of people rushing around in every direction, as the loud beeping of horns belonging to the vehicles zipping to and fro filled the air.

It was only when she was a few yards away that Bella stopped and looked back to catch a glimpse of Sister Ruby, who was now slowly making her way across the street to her friend's grocery shop. She raised her hand and touched the left side of her face, amazement filling her eyes. "She never made a rude comment about my ugly birthmark," Bella said softly to herself. "Nor did she look at me as if I were an alien or something. I think I'm going to like it here in Port Antonio. Maybe for once in my life, I can feel like a normal person."

Bella felt optimistic as she strolled down the street, stopping every few feet to rest, the sweat running down her face and back. Sister Ruby had called it right: it was a very hot, humid day.

Finally, Bella came upon the big blue and white house. She walked up to the tall white double-swing gate and called, "Hello? Mrs. Moon?" Not getting a response, Bella picked up a small stone lying close by and gently knocked on the gate with it. "Mrs. Moon?"

Just then the front door opened, and a pleasant-looking senior lady ambled from the house toward the gate, where Bella stood. "Hello there," she greeted Bella through the gate. "You were calling me? I'm Joyce Moon."

"Yes, ma'am. My name is Bella. Sister Ruby told me that you may have a room to rent. I'm new in town."

Mrs. Moon glanced down at Bella's suitcase before looking back at her face, which Bella quickly turned away to avoid making eye contact. "If you're a friend of Sister Ruby, then I have a room for you." She proceeded to unlock and open the gate.

Bella didn't dare tell her that she had just met Sister Ruby.

"Come in, baby." Mrs. Moon stood to the side as Bella dragged her suitcase into the driveway. "It just so happens that a nice pastor and his wife who were passing through town left this morning. So, the room is available for you."

Bella nodded her appreciation, then asked a very important question. 'How much is it for the room, ma'am?"

Mrs. Moon's kind eyes sparkled as she looked at the shy young lady. "We'll figure out something that fits your budget, sweetheart. It's not about money for me. I don't want you out there on the streets. How is that?"

"Thank you." Bella's grin spread from ear to ear and remained for a few seconds before it disappeared. Self-consciously, she looked down, and her eyes landed on her own sandals.

Mrs. Moon caught Bella's gesture before she turned around and closed the gate. "Let's get you settled inside." She walked back to the house, with Bella closely behind her.

Once they were inside, Bella's eyes traveled over the house as they made their way down a long hallway, passing the beautifully furnished living room on the right and the spacious, homey kitchen on the left. It was a very nice house.

Finally, Mrs. Moon entered a bedroom at the back of the house. "And this will be your room. I just changed the sheets and cleaned it up this morning."

Bella entered the large, airy bedroom, and her eyes lit up with approval. The full bed was neatly made up with bright floral sheets and two matching fluffy pillows, and two bedside tables stood on either side. There was a beautifully crafted wooden dresser on one side of the room and a huge matching wardrobe on the other.

Various paintings of exotic flowers, gushing rivers, and captivating landscapes, as well as framed family portraits, lined the pink walls, while light yellow and white curtains swayed gently at the two open windows.

"It's very nice, Mrs. Moon. I'm glad Sister Ruby sent me to you. Thanks again."

"Don't even mention it. I welcome the company in this house, which is why I began taking in boarders after Mr. Moon passed away six years ago and our daughter moved to Westmoreland. The bathroom is through that door." She pointed to a door beside the closet, which Bella noticed for the first time. "After you unpack and freshen up, I'll show you the rest of the house." She smiled and left quietly, pulling the door closed behind her.

Bella moved over to the bed, kicked off her sandals, and threw herself down on it. She was exhausted from not getting much sleep the night before and from making the trip to Port Antonio. Her eyes closed, Bella inhaled the clean smell of the bedsheets, and it wasn't long before she dozed off.

The smell of fried fish tickled Bella's nostrils. She sniffed and opened her eyes, her stomach growling in response. It took a few seconds for Bella to remember she was in her rented room at Mrs. Moon's house in Port Antonio.

Yawning, she stretched her arms over her head before she rolled to the edge of the bed and got up. She unzipped her suitcase and backpack and unpacked the few items she had brought with her.

Bella took her bath soap, toothbrush, and toothpaste into the bathroom and placed them on the edge of the sink. After taking a welcome shower, she dried off with one of the two clean towels Mrs. Moon had set on top of the toilet tank. She walked back into the bedroom, put on one of her summer dresses and a light sweater over it. The scars on her legs and across her back were fully covered. Once she was dressed, Bella left her room, in search of Mrs. Moon.

She followed her nose to the kitchen, where she found Mrs. Moon humming as she turned something in a frying pot on the stove.

"Hi, Mrs. Moon," Bella said shyly as she lingered by the kitchen door.

"Hey, Bella. I see you got yourself some rest." Mrs. Moon glanced up at Bella and smiled.

Tugging her hair down toward her face, Bella turned slightly to her right so the birthmark on the left side of her face wasn't that visible.

"I'm almost finished with these festivals to go with those escovitch fish," Mrs. Moon said, referring to the slightly sweet fried dumplings and the fried fish. She nodded at a plate with fried fish on it on the long wooden dining table in a corner of the big kitchen. "I hope you'll join me for dinner."

Bella's mouth watered instantly. "Thank you, ma'am."

"Go and have a seat, dear." Mrs. Moon waved over at the table, then turned back to the stove to remove a golden-brown festival from the pot to a plate close by.

Bella did as instructed, her eyes glancing around the beautiful, homey kitchen.

"So, Bella, tell me a little more about yourself. You seem so very young to be out there all by yourself," Mrs. Moon remarked as she went to get juice from the refrigerator.

Bella remained silent for a few seconds. *How much should I tell her? She seems like a nice, friendly lady, but I'm not ready to tell her about what I've been through.* Bella self-consciously tugged on the neck of the shirt.

"Sorry. I didn't mean to get into your business." Mrs. Moon placed a plate piled high with festival on the table in front of Bella. "You don't have to say if you don't want to, my dear."

"It's all right," Bella replied and began to tell Mrs. Moon a shortened, more pleasant version of her life story. "My mother died a little over a year ago from a heart attack, and my father two weeks ago from natural causes. Being an only child and now an orphan, I wanted to make a fresh start for myself, so I decided to come to Port Antonio. My mother had a friend who lived here, and she had told us how great it was here."

Mrs. Moon placed a jug of ice-cold lemonade on the table and gingerly lowered herself into a chair across from Bella.

"And here I am," Bella concluded.

"Yes, here you are." Mrs. Moon put a big fish on her own plate, followed by two festivals. "I'm sorry about your folks, Bella. And I'm happy to have you here."

Bella nodded, her hands in her lap.

"Please help yourself, my dear." Mrs. Moon pointed with a festival at the pile of escovitch fish. "Don't be shy now."

Bella timidly did as she was told and put a fish and a festival on her plate, her eyes flickering everywhere but at her company at the table.

As they ate, Mrs. Moon took the time to tell Bella about her late husband, their courtship almost fifty years ago, their marriage, and his peaceful passing. Her face lit up when she spoke of their only child, Sophia.

"Now, that girl was smart as a whip since the day she was born." Mrs. Moon's face glowed with pride. "And her papa spoiled her like no tomorrow." Mrs. Moon laughed lightly. "Boy, what a blessing and joy Sophia brought to our lives. You know, she teaches English at St. Mary High School."

Bella listened as she ate and couldn't help comparing herself to the well-loved Sophia. The girl whose father doted on her while her own father beat on her. The girl who seemed to have grown up stress free and carefree, while she had been mocked and bullied. While Bella wouldn't exchange her beloved mother for anything in the world, she wished she had a father like the late Mr. Moon.

"You do have a Heavenly Father who loves you, Bella," Mrs. Moon said as she bit off a piece of festival.

"Huh?" Bella glanced at Mrs. Moon briefly, a puzzled look on her face.

Mrs. Moon swallowed the food in her mouth and said, "You said you wish you had a father like my Adolph."

Bella's eyes widened; she had no idea that she had spoken her thought aloud. "Oh . . . sorry."

"Nothing to be sorry for, sweetheart. Just remember, God loves you very much. Psalm sixty-eight, five, says, 'A father of the fatherless, and a judge of the widows, is God in his holy habitation.'"

Bella snorted; her face twisted up like she was sucking on a Vidalia onion instead of the tasty festival. "Of course He is," she said, sarcasm dripping from her words like slow molasses. "He's definitely *my father*." She had long ago lost her faith in God, who had done nothing to protect her from her abusive father.

Mrs. Moon was rendered speechless. "Hmm . . . well . . . I know you—"

"Thanks for dinner, ma'am." Bella shoved the almost full plate away from her, pushed her chair back, and rose to her feet. "Do you need me to help you with the dishes?" There was now coldness in the eyes that were staring over Mrs. Moon's head.

"That's okay, baby. I'll do them after I'm finished with my dinner."

Bella's head bobbed. "I'll see you later." She moved toward the door.

"You are free to go and watch the TV in the living room." Mrs. Moon's words halted her steps.

"That's all right. I think I'll just go to my room." Bella shuffled away, leaving Mrs. Moon alone at the table.

Bella woke up the next morning more rested than she had been in a long time. She showered and dressed, then left her bedroom to search for Mrs. Moon. "My behavior last night was unbecoming," she mumbled softly to herself. "But it just rubbed me the wrong way when Mrs. Moon began talking about her supposedly Heavenly Father. Mark you, the same father that caused me to be born looking like Godzilla. The same father who didn't prevent my mother from dying, possibly at the hands of her own husband. The same *Heavenly* Father who never helped as my *earthly* father brutalized me for years. That father? Yeah, right."

Bella went from one room to the other, taking the time to look around the four-bedroom house, as she had never got a chance to do so the night before. But she still didn't find Mrs. Moon. Just then, she heard soft singing coming from the back of the house, and she followed the voice.

Mrs. Moon was in her little vegetable garden, which was filled with tomatoes, peppers, mint, cabbage, callaloo, chayote, and cucumber.

"I'm sorry about last night, ma'am," Bella said as she went and stood at the edge of the garden.

"Don't worry about it, dear." Mrs. Moon picked a big, ripe tomato and put it in the basket by her feet. "We all have ghosts from our past. I'm praying that one day you'll see that God is able. So, what do you have planned for today?"

"I need to get a job. So, I was thinking I would walk into town and check with a few places." Bella frowned. The thought of asking for a job while people scrutinized her was unsettlingly. But she needed a job.

"I think that's a good idea," Mrs. Moon told her. "You can tell them that you're staying with me. Most people around here know me."

"Okay, ma'am."

"But eat some breakfast first. I left yours on the stove."

"You did?" Bella asked in surprise. "For . . . for me?"

Mrs. Moon nodded and smiled at her sweetly.

"Thank you, ma'am." Tears of gratitude welled up in Bella's eye. "That's very nice of you." Bella was starved, and so she hurried into the house. In the kitchen she sat by herself, a big grin on her face, feeling like a queen. She chewed slowly as she savored the tasty fried fritters with callaloo and saltfish and chocolate tea. After breakfast, she left the house with her backpack on her back.

Bella walked slowly, enjoying the warm, sunny weather. She took in the nice, well-kept houses sprinkled with an array of beautiful flowers and fruit trees in the front and back yards. Bella smiled contentedly. However, as soon as someone looked at her, she would drop her head and hurry her steps, assuming they were staring at her face.

After arriving in town, Bella did a little sightseeing, walking slowly through the streets, which were full of moving, busy bodies. She walked until she found herself in front of the small grocery shop that Sister Ruby had told her she frequented.

"I wonder if Sister Ruby is inside," Bella said aloud. "I need to thank her again for telling me about Mrs. Moon." She walked into the shop. It was empty except for the pleasant-looking elderly lady behind the register.

"Hello, dear," the lady greeted. "You're new in town."

Bella gave her a quick, surprised look. "Yes. I'm Bella."

"I've been living here all my life, so I know a new face when I see one."

At the mention of the word *face*, Bella turned away slightly and brushed down her hair, trying to hide the birthmark. "Hmm . . . I came to see if Sister Ruby was here. Yesterday she told me she is here often."

"Ah, Sister Ruby." The lady came from behind the register to stand in front of Bella. "I'm Mertella. Sister Ruby and I have been friends for over fifty years." She stretched out her right hand.

Bella briefly took the hand before dropping it, her eyes fixed on the tiled floor, and said, "Nice to meet you, Ms. Mertella."

"Sister Ruby has her grandchildren today, so I don't think she's coming by. Maybe tomorrow." Mertella walked outside, with Bella behind her, and took a seat on the small bench right in front of the store. She patted the space beside her for Bella to sit.

Bella hesitated before she perched on the edge of the seat, her back almost facing Mertella, the birthmark gladly hidden from sight.

"So, have you been to Port Antonio before?" Mertella's voice was soft as she tried to put Bella at ease.

Bella gave her the same condensed story she had told Mrs. Moon, the one minus the real, ugly truth of her life. "I've been here only a day, but I like it so far. I think if I can get a job, I'd like to stick around. At least for a while."

"I can tell you're very young. No college?"

Bella nodded. "Yes. That's in my plan as well. After I save enough money, I do want to go to college. I promised my mother."

Mertella reached over and patted Bella's hand. She noticed how quickly Bella moved it away. "That's nice to hear. You know, education is the key to success. You know we have that fancy college over there in Passley Gardens?"

"Yes, ma'am. I heard CASE is a good college." Bella's eyes were filled with sadness as she spoke about the College of Agriculture, Science and Education. "I want to do it for Mama."

"And for you too. You have a great—"

"Ms. Mertella, I'm going to get some milk." A customer had approached with a big brown bag over one shoulder and a wiggling baby over the other. "Can you please come and ring me up?"

"Of course, my dear." Mertella groaned a little as she raised herself up. "Bella, I'll be right back." She entered the store with the lady and her baby.

As Bella waited on Mertella, her mind drifted to her mother. How she wished Agatha were there with her. "I don't really want to go to college, Mama," Bella said under her breath. "They are only going to make fun of me, like they did in high school. But you wanted me to, so I'll try to endure it for you."

So caught up in her thoughts, Bella didn't see the customer leaving. She jumped when Mertella sat down beside her, then quickly swiped her hand across her damp eyes.

"I'm sorry I scared you," Mertella remarked. "Are you okay?"

Bella bobbed her head. She opened her mouth to speak, but just then two customers walked up.

Mertella got up again, then took a few steps to go inside before she stopped and turned back around. "Bella, do you want to give me a hand inside?"

"Huh? Well . . . sure." Bella followed Mertella into the shop. She went and stood by the register. As Mertella rang up the items for the first customer, Bella packed them in black plastic bags. It wasn't long before both customers had got served.

Soon other customers came in, and Bella ended up spending the day working with Mertella—packing groceries and learning to use the register under Mertella's direction. By the close of shop, she felt happy that she had helped out. It certainly had taken her mind off her mother and her circumstances.

"Here you go, sweetheart." Mertella's took cash from the register and stretched her hand out toward Bella. "Thank you for helping me out today."

"Oh, you're paying me?" Bella glanced from the hand with the money to Mertella's face before looking away.

"Of course. You did a full day's work. Please take it."

Bella timidly took the money. "Thank you, ma'am."

"You're welcome. And I would like to offer you a job helping me out, if you want it."

"Really? Yes, I would like that."

"I can't pay you that much, but it's something until you get a better job."

Bella gave her a little smile and nodded. "It will do for now. Thank you."

Mertella returned the smile. "So, I'll see you bright and early tomorrow."

Bella helped Mertella close the shop and watched as the woman walked to her small house behind it. She felt more comfortable about being in Port Antonio now that she had gotten a little job. This would help her pay for her room and board, and hopefully, she could still save a few dollars toward her college fund.

Chapter Six

Two months went by, and Bella was settling down in Port Antonio. She was working at the grocery store, packing boxes, stocking shelves, and cleaning up. She avoided direct contact with the customers as much as possible and worked the register when Mertella took a break.

She enjoyed living with Mrs. Moon, who made breakfast and dinner every day. Bella tried to give Mrs. Moon a little more money, but she wouldn't hear of it.

"I want you to save so you can start college next year," Mrs. Moon had told Bella. "I don't care if it's only one class. Okay?"

Bella had agreed. It was her mother's dream for her to go to college, and she would try to fulfill it.

As Bella entered the house one Saturday evening after work, loud laughter filtered out from the living room. *It seems as if Mrs. Moon has company*, she thought as she tiptoed down the hall, hoping to pass the living room without being seen. The door was wide open, as usual, and the laughter got even louder as she got nearer. One step, two steps, three steps—

"Bella, is that you?" Mrs. Moon's voice stopped Bella in her tracks.

Bella took a deep breath. "Yes. Mrs. Moon," she replied from the doorway of the living room, her body still faced forward.

"Come in for a minute, dear. I want you to meet my daughter, Sophia."

Bella knew there was no way out. So, she turned and entered the living room, her head hanging low.

"Hello, Bella. Mama has been telling me a lot of good things about you," Sophia greeted.

Bella looked up at her, and for some reason, she didn't look away. Sophia was a tall, beautiful woman in her early thirties and was dressed in a fancy-looking beige pantsuit, with her straight hair resting on her shoulders. But it was her face that captivated Bella. It was smooth like toffee. Flawless, without a blemish or a hideous birthmark.

"Bella?" Mrs. Moon got up off the couch and walked over to Bella, concern etched on her face.

Bella finally looked away from Sophia and gazed down at the floor. "I'm okay. Nice to meet you, Sophia," she said, feeling uglier than she had in a long time. "Well, see you later." She practically ran from the living room to her bedroom.

Bella dropped her bag on the floor, kicked off her sandals, and strolled over to the dresser mirror. Tears ran down her face as she looked at the angry, hideous birthmark that spoiled her face. "Why can't I look like Sophia?" she asked the reflection in the mirror. "Why can't I be normal?"

But the questions were left unanswered, and that night Bella showered and got in bed without eating her dinner. They were still unanswered as she cried herself to sleep and when she woke up the next morning.

It was Sunday, and the grocery store was closed. According to Mertella, Sunday was reserved for the Lord. And so she spent the entire day at church.

Mrs. Moon also attended Sunday school and church service, leaving Bella alone to sleep as late as she wanted, before eating breakfast, then watching television. Bella always refused the invitation to church.

This morning, however, would be different. Hungry, Bella headed to the kitchen, knowing Mrs. Moon would already have left for church and hoping she had taken Sophia with her. She breathed a sigh of relief when she passed the empty living room and found the kitchen to be the same.

Bella's mouth watered as she loaded her plate with the soft-boiled green bananas and salt mackerel that Mrs. Moon had left on the stove. She poured a cup of mint tea and took her place at the kitchen table. In record time the plate was almost clean.

"Good morning. Did you save some for me?" Sophia asked teasingly as she entered the kitchen.

Bella tensed, and her hand stilled with the cup of tea at her mouth. She bobbed her head.

"I'm so hungry." Sophia grabbed a plate and strolled over to the stove. As she dished out her food, she tried to make conversation with Bella. "I thought you went to church with Mama."

Bella shook her head, even though Sophia had her back turned to her.

Not getting a response, Sophia looked over at her. "Bella?"

"No," Bella shrieked. She cleared her throat loudly, then added. "I don't really attend church."

"Oh, I see. I don't get to go as often as I would like, because of my job. But I do enjoy going to church." Sophia took a seat across from Bella. "I've been working some long hours this week, so I told Mama I was going to sleep in this morning."

Bella nodded and shifted uncomfortably in her chair. Her eyes were focused on her plate, but she could feel Sophia staring at her. Consciously, she leaned her head away, with one hand over the birthmark.

"I'm sorry. I don't mean to make you uncomfortable," Sophia said, "but I can't help noticing how you are trying to hide the birthmark on your face. You're still a beautiful girl, Bella."

"I'm ugly, "Bella snapped. "I'm a freak."

Sophia gasped loudly. For a few seconds she was unable to find words to say to Bella. Then she tried. "That's not true at all, Bella. I just met you, and I don't think you're a freak."

Bella pushed back her chair. "I . . . I have to go." She stood up and took her plate and cup to the kitchen sink. *I'll come back and wash them when she's gone.*

"Bella, please wait a minute," Sophia said as Bella moved toward the door.

Bella paused, her back to Sophia, but she didn't turn around.

"If you hate that birthmark so much, I can help you cover it up," Sophia told her. "I was a makeup artist while attending college, and I still do some weddings and special occasions for my friends and coworkers."

Bella felt a shiver of hope leap in her belly. Was that even possible? She turned to Sophia and peered at her face. She noticed that Sophia's fresh face was still even and smooth but not as perfect as the night before. "You can do that?" Bella's voice was a little above a whisper. It was as if she feared that speaking louder would erase what Sophia had just said.

"How about I show you instead?" Sophia pushed her chair back.

"No, please finish your breakfast first," Bella replied, stopping her. "You said you were hungry."

Sophia smiled. "Thank you. Meet me in my room in twenty minutes. Okay?"

"Okay." Bella's mouth turned up in a little smile before she scurried away from the kitchen, her heart somersaulting in her chest.

After watching the small clock that was mounted on the wall in her bedroom for twenty minutes, Bella knocked on Sophia's bedroom door.

"Come in, Bella," Sophia shouted. "The door is open."

Bella stepped through the doorway and went in. She barely glanced around the room, as she was so focused on Sophia, who was standing in front of her dresser. In front of her were various brown bottles and brushes.

"Now, have a seat right here." Sophia pointed to a chair beside the bed.

Bella sat down with her back to the mirror, her body trembling. Was there actually makeup that could camouflage this repulsive birthmark that she had lived with all her life?

"It's really good that you and I have the same complexion," Sophia said to Bella. "A lot of this makeup I haven't used, but my coworker sells Avon, so I'm always buying new stuff." She sat on the edge of the bed, facing Bella.

Bella's eyes flickered nervously around the room, and she rubbed her fingers together.

"I want you to close your eyes." Sophia was trying to get Bella to relax. "When you open them again, you'll see the result."

Bella gladly obliged.

"I'm going to start with this liquid concealer." Sophia used a sponge and evenly applied the concealer to Bella's face. "Next, I'm using this lasting liquid foundation." She skillfully applied the foundation, putting a little extra on the birthmark, which Bella loathed. "And to finish it off, I'm now applying some flawless pressed powder."

Bella barely breathed as Sophia worked. She heard her voice but didn't pay much attention to the words. She wanted to pray and ask God to make whatever Sophia was doing work, but she knew her prayers were useless. *I guess I'll have to wait and see.*

"Now I don't use this blush a lot, but it will look great on your complexion." Sophia continued to work to Bella's face. "Close your lips. I want to see how this lip gloss looks on you. Bella?"

"Huh? Sorry. What did you say?"

"Close your lips please."

Bella did as instructed, and it felt as if Sophia was drawing a line around the edges of her lips with a pencil of some sort. Then something sticky was being applied to her lips. But she wasn't concerned with her lips. Her focus was on her face, which had brought her so much heartache over the years.

It seemed as if Sophia was working on Bella for years instead of a few minutes. She wanted to ask her how it was going, but she kept quiet.

"All right. I'm done." Sophia's voice was filled with excitement. "Open your eyes slowly."

Bella breathed in deeply and exhaled loudly before she slowly opened her eyes. She peeked at Sophia's face and caught the twinkle in her eyes. She then looked away.

"Turn around and look in the mirror now, Bella."

But Bella stood up instead and walked over to the mirror. Her eyes bugged out, and her mouth popped wide open. Staring back at her was a flawless, beautifully made-up face. The hideous birthmark seemed to have disappeared. "Oh, my God." Her hands went up and lightly touched the area that was once flawed. "Oh, my God," she repeated.

"Oh no, you don't," Sophia warned when she saw the tears welling up in Bella's eyes. "You better not ruin my hard work."

Bella sniffed loudly, willing the tears away. She tilted her head to the right so the sunlight coming through the window was on the left side, the side where the birthmark was. It didn't show.

Sophia watched Bella in silence, a big grin on her face and unshed tears in her eyes. Sophia felt as if a piece of hard dough bread was lodged in her throat.

"I'm not that ugly anymore," Bella said aloud. "I don't look like a peel-head John Crow now." John Crow was the local name for a vulture in Jamaica, and it had been one of Bella's father's favorite names for her.

The grin fell from Sophia's face. She walked up behind Bella and rested both hands on Bella's shoulders. Her eyes met Bella's, and for the first time, Bella didn't look away. "John Crow? Bella, even without the makeup, you were never an ugly girl. Yes, you have a birthmark on your face. And I can understand you being conscious of it, and I have a feeling you were teased about it too. But to say you looked like a John Crow?"

Bella hung her head. "Papa thought so. He called me a John Crow for as long as I can remember. And please don't let me tell you the other names he had for me."

"I think Mama said he died recently?" Sophia asked through her teeth.

"Yes."

"Good riddance. May he rot in hell."

Bella looked up and met Sophia's eyes through the mirror. They stared at each other for a few seconds before they both burst into laughter. Bella was laughing so hard, she had to sit down on the edge of the bed.

"I think I wet myself," Sophia said from the floor, where she now sat.

"Me too." Bella laughed so hard that her side hurt, and she had to hold it with one hand.

Finally, the laughter died down, and Bella took deep breaths while gently using her fingertips to wipe away the tears that had leaked out of her eyes. It was like a jolt of happiness had hit her. For the first time, she didn't feel like a freak.

Chapter Seven

"Good morning, Mrs. Moon. What's for breakfast?" Bella asked as she danced into the kitchen the next morning, a huge Kool-Aid smile on her well-made-up, pretty face. Sophia had given her a few quick lessons on how to apply the makeup herself, and while her handiwork was not as perfect as Sophia's, it did the trick. The birthmark was hidden.

"Well, well, well. Let me see." Mrs. Moon moved from the stove to where Bella stood. Her eyes sparkled as she looked up at the beautiful young lady. Yesterday after church she had gone with some church members to visit an ailing friend, and where they had had dinner before heading back to Sunday evening worship service. Sophia had informed her of Bella's transformation with the Avon makeup last night, when she got home.

"Bella doesn't need makeup to feel pretty," Mrs. Moon had said. "I'll be praying that one day she'll look inside and see that true beauty comes from within."

But now looking at the glow that came from Bella, Mrs. Moon was glad that Sophia had helped Bella with the makeup transformation. "You look beautiful. And so you know, I thought so from the first day I met you."

Bella nodded, her thirty-two teeth glistening. "Thank you."

"It's great to see your head held high as you look me in the eye. Come here." Mrs. Moon grabbed Bella to her ample bosom in a big hug.

Bella stayed in the warm embrace for long moments, her mind going back to the hugs that her mother had given her, especially when she'd come home crying from school after being bullied.

"Grab a seat," Mrs. Moon said after they broke the hug. "Sophia left early this morning because she had to go to work. She said to tell you she'll call you later."

"Okay. Thank you." Bella floated over to the table, the wide red skirt flaring around her knees. Tucked into it was a red and white polka-dotted blouse that she had bought after getting her first paycheck. The low-heeled, strappy white sandals completed the look.

"Oh, by the way, I like those cute little earrings you got on." Mrs. Moon added some callaloo and saltfish to the boiled green bananas that were on the plate she was preparing for Bella.

Bella reached up and felt the gold-plated knob in her left ear. "Mama bought them for my sixteenth birthday and took me to pierce my ears. She wanted me to feel pretty." Bella smiled sadly. "She didn't know earrings on a monkey can't make her pretty. That's what my father told her after we got home."

Mrs. Moon put the food in front of Bella and took her seat across from her without saying a word.

"I grabbed the earrings out of my ears, and I never wore them again. Until now."

"Because now you feel pretty." Mrs. Moon took a sip of her peppermint tea, staring at Bella over the rim of her cup.

"Yes. Now I don't feel as if I look like a monkey."

"I don't wish to speak ill of the dead, but it sounds like your father was the one who was the monkey. As a matter of fact, make that an ape."

Bella hooted with laughter, and Mrs. Moon joined in. Once they caught their breath, they ate their breakfast in a comfortable silence before Bella left for work at the grocery shop.

As Bella walked to work, she was aware of people looking at her. But instead of looking away and lowering her head, Bella smiled and even said a few good mornings. The ugliness of her life was now fully hidden: the makeup covered the birthmark, and her long clothing hid the scars on her body from the beatings.

Even Mertella complimented her on her new, radiant look, but she was also quick to add that Bella was beautiful with or without the birthmark being exposed. "You have a good heart and a kind soul. And that's beauty from inside."

Bella thanked her and went to help a customer. Throughout the day she received numerous compliments and relished all of them. In fact, two young men even invited her out that evening. Though flattered by the attention, Bella quickly declined. The makeup was one thing, but dating was on a whole other level. She wasn't ready for all that.

Over the next few weeks, Bella went through life in a state of bliss. She enjoyed her job at the grocery store with Mertella, and living with Mrs. Moon felt like home. But what she really enjoyed was making up her face and transforming herself from a caterpillar to a beautiful butterfly. Bella got so dependent on her makeup that she refused to go outside her bedroom without it. She washed it off before going to bed and put it on before leaving her bedroom. Anyone who had not known her before her introduction to Avon could not tell that she had a birthmark.

This was true for the couple who was sitting in their car across from Mrs. Moon's house as Bella left for work that Saturday morning.

"What do we have here? It seems as if our luck has finally taken a turn for the better. Isn't she beautiful?" The woman took a pull on the lit joint that the man had given her, then blew out the smoke through glossy ruby-red lips.

The man behind the steering wheel nodded, pulling on his right ear, his eyes locked on Bella as she walked up the road. "It seems as if she's also staying with our friend Mrs. Moon."

"Good. We don't have to make up an excuse why we aren't staying in that pathetic little house." The woman turned up her nose, as if she smelled something that stank. "Plus, that would be even better for us. Follow her and let's see where she goes."

The man started the car and drove slowly behind Bella, keeping a safe distance. They watched as she smiled and greeted a few people she passed on the street.

"She's friendly too. That's nice." The woman glanced over at the man, and he bobbed his head.

Once they got to the square, they watched as Bella crossed the road to the grocery store. "Is that where she works?" The woman snorted.

"If it is, I doubt she's making much working in that little store."

"Good. That will work well in our plan."

"Are we going into the store?" The man took the joint from the woman and puffed on the little bit left.

The woman shook her head. "No. Let's go and get some breakfast, then find something to do until this evening. We'll stop by to say hi to Mrs. Moon, and hopefully, she'll be there."

The man grinned. "You are such a smart woman." He reached over and caressed her leg. "She'll trust us more if Mrs. Moon introduces us."

The woman winked. "Everything rests on this, baby. You know we have been looking for a while. We have to find the perfect girl to do this."

"And we will. Don't worry, sweetheart." He drove off so they could get some breakfast and go over their plan for the beautiful young girl they had just seen.

Later that evening, the woman and the man knocked on Mrs. Moon's gate.

Mrs. Moon beamed as she opened the gate to her visitors. ""Hello, Reverend and Mrs. Ozzy. I didn't know you guys were going to be in town."

"We were at a convention in Somerset Falls today," Mrs. Ozzy said, "so we decided to stop by and see you before we head back home."

"Okay. I thought you were planning on staying with me again," Mrs. Moon replied. "I was going to tell you that the room is not available. It's rented to a delightful young lady who has been with me for a while now." The Ozzys had stayed with Mrs. Moon a few times when they were in the neighborhood or the surrounding area, doing the Lord's work.

"That's wonderful. I'm glad you have some company in the house," Reverend Ozzy said, then kissed Mrs. Moon on her plump right cheek.

"We have grown so close. It's like having my grand-daughter here."

Mrs. Moon walked toward the house, and the Ozzys followed. When she reached the veranda, she said, "Please have a seat." She motioned to two chairs, and the Ozzys sat down. "Can I get you something to drink? Some lemonade or a glass of ice water?"

"Water for me, please," Mrs. Ozzy replied in a chirpy voice.

"I'll have the same, Mrs. Moon." Reverend Ozzy's grin stretched from ear to ear, making the long scar that ran down his right cheek more pronounced.

"I'll be right back." Mrs. Moon hurried inside the house.

The Ozzys each took a glass of ice water from the tray Mrs. Moon held when she returned.

"So how was the convention?" Mrs. Moon asked as she lowered the empty tray onto the veranda table, then took a seat across from the Ozzys. "You two are so dedicated to the work of the Lord. God bless you."

"Thank you," Mrs. Ozzy said modestly. "Where He leads us, we'll follow." And she proceeded to tell Mrs. Moon about the convention that never took place. "The Holy Spirit moved in such a powerful way, and many souls were saved for His kingdom."

"Hallelujah." Reverend Ozzy raised his hand in the air, shaking his head from side to side.

"And you know Reverend Ozzy delivered that Word. Glory!" Mrs. Ozzy rocked to the left, then to the right.

"Praise the Lord." Mrs. Moon's eyes sparkled with excitement, as they usually did when she was discussing the Lord. "I can't wait to take in one of Reverend's sermon." She missed the quick look exchanged by the Ozzys. "Please let me know when you're coming back this way to preach."

"Will do, my sister," Reverend Ozzy promised and pulled on his right ear, his jaws stretched wide from his cheeky signature grin.

The three adults were still deep in conversation when Bella opened the gate, crossed the yard, and stepped up onto the veranda. "Good evening, everyone."

"Hi, Bella. Please come and meet Reverend and Mrs. Ozzy." Mrs. Moon made the introduction. "They stayed with me for a few days before you came here."

"Yes, I remember." Bella smiled as she shook hands with the Ozzys.

"It's nice to meet you," Mrs. Ozzy remarked. "You're such a beautiful young lady."

Bella blushed and said, "Thank you."

"So, Bella, tell us a little about you." Reverend Ozzy's kind eyes met and held hers.

The Ozzys listened as Bella rushed through the short version of her life story, not giving away much of her past.

"I'm sorry you have lost your parents, Bella." Mrs. Ozzy's exquisite face frowned. She flipped her long, straight hair over her shoulder and graciously crossed her delicate ankles. "We are here if you ever want to talk or need anything."

"Yes, we'll always be available for you, Bella," Reverend Ozzy confirmed. He noticed how Bella was staring at Mrs. Ozzy with fascination.

"Thank you," Bella responded. "You're both so kind."

"Any plans for college, Bella?" Mrs. Ozzy asked. "You know, a good education is the key to a successful career."

Bella nodded and said, "Yes. I do plan on enrolling at CASE as soon as I save up enough money to do so."

Reverend Ozzy gave her a thumbs-up. "Good for you, my dear. I'll be praying for you."

The four laughed and talked until night fell.

"Well, we better get going now," Reverend Ozzy finally said, rising to his feet. "We have a long drive to St. Thomas."

The Ozzy's bid goodbye to Mrs. Moon and Bella and left.

"Let's see if we can get a room tonight at the Jamaica Palace Hotel," Mrs. Ozzy said when they drove away from the house. "I'm tired."

"All right," Reverend Ozzy agreed and headed to the hotel. They were lucky and got a room with a beautiful, picturesque view. After showering, the couple ordered dinner. As they ate, they discussed Bella.

"Did you see those cheekbones and that gorgeous, healthy skin?" Mrs. Ozzy asked. "She's also an intelligent young lady."

Reverend Ozzy bobbed his head. "Plus, she's an orphan and is trying to save money for college. She'll probably be ninety years old when she starts if she continues to work at that little grocery store."

"So money is important to her now, and we're going to offer her so much, she can't refuse."

"She's the one," Reverend Ozzy agreed. "We start working on her now. Time is of the essence."

Early that Sunday morning the couple went home, and in the late afternoon Mrs. Ozzy called Mrs. Moon's house. Bella answered the telephone.

"Hello. Is this Bella?" Mrs. Ozzy asked.

"Yes."

"Bella, it's Rachel Ozzy. How are you? It was great meeting you yesterday."

Bella's eyes lit up. "Hi, Mrs. Ozzy. It was nice meeting you and Reverend Ozzy as well."

"I wanted to ask Mrs. Moon something, but I assume she's not there." Mrs. Ozzy knew Mrs. Moon would be at church at this time. She had called hoping Bella would answer the phone.

"No, she's at church," Bella told her. "I can have her call you when she comes back."

"That's fine. I'll just call Mother Nash from our church. Bella, let's exchange numbers so we can keep in touch. You're such a lovely young lady."

"I don't have a cell phone," Bella admitted. "I'm saving for college and hope to start this September."

"I admire your dedication to further your education. Listen, I have a prepaid cell phone here that I'm not using. I can give it to you. In fact, it has some money on it, and when that's finished, you can add some more credit. What do you say?"

"You'd really give me a cell phone?" Bella sounded surprised. "That's so nice of you."

"The Lord blessed me, so I can bless someone else. I'll mail it off for you tomorrow. Here, take my number, and make sure I'm the first one you call on it."

Bella got her new cell phone a few days later, and she was so excited. She called Mrs. Ozzy, and they spoke for a while. Over the next four weeks, Bella got a call from Mrs. Ozzy almost every day.

"Bella, you're such a lovely young lady," Mrs. Ozzy would say. "You have such a wonderful life ahead of you."

Bella beamed each time. Mrs. Ozzy was throwing out the compliments like bread crumbs, and she picked at them like a starved little birdie.

As they got to know each other, Mrs. Ozzy revealed to Bella that she was only twenty-six years old, just six years older than Bella.

"Wow. You're a very young first lady," Bella remarked. "And it's just awesome how committed you are to helping others and doing God's work. I want to be like you one day."

"Thank you, dear. Think of me as the older sister you never had."

Bella liked that a lot. As the days passed, she grew more comfortable with Mrs. Ozzy, and their relationship got closer and closer.

Mrs. Moon was happy that the first lady had taken a liking to Bella, and told her as much. "She's a great role model for you, Bella. I'm glad you have someone like her in your life."

"Me too, Mrs. Moon," Bella replied enthusiastically. "I admire her so much. She's such an awesome woman."

Chapter Eight

A few weeks into their relationship, Bella called Mrs. Ozzy, but she didn't answer, so Bella left a message. She waited for a call back but never got one. Concerned, Bella called her again the next day and got her voice mail.

She left a message. "Hi, Mrs. Ozzy. It's Bella again. I hope everything is okay."

A week and a half went by, and Bella still hadn't got a return call from Mrs. Ozzy. But then her cell phone rang while she was at work that Saturday morning.

"Mrs. Ozzy? Are you okay?" Bella asked when she answered the phone.

"I'm hanging in there." Mrs. Ozzy's voice was low and flavored with sadness. "I've been under the weather lately, so we decided to get away and come to Port Antonio for a day or two."

"That's great. I can't wait to see you." Bella was over the moon to see the woman she had come to admire so much.

"We're leaving in a few minutes and should get there later tonight. I hope you'll join us for lunch tomorrow at the Hotel Mockingbird Hill. Take a taxi and we'll give you back the money. Also, please don't tell Mrs. Moon. I don't think I'm in the mood to see her on this trip, and I wouldn't want her to be upset."

After work, Bella took some money from her pay and bought a bright yellow dress that rested at her ankles and had long puffy sleeves. *I bet Mrs. Ozzy will like this*, she thought as she walked home with her purchase.

The next day, after Mrs. Moon had left for church, Bella carefully applied her makeup and pulled her hair back in a long ponytail. She put on her new dress, which fit her perfectly, then strapped on a pair of white sandals. Once dressed, Bella walked out to the street and hailed a taxi.

She got one in no time, and ten minutes later they were pulling up in front of the hotel. Bella paid the driver and got out. She felt important as she glided into the hotel lobby. She looked around for the Ozzys, as they were to meet her there, but she didn't see them. Bella waited a few minutes, wondering if maybe she had heard the wrong hotel when Mrs. Ozzy told her.

"Let me call her," she said softly to herself.

Reverend Ozzy answered the phone. "Hi, Bella. I was just going to call you. My wife is not feeling well, so we decided to have lunch in our suite instead. Can you please come up?"

"Sure." Bella hung up after she got the room number. She followed the signs posted on the wall and took the elevator to the Ozzys' room.

Mrs. Ozzy opened the door when Bella knocked. Her eyes were red, as if she had been crying.

Bella gave her a hug and said, "You're still not feeling well?" She stepped into a small living room area off the bedroom. Reverend Ozzy was sitting on a long black couch, looking despondent.

"What's wrong?" Bella asked after sitting on a chair across from the couch.

"I got some bad news a few days ago." Mrs. Ozzy slowly lowered herself down beside Reverend Ozzy. "I had another miscarriage." She burst into tears, and Reverend Ozzy lowered his head, wiping his wet eyes with his fingers.

"Oh, no. I'm so sorry."

"This is the third one, and it was very bad," Mrs. Ozzy said. "I had other medical complications from it, and I won't ever be able to have kids."

"I wish there was something I could do to help." Bella's shoulders slumped from despair.

"Maybe you can, darling." Mrs. Ozzy blew her nose into a tissue she had in her hand.

"I can? How?" Bella leaned forward.

"Well, Reverend Ozzy and I were wondering if you could be a surrogate mother for us."

Bella's mouth opened wide, and her eyes even wider. She glanced over at Reverend Ozzy, and he nodded. "Say what?"

"I know it's probably too much to ask, but hear us out, please?" Mrs. Ozzy said in a low voice. "This would be a traditional surrogacy, because we'll have to use your egg, as my ovaries and womb were removed. So you'll be the egg donor and the surrogate for the embryo. You'll be impregnated using a process known as artificial insemination. We have a wonderful doctor at the Princess Margaret Hospital. He will transfer sperm that is taken from Reverend Ozzy into your uterus."

Bella blushed and lowered her head.

"Once you're pregnant, you'll stay in one of the apartments that we own in St. Thomas. This we'll give to you after the baby is born. You can live there and commute to the College of Agriculture, Science and Education, as you had planned, or you can sell it and buy another apartment in Port Antonio."

"What? You'll give me an apartment?"

"We certainly will. We'll also give you five hundred thousand dollars," Reverend Ozzy said. "This you can use to go to college. And I think you'll need a car to get to work and school, so we'll buy you a brand-new one."

Bella's head was spinning. "I can't drive," she mumbled.

"We'll pay for driving lessons for you too." Mrs. Ozzy smiled for the first time since Bella had entered the room. "You'll be giving two people something they want more than anything in the world. I know we're asking a lot, as this will be your baby too. But we'll raise him or her, and you can come and visit us anytime you want. We want you in our lives. As one family."

The word *family* resonated in Bella's head. She had come to think of Mrs. Moon and Sophia like family. Now this pastor and his sophisticated wife wanted her to be a part of theirs too.

"Bella, I know the Lord has chosen you to carry this baby," Reverend Ozzy informed her. "He told me you were to be like the Virgin Mary. Do you know about her?"

Bella's face flushed. She remembered a conversation she had had with Mrs. Ozzy, and she had asked her if she ever had a boyfriend. Bella had admitted that she never had a boyfriend and she was a virgin. "Yes. I used to attend church with my mother." Her voice sounded like there was sandpaper in her throat.

"So you see, Bella, the Lord has chosen you to help us with this gift of life." Mrs. Ozzy got up and went to stand in front of Bella, then took her hand in hers. "Will you help us please?" The tears came back and trickled down her face.

"Hmm . . . this . . . this is a lot to take in," Bella stammered. "I have to think about it."

"Of course." Mrs. Ozzy leaned down and kissed Bella on the cheek. "This is a big decision. But I want you to know no matter what you decide, I'll still love you. You're important to me."

That night Bella twisted and turned before falling into a troubled sleep.

You'll never get a man with your ugly behind. Burchell Pigmore's harsh words hammered into Bella's subconscious mind. *Thank God. You won't have any spawns.* His nasty laugh echoed in Bella's head.

"No, no, no," Bella murmured in her sleep. She turned on the bed, sending the bedsheet to the floor.

I'll still love you. Now it was Mrs. Ozzy's words in her head. *You're important to me.*

Bella rolled over onto her side, a smile on her sleeping face. "You're important to me too."

You're a monster with that thing on your face! Burchell's voice.

You're gorgeous, Bella. Mrs. Ozzy's voice.

I know the Lord has chosen you to have this baby. Reverend Ozzy's voice.

The voices went in and out, clashing, bouncing off each other, pounding at Bella's head.

"Stop!" Bella jumped out of her sleep, her heart racing in her chest, perspiration dampening her face, and her nightgown clinging to her body. She took a few deep breaths before she got off the bed and walked from her bedroom to the kitchen. There she gulped down a tall glass of water.

Bella then returned to her room and sat up on the bed, her back against the pillows that rested on the headboard. She had a lot to think about. "Now I get the chance to prove you wrong, Papa," she mumbled. "I'm getting the opportunity to have a baby, *my* baby."

Just then Bella remembered one of her mother's little pep talks about fornication. "I want you to wait until you find a nice, godly husband to share your body," Agatha had told her repeatedly.

Sure, Mama, Bella had thought sarcastically. *The men are knocking down our door because I'm so gorgeous.*

Suddenly Bella got off the bed and walked over to the dresser. She slipped the nightgown over her head and allowed it to fall at her feet. Her eyes locked on the long scar across her tummy from the buckle of Burchell's thick leather belt. She turned around and looked over her shoulder at the maze of scars on her back. It looked like the map of Jamaica. "It's a miracle that after all those beatings, it's not worse," she muttered. She turned around to face the mirror and opened her mouth wide; all her teeth were still there. Her hands ran over her ribs, which had taken hard, heavy blows but were never broken.

"In a few months I'll be twenty-one years old," Bella said to her reflection in the mirror. She touched her unblemished face. "I'll never get married. What would my husband think when he sees my body, and after I wash the makeup off my face? I would have to reveal the birthmark at some point, right?"

Just then Bella's eyes grew big. "Oh, Lord." The Ozzys didn't know about it, either. Should she tell them? Would it make a difference in terms of them choosing her to be their surrogate mother? Would they still want her to have the baby?

"Mama, why do I have a birthmark and you don't?" Bella remembered asking Agatha after she was mocked by some boys at school who had accused her of being marked by the devil.

"I think when I was pregnant, I had a craving for milk and rubbed my face," Agatha had responded. "That's why you have that milk-white beauty mark on your pretty face."

Bella had wanted to roll her eyes at the "beauty mark" comment. Only her mother had thought her birthmark was a beauty mark.

"So it's not a genetic trait," Bella whispered into the early dawn now, staring up at the ceiling, where shadows from the trees and moonlight outside danced. "There is no need to tell the Ozzys anything, because my baby won't be disfigured like me. I just have to make sure I don't crave milk or anything else and rub my face while I'm pregnant."

Before Bella made a final decision, though, she first had to address some unanswered questions nagging at her. Would she be able to give her baby away to the Ozzys? And how often would she get to see the baby?

Chapter Nine

"Hi, Mrs. Ozzy," Bella said into the phone two days later. "I have a few questions about what we discussed and was hoping we could meet and talk."

"Of course, darling," Mrs. Ozzy replied, her happiness transparent over the telephone. "The fact that you're thinking about it means so much to Reverend Ozzy and me. We have some church activities today, but we could drive up tomorrow. How does that sound?"

"That's fine. I'll meet you at the house after work?"

"No, no, no," Mrs. Ozzy said quickly. "Please remember not to say anything to Mrs. Moon, at least not yet. These older women don't really understand things like surrogate mothers and artificial insemination."

Bella hesitated. She didn't like keeping something like that from Mrs. Moon and Sophia. But maybe she could wait awhile before telling them. "I guess that's okay."

"Great! So we'll meet back at the hotel. Thank you so much, Bella."

The Ozzys came back into town the next day, and Bella met them in the hotel restaurant after work.

"Bella, so nice to see you." Reverend Ozzy kissed her cheek lightly. "Thank you for coming." He stepped aside to make room for Mrs. Ozzy.

"Hi, sweetheart." Mrs. Ozzy did the same as her husband. She pulled away and stared at Bella's smooth mocha face. "I think you look more beautiful every time I see you."

Bella blushed and said, "Thank you."

"Let's sit down," Reverend Ozzy urged as he pulled back a chair for Bella to sit, then another for Mrs. Ozzy. Then took his own seat around the table. He lifted his hand in the air to signal to the waiter that they were ready to order.

"So, Bella, you have some questions for us?" Mrs. Ozzy asked after the waiter had left with their orders.

"Yes. I went to the library and did some research on artificial insemination and how it's done. So I won't have to . . . uh . . . I mean, I'm not going to, like, sleep with Reverend Ozzy. Right?"

"Only if you want to." Reverend Ozzy grinned and tugged on his right ear.

Bella gasped loudly, and Mrs. Ozzy glared at him.

"Hey, I'm only kidding." Reverend Ozzy held up both hands. "I'm just trying to lighten the mood."

"Bella, the process our doctor will be using is intrauterine insemination," Mrs. Ozzy said. "That's IUI, and you may have read up on it. Reverend Ozzy's sperm will be placed directly in your uterus near the time of ovulation. That's all."

Bella nodded and said, "You said I would get to be in the baby's life. Did you mean that? How often would I get to see the baby?"

"We absolutely mean it, Bella," Mrs. Ozzy told her. "You'll be living in your new apartment, which is just a few miles from our house. So you can come and visit anytime you want and see the baby whenever you want. Maybe you could even come and work at the church after college. Wouldn't that be awesome?"

"And I'll help you with that," Reverend Ozzy added. "We always need good workers for the Lord at church. But if you would rather do something else, I know a lot of people. I'll get you a wonderful job."

Bella's face lit up. She rested her elbows on the table and leaned forward. "I would like that very much."

Mrs. Ozzy nervously wrung her hands together. "Does this mean you'll do it?"

Bella smiled. "I'm getting the chance to live a good life and to fulfill my mother's dream for me to go to college. I'm also putting Papa to shame by having my own baby, who will be raised by two people I've come to love and respect very much. I mean, over the past few years, I thought God had forgotten about me. But now I can't help feeling like He's making everything right. Yes, I'll do it."

"Hallelujah!" Reverend Ozzy pumped both fists in the air, ignoring the curious stares of the other patrons.

"Look at God." The tears trickled down Mrs. Ozzy's face. "You won't regret this, Bella. I promise I'll be the best mother ever."

"We're family now, Bella." Reverend Ozzy reached out to take Bella's hand in his. "God is going to bless you ten thousand times more than you have blessed us. Thank you."

The Ozzys discussed the artificial insemination process some more with Bella until their food arrived. As they ate, Bella asked questions about the Ozzys' church and their personal lives. The Ozzys' laughter filtered across the restaurant and created a comfortable ambiance, all due to the excitement of what was to come—the birth of their child.

"Bella, please remember not to tell anyone about this," Mrs. Ozzy said after dinner. "It's just between us for now. Okay?"

"Sure," Bella agreed.

"Here, Bella." Reverend Ozzy handed Bella money across the table.

"That's for you to take a taxi to the Princess Margaret Hospital in St. Thomas for our first consultation with the doctor," Mrs. Ozzy told her. "After that, we'll show you your apartment."

"Wow. This is really happening, isn't it?" Bella was elated.

Bella took a day off the next Friday, telling Mertella and Mrs. Moon that she had been invited to a rally at the Ozzys' church in St. Thomas. Bella felt bad for lying to Mrs. Moon, but she was beginning to agree with Mrs. Ozzy that Mrs. Moon wouldn't understand what she was getting ready to do. And she had to have this baby, her baby.

As Bella sat in the back of the taxi as it sped to St. Thomas, she stared out the window at the beautiful scenery, the green fields with all kinds of fruit trees growing, including mango, banana, apple, and orange. They passed by people who were walking along the road and vehicles going up and down it.

It took an hour and forty-five minutes to get to the hospital. As the taxi drew closer, Bella began to get nervous. However, there was a touch of excitement at what was to be. "My baby," she muttered. "Someone who will love me unconditionally and won't care about my birthmark." It was a love that Bella craved and deeply wanted.

The taxi pulled up in front of the hospital, and Bella paid the cabbie before getting out. She walked into the reception area, and the Ozzys were there waiting for her.

"Bella." Mrs. Ozzy hugged her. "How was the ride?"

"Very nice," Bella responded, then hugged Reverend Ozzy.

"Well, Dr. Zandt is waiting for us in his office. Let's go." Mrs. Ozzy took Bella's hand in hers, and they walked down the corridor, with Reverend Ozzy following.

All three of them entered an elegant office, and Reverend Ozzy closed the door behind them. There was an Asian man sitting behind a large executive desk about ten times his size.

"Hello, Mrs. Ozzy." Dr. Zandt smiled, showing tiny teeth that looked like fangs. "And you must be Bella," he said with flair, waving a hand in the air. He sashayed around the desk and came to stand in front of Bella. He was wearing a red and white polka-dotted jacket and skinny white pants.

"Hi." Bella looked at him with apprehension. There was something about Dr. Zandt that didn't sit well with her. But she couldn't put a finger on it right then.

"I say, you guys picked the perfect mother for your baby, Rev." Dr. Zandt winked at Reverend Ozzy.

Reverend Ozzy gave him a stern look and replied, "Bella is a lovely young lady with good principles. My wife and I are very happy she has agreed to be our surrogate mother."

"Let's sit down and talk," Mrs. Ozzy said as she looked pointedly at Dr. Zandt.

"Okay, okay." Dr. Zandt rolled his eyes dramatically. "Let's not get so uptight." He danced back to his chair and sat down.

The Ozzys and Bella took seats facing him.

"Bella, I want to start with some initial questions," Dr. Zandt announced. "When do you usually get your period? How frequently, and how long does it last?"

Bella flushed and looked down at her lap. But she answered all Dr. Zandt's questions in a low voice.

"Thanks, Bella. Today we're going to take some blood for an infectious disease screening. I'll also be doing a blood test that will detect an increase in progesterone, which means you're ovulating."

Bella hung her head even lower. She had read about this at the library.

Dr. Zandt continued, "You're young and appear to be healthy, but I still want to do a physical exam to make sure your heart is strong enough to endure a pregnancy and so forth."

They all listened as Dr. Zandt walked them through everything from beginning to end. The Ozzys asked questions, which Bella knew was more for her benefit, as she was sure they had heard all this before at their own consultation.

Next, Dr. Zandt's nurse came and took Bella to a private room, where she took Bella's blood. After that, Dr. Zandt came in and did the physical exam.

After they left the hospital an hour later, the Ozzys took Bella to a beautiful apartment building in Morant Bay, on the outskirts of town. A paved walkway lined the freshly manicured grass and led to a three-story brick building. The apartment where Bella would be living was on the first floor.

"Wow, this is very nice," Bella exclaimed when they entered the exquisite furnished, two-bedroom apartment. She looked around, in awe.

"You'll stay here once you get pregnant," Mrs. Ozzy told her. "Then it's all yours after the baby."

"I can't thank you enough." Bella looked over at the Ozzys. "You're changing my life, you know that?"

"No, thank *you*," Reverend Ozzy said. "You're the one changing our lives, and for the better. We'll forever be grateful for having you in our lives, Bella."

Bella nodded. "I'm looking forward to visiting your house when I move here and also your church."

The Ozzys exchanged a quick look.

"Hmm . . . Bella. We would prefer not to do that just yet," Reverend Ozzy revealed as he came and stood in front of her. "I have some elders in my church who, like Mrs. Moon, wouldn't understand what we're doing. Mrs. Ozzy and I would prefer to wait until the baby is born before we introduce you to the entire congregation."

"We don't want to be judged or for anyone to judge you." Mrs. Ozzy came to stand beside her husband. "Once the baby is here and we explain that you were our surrogate mother, then they'll be more accepting. Do you understand, sweetheart?"

"Sure. I understand," Bella said. "We'll tell everyone, including Mrs. Moon and Sophia, after our precious baby is here."

The Ozzys ordered Chinese takeout and ate dinner with Bella before leaving the apartment. "We have an early prayer meeting in the morning," Reverend Ozzy explained as they took their leave.

By herself, Bella did another walk-through of the apartment, rubbing her hand over the soft beige leather couches and touching the colorful artwork hanging on the walls. She went and threw herself down on the king-size bed and giggled as she rolled from one end to the other. Once she had settled down, she stared up at the ceiling, wrapped up in happiness the likes of which she had never known before. It wasn't long before Bella slipped into a deep sleep and had a troubling dream.

She was back in Frankfield and was sitting on the veranda. She felt someone beside her and looked over to see Agatha sitting in the chair. She wasn't looking at Bella and seemed very sad.

Mama, what's the matter? Bella asked.

But Agatha only wrapped her arms around her stomach and rocked from one side to the other.

Mama? Bella reached over to touch Agatha, but she got up and walked away, then paused to speak over her shoulder.

Be careful of wolves in sheep's clothing, my daughter.
Then Agatha disappeared.

Bella jumped out of her sleep. She lay there and thought back on the dream, puzzled that her mother didn't seem happy for her. "I'm helping a pastor and his wife to have a child they want, Mama," Bella said aloud. "I can live in this nice neighborhood or buy my own apartment in Port Antonio. I'm getting the money to go to college, as you wanted me to do, Mama."

Bella got off the bed and began to pace the carpeted floor. "Don't you see this is a dream come true? I'm going to have a baby, your grandchild. Why aren't you happy for me, Mama?" She paused, as if expecting an answer from Agatha. But there was none.

Bella couldn't help thinking that Agatha's warning was like a dark cloud hanging over her head. Were the Ozzys really wolves in sheep's clothing?

Chapter Ten

Early the next morning Bella went back to Port Antonio to wait on the call from the Ozzys with her blood results. As instructed by Dr. Zandt, she would also be using an ovulation calculator, which would tell when she was most likely fertile.

Mrs. Ozzy called a week later to tell Bella that her blood results were okay. Dr. Zandt had given them the go-ahead to move forward with the procedure.

"I'd like to set up an appointment to get it done in two months," Mrs. Ozzy informed Bella. "Is that okay with you, Bella?"

"Yes, that's okay. But I have to tell Mrs. Moon something. I mean, I'll be gone for a few months during my pregnancy. Sophia too."

"I know, and we don't want to worry Mrs. Moon, so Reverend Ozzy and I will be down to speak with her."

"Oh, you're going to tell her what's going on?" Bella felt relieved. Now everything would be out in the open. And if Mrs. Moon objected, she would tell her that she had already made up her mind.

"Not yet. Remember, we agreed to wait until after the baby was born to tell anyone else. We're going to tell her that you'll be working with us for a while," Mrs. Ozzy said. "It's not really a lie," she quickly added. "I mean, you're working with us so we can be parents, right?"

Bella frowned and remained silent. *It's not really a lie, but it's not exactly the truth, either.* Then Agatha's words from her dream came back to her: *Be careful of wolves in sheep's clothing, my daughter.*

"Bella? Are you there?"

"Yes, I'm here." Bella sighed loudly. This was money for college, an apartment, and a new car. But, most importantly, this was her baby. A dream she had never known would come true. "Sounds like a plan to me. I'll see you when you and Reverend Ozzy get here."

The Ozzys arrived at Mrs. Moon's house the next day. They informed Mrs. Moon that Bella would be working as an assistant in their ministry for a few months.

"We're growing so fast," Reverend Ozzy said. "We need more people to work with us to spread the gospel and win more souls for the kingdom of God."

"This would also totally renew Bella's faith in God," Mrs. Ozzy added. They all knew that Bella didn't like church much, and she had admitted that God didn't hear her prayers.

Mrs. Moon's face became sad, and she said, "I'm going to miss her. Bella is now family, you know. But I'm happy she'll be learning about the ministry, and I agree it will strengthen her walk with the Lord."

"Plus, it will only be for a few months. Definitely less than a year." Reverend Ozzy flashed his grin. "And you can come and visit us also, Mrs. Moon."

Mrs. Moon face lit up. "Really? Then it's okay with me." She was now satisfied with the plans for the young lady she had grown to love like a granddaughter. "Bella is in fine hands, and I think this will be good for her."

Bella herself told Mertella about the assistant job with the Ozzys.

"It's nice that they took such a liking to you, Bella," Mertella told her. "Just remember, if things aren't working out in St. Thomas, you now have a home here. You hear me, hon?"

"Yes, ma'am. Thank you." Bella felt bad for not telling the whole truth, but the Ozzys had said it was best this way, at least for now.

It was a Sunday afternoon when Bella left for St. Thomas two months later to live in the apartment. The procedure was scheduled for the next morning, at 8:00 a.m.

With Mrs. Ozzy holding her hand and her eyes tightly shut, Bella felt some light pain as Dr. Zandt did the procedure the next morning at the hospital. But this was like a little pinch in comparison to a kick in the ribs from her father's work boots, which she had received numerous times.

"All done," Dr. Zandt announced after just a few minutes. "Now you'll stay here in this room, as I told you, for about thirty minutes."

"Maybe we should do forty minutes," Mrs. Ozzy said with excitement in her voice. "I mean, just to make sure."

"That's all right. I was so nervous I didn't get much sleep last night," Bella told them. "I think I'll take a little nap while we wait."

Bella's nap lasted an hour. Reverend Ozzy woke her up. He told her that his wife had an emergency at home but would be back to see her soon. He then took her back to the apartment.

"In bed you go," Reverend Ozzy told Bella as soon as they walked through the door.

"I feel fine, Reverend Ozzy." Bella went and sat on the couch. "Remember, Dr. Zandt said I could resume normal activities now."

"Okay." Reverend Ozzy smiled at her. "It's just that I'm about to be a father. It's hard wrapping my mind around it sometimes."

"Dr. Zandt said we'll know in fourteen days, when I do the test to find out," Bella reminded him.

"That's right. But I just know in my spirit that everything went okay," Reverend Ozzy said. "The Holy Spirit never lies. I'm going to order some dinner for you, and I can stay with you for a day or two, to make sure you're fine."

"No, no. I'm fine." Bella lifted her legs onto the couch and lay back. "I know the fridge and cupboards are packed, and I have my cell phone. I'll call if I need anything."

Reverend Ozzy said, "Are you sure? I don't mind—"

"I'm sure. Please go and see to your church. I'll order something to eat later."

Reverend Ozzy left after Bella promised to call if she needed them.

Bella lay on the couch, with her hand on her flat stomach and a grin stretching from one ear to another. She could be having a baby in nine months.

The reality set in as the days went by and Bella approached that fourteenth day and her next doctor's visit, when she would learn from Dr. Zandt if she was pregnant. The Ozzys called her every day, but it was mostly Reverend Ozzy who visited and took Bella to the supermarket to get items that she needed.

"Is Mrs. Ozzy all right?" Bella asked him one morning when he came by.

"Yes, she is. She's sorry she couldn't make it this morning, but a church sister she's very close to was hospitalized last night, and she wanted to be there for the family."

"That's Mrs. Ozzy. She's always thinking of others." And it gave Bella even more comfort to know that this generous, loving woman of God would be raising her baby.

"She'll be here with me on Wednesday to take you to the hospital," Reverend Ozzy informed her.

And that Wednesday morning the Ozzys arrived at the apartment bright and early to take Bella to the hospital. When they got there, Dr. Zandt was waiting in his office, this time wearing a deep purple and white suit.

I wonder if he ever wears normal suits, like other doctors, and a white coat, Bella pondered as they sat in Dr. Zandt's office.

"So today is the day," Dr. Zandt exclaimed and rubbed his hands together like a kid at the carnival. "I gotta feeling that today gonna be a good day!"

"We certainly hope so, Dr. Zandt," Mrs. Ozzy said. "Can we get on with the tests please?"

"Most definitely." Dr. Zandt looked at Bella and said, "So, Bella, I'll be doing a urine test, or a UPT, and a sonogram to confirm if you're pregnant." He went on to explain what a sonogram was and how it worked.

Bella was instructed to leave a urine sample in the bathroom and was taken to a room by the same nurse who was there for the AI. Moments later Dr. Zandt joined them and did the sonogram. Once she was dressed again, Bella joined the Ozzys in Dr. Zandt's office to wait on the results.

Silence lingered in the office, with each person in their own thoughts, as they waited. Bella noticed that Reverend Ozzy held Mrs. Ozzy's hand in his and that his head was slightly bowed, as if he was praying.

Please let me be pregnant, Lord, Bella prayed silently. *If not for me, then for the Ozzys. These people have dedicated their lives to you. I'm begging you to help them.*

"Ta-da!" Dr. Zandt burst through the office door, his arms wide open and his head thrown back in an exaggerated manner. "I got it here." He waved a piece of paper in his hands. He closed the office door, then skipped over to his monstrous desk.

All three pairs of eyes followed him, but no one said a word.

Bella folded her hands over her stomach and waited.

"Well?" Reverend Ozzy said finally. "What are we waiting for? The Second Coming?"

Dr. Zandt rolled his eyes dramatically. "Being the great doctor that I am, it's with great pride that I inform you that Bella is pregnant! Hello!"

It seemed as if a gush of water flooded Bella's head. The Ozzys animated talking and laughter sounded like it was a thousand miles away. *I'm pregnant*, she thought. It was one thing for Bella to wish she was pregnant, but now that it was official, it took things to another level.

"Bella, are you okay?" Mrs. Ozzy was by her chair, bent over, with her face close to Bella's.

"Huh?" Bella looked over at her. "Oh, yes. I'm fine. It just hit me that I'm carrying a life inside me. I mean, this is real."

"Yes, it is, darling." Mrs. Ozzy kissed her on the cheek. "I'm so happy."

"Thank you, Lord." Reverend Ozzy yelled.

Over the next few weeks Bella's body began to change as it prepared for motherhood. Her breasts got tender, sore to the touch, and felt heavy. She had minor cramping here and there and was hungry all the time. She also had nausea in the mornings and would throw up for what seemed like hours.

Her flat stomach got bigger and bigger, as one month ran into the other. When she was five months pregnant, the Ozzys hired an older lady to come during the day to help Bella with the household chores and to cook, despite Bella's protests.

"I'm fine," Bella told Mrs. Ozzy. "I don't need any help."

"Yes, you do," Mrs. Ozzy insisted. "I don't want you to do any heavy lifting or anything strenuous."

Reverend Ozzy agreed, and Bella relented.

Mrs. Ozzy rarely visited over the next few months, but Reverend Ozzy was at the apartment often to check on Bella. He was also there to take Bella to her doctor's visits. Bella thought it a little odd that the first lady seemed to have more obligations than the pastor, but she didn't dwell on it too much.

Mrs. Moon called Bella often and wondered why she hadn't visited, but both Bella and Mrs. Ozzy always had an excuse. They were traveling here and there, or they had a retreat, a rally, or some other work of God to plan.

Bella also kept in touch with Sophia and told her the same as she did Mrs. Moon. Sophia was so busy as an English teacher at a new school and didn't probe too much. And even though Bella hated lying to Mrs. Moon and Sophia, she only had to look down on her enlarged stomach to feel that her actions were justified.

Once they see the baby, they'll understand, she would tell herself. Gradually, Bella stopped taking and returning Mrs. Moon's and Sophia's calls, as instructed by Mrs. Ozzy.

It wasn't long before Bella's due date drew close. Her twenty-first birthday came and went with no recognition. Everything was centered on the baby.

Reverend Ozzy practically moved into the guest room the week prior to Bella's due date, which was a good thing when Bella's water broke one morning, two days before the due date Dr. Zandt had given them.

Bella had been feeling mild contractions but had thought nothing of it as she got dressed that morning and applied her makeup. She knew she had two days to go, but it was soon apparent that she was in labor. As Reverend Ozzy rushed Bella to the hospital, he called Mrs. Ozzy.

"Mrs. Ozzy is on her way, Bella," he announced when he ended the call.

The next call was to Dr. Zandt, who, luckily, was at the hospital, and so he was waiting for them when they got there. Bella was rushed to a room, and Dr. Zandt's nurse helped change her into a hospital gown.

"We have some way to go, Bella," Dr. Zandt told her after he examined her. "You're not fully dilated. I'll give you something for the pain if it gets too bad. Just let me know, okay?"

"No, no, no. I'll manage." Bella breathed deeply through her mouth. "I don't want anything that may harm the baby."

Three hours later Mrs. Ozzy rushed into the room. "Thank you for waiting on me." She had perspiration running down her face, as if she had run to the hospital instead of driving. "There was an accident on the way, and the police stopped traffic for a while."

"You're here now, darling," Reverend Ozzy replied. "You'll get to see our baby born."

Both Bella and the Ozzys didn't want to know the sex of the baby, so this was going to be a surprise to everyone.

Dr. Zandt floated into the room, as if he was walking on hot air. This time he had on a white coat over his red and yellow plaid suit, no doubt to avoid it being soiled during the birth. "Alrighty! Let's see where we are, Bella."

He examined Bella. "I think we're ready, darling," he said to her.

Bella nodded her head and clenched her teeth as another pain hit her. Not once did she ask for pain medication, as Mrs. Ozzy had suggested. Instead, Bella rode out each contraction with her eyes closed against the pain. Her threshold for pain was very high from all the brutality she had suffered at her father's hands.

With the Ozzys on either side, each holding one of Bella's hands, Dr. Zandt and his nurse focused on delivering the baby.

"We're almost there, Bella. I can see the head. Push for me," Dr. Zandt coached.

Bella gritted her teeth and pushed with all her might. Through all the huffing, puffing, pushing, and perspiring, some of her makeup ran down her face, but enough remained in place to keep the birthmark her secret.

"I got the head. Just a few more pushes, Bella," Dr. Zandt remarked.

The agonizing pain was getting really bad. Bella wanted the baby out now.

"You can do this, Bella," Mrs. Ozzy whispered in her ear. "At the count of three, give one big push. One . . . two . . . three."

Bella closed her eyes tight, bit her lips, squeezed the hands of Mrs. Ozzy and Reverend Ozzy, and dug deep down for a giant push.

"It's a girl," Dr. Zandt announced as the baby entered the world. After he cut the umbilical cord, he stood up and lightly slapped the baby's bottom, and she took her first cry. He then placed the baby in the blanket that the nurse held so she could clean her up.

"You did great, Bella. Here. Drink some water. You'll see your daughter as soon as the nurse cleans her up." Mrs. Ozzy put a glass to Bella's mouth after Reverend Ozzy helped her lift her head off the pillow a little.

Bella drank greedily and emptied the glass before settling back on the bed. "My baby?"

"She's coming," Reverend Ozzy responded soothingly.

But Bella soon began to feel groggy. Her eyes were droopy, and her head felt like it wanted to float away. She glanced up at Mrs. Ozzy, and her blurry face went in and out of Bella's field of vision. "I . . . I . . . don't feel . . ."

Bella thought she heard Dr. Zandt saying something, but it sounded like an echo from another planet. She wanted to open her eyes, but she didn't have the strength. She was so tired.

Bella slid into a deep sleep and missed the strange look on the nurse's face as she cleaned up the infant.

Chapter Eleven

"Mrs. Ozzy?" Bella whispered as she opened her eyes and glanced around the small, sterile white hospital room. The light in the ceiling seemed like a bright floodlight dangling a few inches away from her. She turned her head slightly to the right and winced at the pain in her head. "Reverend Ozzy?"

The memories of giving birth came rushing back, and Bella's hand went to her tummy. "Where is the baby?" Her voice was hoarse, and her throat was so dry. "Where is everyone?" Bella rolled over onto her side.

"Wait a minute, young lady." Dr. Zandt hurried to Bella's side. "I think you need a few more minutes before getting off that bed."

Bella ignored him and pulled herself up into a sitting position, her legs dangling over the edge of the bed. "What time is it? Where is my baby? Where are Reverend and Mrs. Ozzy?"

Dr. Zandt looked down at Bella over the rim of his glasses, and for a second, a look of sympathy flashed across his face. "The Ozzys have gone home. There was an emergency, and they had to go."

Bella's eyes bugged out, and her head began to pound even more. "They took my baby?"

Dr Zandt sat down beside her on the bed. "I thought the baby belonged to them. Weren't you just the surrogate mother?"

"No. I mean, yes. It's their baby. I did this for them, but I'm also going to be in the baby's life." Bella rubbed her forehead, breathing loudly through her mouth. Giving birth certainly had given her a monster of a headache. "What time is it?"

Dr. Zandt glanced down at his watch and replied, "It's almost seven o'clock in the evening. You slept for a while, but you'll start feeling better soon. After all, you just gave birth to a beautiful little girl."

Bella smiled sadly. "I wish I had got to see her before they took her home. But I'm sure they'll bring her to see me tomorrow."

Dr. Zandt nodded and replied, "I want to quickly go over a few things with you. You will get some afterbirth pain, but these cramps will go away in a few days, okay? Also, there will be some vaginal discharge as the body gets rid of the blood in the uterus."

"I still feel so sleepy." Bella pulled her legs back onto the bed and was about to lie down when Dr. Zandt stopped her.

"I called a taxi to take you back to your apartment. My nurse will be in shortly to help you get dressed."

"Oh. I thought I was staying here until tomorrow." Bella looked at him. "My head is hurting. I don't feel too well."

"It's just the stress you went through giving birth. You'll be more comfortable at home."

"Okay." Bella's body was sore, and the room was spinning a little. But Dr. Zandt was right; she would be comfortable in the nice apartment that the Ozzys had given her.

Dr. Zandt's nurse came in and helped Bella change back into her maternity dress, and she had to practically hold up the weary young woman in the process. "Slip these on your feet." She assisted Bella in putting on her sandals, while Dr. Zandt stood in a corner of the room and watched.

"All set?" Dr. Zandt asked.

The nurse nodded.

"Great!" He clapped his hands in glee, as if he had just won a million dollars. "Take her out to the taxi. Bye, Bella. I wish you all the best."

Bella nodded and leaned against the nurse as she was led from the hospital room, down the corridor, and out through the back exit. A battered old car was waiting with its engine running.

Bella stopped, puzzled.

"It's all right. We know him, and he'll get you home safely." The nurse escorted Bella to the car and opened the back door. "Be careful now," she said as Bella dragged herself onto the stained back seat. She threw Bella's backpack on her lap and slammed the rickety door closed. She then walked to the driver's window, handed him money she took from the pocket of her scrubs, then strolled back into the hospital.

"Address?" the driver asked in a high-pitched voice, which only intensified the knocking in Bella's head.

Bella told him and slumped across the back seat as the car pulled away. With her eyes closed, she tried to conjure an image of her daughter, but she hadn't even gotten a glimpse of her, and now she was gone. *No, she's not gone. She's with her parents, and you'll see her soon. You're going to see her often.*

"Here," the driver announced tersely about fifteen minutes later.

Bella groaned as she raised herself up off the car seat. With the little strength she could conjure, she grabbed her backpack, pushed the door open, and stumbled out of the taxi. She regained her balance and wobbled up the walkway to the apartment.

It seemed to take forever for Bella to dig into her backpack for the key and open the apartment door. She pushed the door shut once she had stepped inside, and stumbled over to the leather couch, where she literally fell down onto the cushions. She was so weak. In no time at all, her body gave in to exhaustion, and she fell asleep.

When Bella awoke, the moon was making a sluggish retreat and the sun was appearing for its shift. She sat up and was thankful that the sumo wrestler who was sitting on her head was gone. Bella's gaze wandered around the beautiful apartment, and a sense of sadness flooded her being. Her hands moved to her stomach, where her child was for nine months. It was now empty.

Bella walked over to the window and looked out into the early morning. As if they had a will of their own, tears trickled down her face. "Hey, Mama." She rested her head against the windowpane. "I wish you were here." The loneliness wrapped itself around her like a shawl.

Even though Bella had agreed to give the baby to the Ozzys, and she knew in her heart it was the right thing to do, she was surprised how attached she felt to her daughter. It was almost like she wanted to change her mind about giving up custody of her child. "But I can't," she said aloud. "She also belongs to Reverend Ozzy. Plus, I can't take care of her."

She stayed by the window, deep in thought, until she heard voices coming from the other apartments as people awoke. Only then did she go into the bathroom and have a much-needed bath. With the towel wrapped around her body and her face naked of makeup, Bella peered at herself in the mirror, her eyebrows knitted in a frown. The white birthmark looked even bigger and more hideous than before.

Filled with dismay, she looked away. "I'm so ugly," she muttered and lowered herself onto the closed toilet seat.

She began to sob. "Lord, please don't let my daughter be as ugly as me. The Ozzys won't want her, and people are going to tease her."

Bella's emotions were all over the place as she cried uncontrollably. When the crying subsided, she stood up and washed her face. Once she was done, Bella reached for her makeup bag and carefully made up her face, watching how the repulsive mark disappeared, replaced by pure beauty. She smiled, admiring her now lovely face, brought to her by Avon.

At around noon, Bella was back at the window, peering out at the driveway, willing the Ozzys to drive up with the baby. She had eaten some Excelsior water crackers and drunk black mint tea for a simple breakfast, and now she was waiting. She wanted to call but didn't want to appear too anxious and upset the Ozzys.

Soon most of the day was gone, and neither had the Ozzys arrived there nor had they called to check on her. That was it. Bella reached for the cell phone and dialed Mrs. Ozzy. The call went straight to voice mail. She hung up without leaving a message. Ten minutes later she called again but got the voice mail again. This time Bella left a message. "Hi, Mrs. Ozzy. This is Bella. Hmm . . . I'm at the apartment. Are you coming to see me today? I would love to see the baby. Okay, see you soon. Bye."

By 8:00 p.m. Mrs. Ozzy still hadn't returned Bella's message, nor did she answer when Bella then called her ten more times. Bella didn't know what to do. Despite all the months she had spent at the apartment, she had never visited the Ozzys' house, so she didn't know where they lived. She was supposed to do so after the baby was born. *Maybe something is wrong with the baby*, she pondered, her breathing speeding up. Alarmed, Bella called Mrs. Ozzy again, but this time she got a recording: "The number you've called is no longer in service."

"What do you mean, not in service? I think I called the wrong number," Bella said aloud, then laughed nervously. She redialed the number but got the same recording. Mrs. Ozzy had disconnected her telephone number. Now Bella had no way of reaching the Ozzys.

The next day Bella went outside, fully made up, as usual, to ask a neighbor if she knew of Worship Center Church of God in Morant Bay. This was the Ozzys' church. She had never visited, because the Ozzys wanted to wait until the baby was born, then introduce her and the baby to the congregation.

"I've never heard of that church, and I've lived in Morant Bay all my life," the neighbor told her. "Are you sure it's in Morant Bay?"

"That's what I was told," Bella replied.

"Wait here a minute. Let me go back upstairs and ask my father. He's a retired pastor who was also born and raised here. He used to travel all over the country, preaching at various churches. He knows every church here in St. Thomas. Shucks, maybe even in Jamaica." She gave a small laugh.

"It's a large church with over three thousand members," Bella added. "The pastor is Reverend Ozzy, and his wife is Rachel Ozzy."

The neighbor frowned, then turned and headed to her apartment.

Bella anxiously paced the ground as she waited.

"What did he say?" she asked moments later, when the neighbor returned.

"My father said that church is neither in St. Thomas nor in Jamaica, for that matter. Also, he has never heard of Reverend and First Lady Ozzy. And trust me when I tell you that he would know of a big church like that. So either you got the name wrong or someone lied to you."

Bella's gut was telling her it was the latter. She thanked the neighbor and went back into the apartment to contemplate what to do next.

Over the next four days Bella fell into a depression. She showered and made up her face, still holding out hope that the Ozzys would show with the baby. She ate enough to keep her strength up, although everything tasted like chalk. But as one day ran into another, all hope of seeing the Ozzys again, and her daughter for the first time, diminished.

Did they lie to me? Have they taken the baby and gone? These were some of the questions Bella kept asking herself, but she always found an answer that explained the Ozzys' absence. Maybe the baby was indeed sick, and they were busy caring for her. But why did Mrs. Ozzy disconnect her telephone number? Something wasn't adding up, but she refused to believe the good pastor and the first lady had deceived her.

In the early morning hours of the fifth day, after another restless sleep on the couch, Bella awoke to someone pounding on the front door. The panic she felt was soon replaced with happiness. *It's the Ozzys with my daughter.*

She jumped up and ran to the door, still wearing her nightgown, and unlocked it without looking through the peephole. A scream became lodged in Bella's throat when she saw the two tall, large, rough-looking men at the door. "Who are you?"

The men stood staring at Bella with perplexed looks on their faces. One man's mouth was slightly agape.

Bella self-consciously crossed her arms. "May I help you?"

"Good God, it's like she has two faces," said the one who was a Hulk look-alike.

Bella's eyes widened before she lowered her head and looked at the ground in shame. She had scrubbed her face last night when she bathed and hadn't yet gotten a chance to reapply her makeup. So the birthmark was visible.

One of the men took one step closer, and Bella moved one step back. "Mmm." He cleared his throat. "I'm the landlord for this apartment, and you have to go."

"Excuse me?" Bella glanced up before quickly looking to the side.

"You heard me. Your rent expired last night. Blacker here"—he pointed to the Hulk beside him—"is the new tenant, and he's ready to move in."

Bella was rendered speechless.

"Hello?" The landlord waved his hand in front of Bella's face, his eyes focused on the birthmark. "You need to pack your stuff and go."

Bella shook her head, willing herself to wake up. But she was wide awake. This wasn't a dream. "You must be mistaken," she replied, her eyes locked on the ground. "This apartment is owned by the Ozzys, and now it's mine. I live here now."

The landlord hooted with laughter, and Blacker chuckled, his belly shaking as if from tremors.

"Listen, Two Face, I don't know what those people told you, but this is my place, which they rented furnished for nine months. Yesterday Mr. Ozzy called and said they no longer need the place and won't be paying any more rent. So I got a new tenant."

Blacker took two steps forward. "Unless you want to stay and keep me company?" He licked his thick black lips with his long tongue as he grabbed his crotch.

"I'll . . . I'll go and . . . uh . . . get my stuff," Bella stammered and dashed inside before closing the door on Thick and Thicker.

Inside Bella reached for her cell phone on the couch and dialed the number she had called dozens of times over the past few days, hoping against all odds that she would hear Mrs. Ozzy's voice instead of that annoying recording. But no luck. The number was disconnected.

Bella walked into the bedroom, where she hasn't slept since she left to have her baby at the hospital. She reached for the suitcase under it and threw it on to the bed. Opening and closing drawers, she quickly flung their contents into the suitcase. Next were the clothes and shoes in the closet, then off to the bathroom for her makeup and other toiletries. She glanced over her shoulder every few seconds to see if the front door was still closed.

Not too concerned that she was leaving something behind, with her backpack over one shoulder, Bella dragged the heavy suitcase out into the living room.

She slipped her feet into the flip-flops by the door and pulled it open. Thick and Thicker were still there waiting.

"I hope you didn't break anything or damage my furniture," the landlord said. "You wait right here while Blacker and I go take a look around." They passed Bella and entered the apartment.

But Bella wasn't going to wait around. She knew she hadn't destroyed anything in the apartment, and the big men made her very nervous. So she dragged her suitcase outside and along the paved walkway, and then she began walking down the street, away from the apartment.

She wasn't sure where she was going, but Bella knew she had to get away.

Chapter Twelve

The sun was already getting hot, and the humidity was rising with it. Sweat began running down Bella's face and back, but she kept walking. Soon she came upon a group of four women sitting under a big tree by the roadside, laughing and talking. They all stopped and stared as she got closer.

Bella lowered her head, angling it away from them, hoping the birthmark wasn't too visible. She hadn't take the time at the apartment to reapply her makeup, knowing that Thick and Thicker were waiting outside for her.

"Are you okay, sweetheart?" one lady asked.

Bella nodded and hastened her steps to get past them.

"Wait a minute." Another lady moved closer to Bella. "You are wearing a nightgown, so we're just concerned about you."

Bella glanced down at the frilly light pink nightgown. Her mouth opened and closed, but no words came out.

"It's all right. I almost do that a few times, but luckily, one of the kids stops me before I leave the house," said the woman who had approached her. The other women chuckled.

Bella smiled shyly and took quick glances at the kind faces. "I had to leave in a hurry and completely forgot to change my clothes. Sorry."

"I'm Dawn," said the same woman.

"My name is Bella."

"Bella, that's my house across the street." She pointed to a white house. "You're free to go and change your clothes on the veranda. No one is home now, and I don't have any dogs."

Bella hesitated but then said, "Okay. Thank you." As she crossed the street to Dawn's house, dragging her suitcase, Bella realized that not once had any of them mentioned the birthmark.

She pushed the tall gate open and entered the yard. On the veranda, Bella lowered her backpack, opened her suitcase, and took out a yellow blouse that could use some ironing and a matching long skirt. She sheepishly looked around and noticed that the neighbors on both sides were a little distance away and their views were blocked by the tall trees and thick shrubs around Dawn's house.

She was quickly pulling the nightgown over her head when she felt something running down her belly. She looked down and saw it was breast milk. Immediately, she felt a tug on her heart for the daughter she had given birth to but had never seen. She let the nightgown fall back into place.

The Ozzys' deception finally caught up with her in that moment, and Bella fell to her knees, in despair. Her whimpering soon got louder, and she began to bawl. "Why me?" Bella asked over and over, looking up at the ceiling. "You can't give me a break, huh? Good God, when will it be enough, Lord? When?"

It took a few minutes for her to get ahold of herself. She wiped the snot and tears from her face with a sleeve of the nightgown, then rose to her feet. She then quickly changed into her clothes. *Maybe I should put on my makeup*, Bella thought. *No. What's the use?* She was feeling ugly again, both physically and emotionally.

But Bella had another problem. Where was she going to live? She hadn't spoken to Mrs. Moon in Port Antonio in a few weeks. Mrs. Ozzy had told Bella it was best she limit her communication with Mrs. Moon as much as possible, so Bella had.

"I was so stupid." Bella felt the tears well up again. "Now what am I going to do?"

"Call Mrs. Moon."

Bella jumped and gave a small yap. She peered around the veranda and out into the yard, puzzled. She was alone, but she knew she had heard a voice. "I can't call Mrs. Moon after all this time." Bella began pacing, wrestling with what to do. "But Mrs. Moon is such a wonderful woman. Maybe she'll understand."

Finally deciding it was worth a try, Bella took out her cell phone and called Mrs. Moon. She nibbled on her lips as the phone rang on the other end.

"Hello." Mrs. Moon sounded like she was singing, her pleasant voice tinkling in Bella's ears.

Bella burst into tears again with the phone at her ear.

"Bella? Bella, is that you, baby?"

Bella sniffled. "It's me, ma'am."

"Oh, Bella. I was so worried about you. I called and called, leaving messages for you, but you never called back. I didn't know what to think. Are you okay? Where are you? Why are you crying?" Mrs. Moon fired off one question after the other.

"I was so stupid, Mrs. Moon. They're liars and thieves."

"Oh, dear Lord. Bella. Where are you now?"

"Morant Bay, St. Thomas."

"Where are Reverend Ozzy and his wife?"

"I don't know, ma'am," Bella responded. "They took the baby and are gone."

"What baby? Bella, what's going on? Listen, you need to come home right now."

Bella's heart leaped with joy when Mrs. Moon referred to her house as Bella's home. "I thought you'd hate me because I never called you back. Mrs. Ozzy said not to. I'm so sorry, Mrs. Moon."

"None of that matters now. I want you to come back, and we'll figure out what's going on. Sophia is here too, and she's also very concerned about you."

"I'll leave now. Thank you, Mrs. Moon."

"Do you have money to get here?"

"Yes, ma'am." Bella had enough money left for the bus from the money that the Ozzys had given her for personal use when she moved into the apartment. She hadn't had to buy anything, because they had provided everything for her while she was pregnant. Now they were gone.

"Bella? Are you there?" Mrs. Moon sounded perturbed.

"I'm here. I'll get directions to the bus and come right away."

"All right, and make sure you keep your phone on. I'll be calling to check on you. See you soon, sweetheart." Mrs. Moon hung up the phone.

With her suitcase in hand and her backpack on her shoulder, Bella hurried off the veranda and into the yard. She walked through the gate and out to the road, where the ladies were still sitting under the tree.

"Now, that's better." Dawn smiled as Bella approached the ladies.

Bella bobbed her head. "Thanks again for allowing me to change on your veranda. Can you please tell me where I can get the bus to Port Antonio? I'm going home."

"That's good to hear," Dawn replied. "We were wondering if you had anywhere to stay . . ." She glanced at the suitcase.

Bella answered, "Yes, I do. I appreciate your concern. All of you."

"My regular taximan should be passing here anytime now. He'll take you to the bus station," Dawn told her.

"Thank you, ma'am, for all your help."

"Bella, we would like to pray for you real quick before you leave. We don't know you or what you're going through, but I can feel in my spirit that you're in a battle that's only going to get worse. But I know with God by your side, you will get the victory."

The other women muttered, "Amen and hallelujah," then stood to form a circle around Bella. Bella hung her head respectfully.

"Heavenly Father, we come to you on behalf of your daughter Bella," Dawn began. "You know her needs and wants, Lord. You know the dark cloud that's hanging over her and the storm that's coming her way. None of this is new to you. And so we ask that you cover Bella under your blood, from the crown of her head to the soles of her feet."

As Dawn spoke, the other ladies prayed softly, knocking on heaven's door for Bella.

"No weapon that's formed against her shall prosper," Dawn continued. "Her enemies will feel the wrath of your hands for trying to destroy your child. Give Bella the victory, Lord. Give her peace, joy, and happiness, which can be found only in you. Walk with her now as she travels home. We ask these mercies in the name of your son, Jesus. Amen."

"Amen," Bella mumbled.

"You'll be okay . . ." A second later Dawn rushed toward the road, waving her hand in the air and calling, "Bruce!"

Bella watched as a Toyota Corolla screeched to a stop in front of Dawn. Dawn walked up to the driver's window and said something to the driver. The man hopped out of the car, and they both walked back to where Bella was standing.

"I'll put the suitcase in the trunk for you." Bruce grabbed Bella's suitcase and strolled off to the car.

"Take care of yourself, Bella." Dawn gave Bella a hug, and the other three ladies did the same.

Bella felt a little weird but returned the hugs before she went to sit in the back seat of the car. Almost immediately the car drove off. Looking back through the rear window, she saw the ladies waving, until the car took a deep turn around the bend.

Luck was on Bella's side, and they made it to the bus for Port Antonio just as the driver was getting ready to pull out of the station. Bruce quickly loaded her suitcase in the back of the bus, and she paid him his fare. She then got on the bus and took a seat at the back.

The ride took around two hours, and Bella slept for most of the trip, except when Mrs. Moon called to make sure she was on her way. When she got off the bus, Mrs. Moon and Sophia were waiting for her. The tears came again as Bella ran over and hugged the women.

"It's going to be all right, Bella," Mrs. Moon whispered in her ear. "God has got you in the palms of His hands, baby."

Then how is it that the Ozzys were able to find me in the palms of His hands? But she dared not voice her thought aloud to Mrs. Moon. It was for God's ears only.

Silence suffused the house. Mrs. Moon sat on the couch, with little rivers of tears running down her plump cheeks, while Sophia's nostrils were opening and closing like butterfly wings, as she squinted her eyes in fury.

Bella had just told them the entire story, leaving nothing out.

"God . . . God is going to get them," Mrs. Moon said in despair. "People that evil must feel the wrath of God's hands."

"I was so stupid." Bella hung her head in shame. "But I thought I was doing the right thing. I wanted to help them and to show Papa he was wrong about me."

"I should have seen them for what they were." Mrs. Moon shook her head from side to side. "I'm a Holy Ghost–filled woman and two demons were in my house and I never even knew it."

Sophia finally spoke. "Because you weren't looking for it, Mama. They said they were pastors, and you let your guard down. That's all."

"Yeah, but some pastors are evil too. That man with that long scar on his face, tugging on his ear like a little *ginnal*," Mrs. Moon said, referring to a con person. "I should have seen him through the Holy Spirit."

"We see them now. And if it takes me the rest of my life, I'm going to find them and get back Bella's daughter," Sophia said.

"It's his daughter too," Bella reminded her in a small voice. "And I agreed to give them the baby."

"That may be true, but *they* told you that you would still be in the baby's life. *They* promised you that they were going to give you that apartment, and it wasn't even theirs." Sophia shot to her feet and began pacing the floor. "*They* told you that they were going to give you the money to go to college, and they did nothing. So in my book, *they* stole your baby."

"But what can we do?" Mrs. Moon asked. "It's obvious they don't have a church by that name, if they even have a church."

"I'm beginning to think they're not even pastors." Sophia looked at Bella. "I think they were in Port Antonio searching for a vulnerable young lady that they could use. Sorry, Bella."

Bella nodded in agreement. She believed what Sophia was saying was true. Everything was all a lie.

"God will take care of those two, Bella," Mrs. Moon said. "I hope one day soon you'll get to see your daughter, but for now we just have to place her in God's hands."

That night Bella twisted and turned, plagued by one nightmare after the other. She saw a faceless baby crying in pain, but try as she may, she wasn't able to move toward her to help. Then Reverend Ozzy appeared, with the long scar on his face, grabbed the baby by her leg, and dangled her over a pit filled with hungry alligators. Bella woke up in a sweat, her heart flip-flopping in her chest.

"Please help her, Lord. Please. I'm begging you, don't let them hurt her." Bella was praying again without even realizing it.

She fell asleep again, and this time Daddy Dearest decided to pay her a visit.

So you went ahead and had your demon spawn, huh? Burchell's face was filled with maggots and other insects feasting on his rotting flesh. *But then it went poof and disappeared.* He bent over and laughed like someone had sprayed him with laughing gas. *Ugly Bella had an ugly duckling, and it's about to die.*

Again, Bella jumped out of her sleep, her body shaking from fright, cold sweat pouring down her face. Fear for her daughter held her in a chokehold, and she had no idea what to do.

"Always pray when in doubt, baby." Her mother used to tell her that when Bella complained about being bullied and was not sure what to do. "God will fight all your battles if you let Him."

So even though Bella had stopped believing in prayer, because she felt God hadn't fought her battles against her bullies and her father and now the Ozzys, she didn't have any other options.

I might as well give it another try, she thought, heartbroken. *What else do I have to lose?*

Bella fell to her knees, rested her head on the edge of the bed, and prayed, "Lord, it's me, Bella. Uh . . . I . . . uh . . . I haven't really prayed in a while, and I think you know why. But I don't know what to do, so I'm asking you, please to help my daughter. I don't know where she is or what the Ozzys have done with her. Please don't let her suffer like I did. Don't let them treat her badly. She's too small and will surely die. Please, I'm begging you to protect her. Thank you and amen."

Bella stayed on her knees for a few more minutes, crying silently for her baby and wondering where she would go from here. One thing was certain; she would never stop looking for her child.

Chapter Thirteen

"Bobby, what are we really going to do with that?" Rachel Osbourne, aka Mrs. Ozzy, pointed to the sleeping baby in the crib in the beautiful nursery, her eyes narrowed and her nostrils flaring in anger. "With that godforsaken birthmark on her face!"

"That is your daughter," Bobby Osbourne snapped. "Remember?"

"My daughter? Oh, no, sir. That's *your* daughter, *Reverend Ozzy*. I can't have kids, remember?" There was a nasty grin on Rachel's pretty face, and her eyes were cold like Popsicles.

"Are we going to keep playing games or use this baby to finish the job?" Bobby's eyebrows went up as he stared at Rachel. "We've had her for a week now. When will you get over it?"

"How am I supposed to act like a mother to that . . . that . . . little monster? Huh? Look at me." She struck a pose in her short shorts, with one bare leg in front of the other. "And look at that thing. How could anyone believe she's my daughter? How did she get that awful thing on her face, anyway?"

Bobby shrugged. "Babies get birthmarks all the time. It's no big deal. Plus, who cares?"

"Bella doesn't have a birthmark,' Rachel continued, as if Bobby hadn't spoken. "I thought she would be so perfect."

"Birthmarks are not usually inherited, Rachel. Again, who cares? We will get rid of her after we get rid of your husband."

Rachel's face lit up. "You're right. I need to stay focused on the plan and all that money we're going to get." She leaped into Bobby's arms, wrapped her legs around his waist, and locked her hands tight around his neck. "We'll be rich, and we'll travel the world." She nibbled on his earlobe.

Bobby gave her a long, hard kiss. "Then it will be just you and me, baby." He playfully slapped her on the behind. "Your husband will be home tomorrow. Make sure you and your newborn are all settled in and waiting for him when he gets here."

Rachel hopped off him, pouting. "Why was it so important for him to get an heir?" she asked, wondering what motivated her husband in this regard. "His father is long—"

The loud ringing of Rachel's cell phone echoed in the nursery. The baby began to cry.

Rachel took up the phone, looked at the caller ID, and sucked her teeth. "He's probably calling to see how his wife and daughter are doing."

"Answer it, and play nice," Bobby hissed before he strolled out of the room.

Rachel rolled her eyes at his back. "Hi, hon."

"Hello, darling." Her husband's voice was breaking in and out. He was calling from Africa. "Is that our little princess crying? Is she okay?"

Rachel rolled her eyes. "Yes, she's fine. Just hungry. I was just going to give her a bottle now. Hold on." She rested the phone on the couch and went over to the crib. She took the crying baby into her arms and reached for the full bottle on top of the chest of drawers. Balancing the baby in the crick of her arm, she picked up the

phone and lowered herself onto the couch. "We're back."
She popped the bottle in the baby's mouth and watched
disdainfully as she began to suck hungrily.

"Aww, my little Gabby was hungry," he said when the
crying tapered off.

Her husband had named the baby Gabrielle and
affectionately called her Gabby. Rachel couldn't care less
and had gladly agreed to the name he had chosen.

"Gosh, I love her so much," he gushed. "My beautiful
little princess. I wish you'd reconsider breastfeeding,
darling."

"We talked about this already. I don't see the difference
between breastfeeding and the bottle, except for me
getting some floppy breasts." Rachel's voice went up a
few decibels.

"Okay, okay. I didn't mean to upset you," her husband
said in his soothing voice. "You know I want the best
for both of you. And, by the way, I love your beautiful
breasts."

Rachel smirked. "Thank you, baby. Don't worry. Our
daughter is healthy, even though she's a preemie." She
made kissing sounds, as if she was kissing the baby.
"She can't wait to meet her daddy in person."

"I'm going to have a serious talk with her as to why she
didn't wait for her daddy to come back home before
she came into the world." He laughed.

Rachel gave a loud fake laugh. "She's going to tell you
that she was too excited to meet her parents."

The couple talked about their daughter for a little
while longer.

"I can't wait to see you tomorrow, darling," Rachael
gushed into the phone. "I miss you."

"I miss you too, babe. See you and our daughter soon. I
love you both."

Rachel hung up the phone and snatched the bottle out of the baby's mouth. The baby started to cry again, but she ignored her and lowered her back into the crib. She then walked out of the nursery into the hallway. "Mattie," she shouted from the second-floor landing of the elegant spiral stairway.

Mattie appeared from the direction of the kitchen, wiping her hands on the white apron around her waist. "Yes, Mrs. Osbourne?"

"The baby is crying." Rachel strolled into the master bedroom, which was next to the nursery, and slammed the door shut. She didn't wait to see if Mattie would attend to the baby, because the housekeeper had been doing so since she had brought her home.

Deep in her thoughts, Rachel lay on her stomach across the king-size bed in the bedroom, her big booty in the air. If anyone had told her two years ago that she would be planning her husband's death now, she wouldn't have believed it. Why did she have to resort to such a drastic measure? Well, because her rich husband refused to touch the twenty million dollars his father had left in his will for his future grandchild.

"Your father is dead!" Rachel had said to her husband, stating the obvious, a few weeks after they got married. "He won't know what you do with the money, nor will he care."

"*I* will know," her husband had retorted, frowning. "That money is for our children, and I won't touch it. It's not like we need the money, anyway, do we now?"

Rachel sighed loudly. Her husband was a very rich man, which was why she had married him. Of course, he didn't know this, because he was too dumb. But why should she settle for what her husband had when there were millions of dollars rotting away in the bank?

And it was this greed that had led to her teaming up with Bobby and formulating the plan to get all her husband's money (and now her supposed daughter's) all for herself. Blood would be shed, and lives would be lost, but those were the usual casualties of war. And this multimillion-dollar war she didn't intend to lose.

Rachel reached for the cell phone beside her on the bed. She speed-dialed Bobby's number. They had more details to work out before her husband came home tomorrow.

Rachel drove to the Norman Manley International Airport in Kingston and parked the BMW convertible illegally in front of the arrivals entrance. She had the top down, and the bright sun was bathing her with its yellow glow. A light wind blew her long, straight hair across her pretty face.

Some passersby gave her curious glances, while a few men openly gawked at the hot beauty in the hot ride. And Rachel just loved it. Ever since she was a child, she had craved being the center of attention, and usually she was.

After peering at the gold watch on her slim wrist, she looked over at the arrival doors; people were exiting the terminal with rolling suitcases and big bags. She listened to the excited squeals as loved ones reconnected with hugs and kisses.

Then she saw him, all six feet of dark handsomeness. He was wearing a casual pair of jeans that hugged his narrow hips, a white T-shirt that showed off the bulging muscles of his torso, and white sneakers. He walked out of the terminal to the busyness outside.

Rachel watched as he fished out his aviator sunglasses from the carry-on bag over his shoulder and placed them on his face. She saw him looking around, searching for his ride, so she stood up in the car and waved excitedly, her ample breasts swinging to the motion.

He saw her, and his face broke out in a big grin before he trotted the short distance to the waiting car. He threw the bag in the back seat. "Hi, darling. I thought Deacon Brown was coming to get me." He opened the passenger door and slid into the car beside his wife, removing the sunglasses.

Rachel sat down and said, "I was missing you so much that I decided to come and get you myself." She leaned over and kissed him passionately.

"Wow. I missed that, and I missed you." He wrapped his wife in his arms, smelling her perfumed hair and feeling her heart beating against his. "I promise I won't be going on another missionary trip until our daughter turns eighteen." He laughed and pulled back to look at her.

You won't be going on another missionary trip because you'll be dead, Rachel thought, but instead, she said, "I'm going to hold you to that. God knows I don't know why you had to run off to that forsaken place, anyway."

He frowned. "When we met, you told me how much you admired the missionary work that I planned on doing. Now it's a problem."

"Well, I . . . I do think it's nice of you," Rachel replied, trying to smooth things over. She couldn't afford to upset him now. "It's just that I miss you when you're not here, and now we have our young daughter to take care of."

"My sweet little Gabby." His brown eyes lit up. "I can't wait to see her and kiss that little pretty face. Good God, I'm a father." He shook his head from side to side, as if in wonder. "I still can't believe it sometimes."

Rachel tried very hard not to roll her eyes. *You're a father to ugly Gabby.* "You better believe it, Papa." She laughed and started the car. After glancing in her rearview mirror, she put on her turn signal and navigated her way into the flow of traffic leaving the airport.

During the two-hour trip home, Rachel listened as her husband gushed about their daughter and the great plans he knew God had in store for her.

"Daddy told me before he died that I was going to have two very important ladies in my life—my wife and my daughter. And he was so right."

It's because of your daddy that you're going to die. "He sounds like he was such a wise man. I'm so sorry he passed away before I could meet him." Rachel reached over and touched her husband's leg with one hand, keeping the other firmly on the steering wheel.

"He'd have loved you. Mommy too."

Rachel highly doubted that but kept her mouth shut.

To Rachel's husband, who was enjoying the scenic view and chatting nonstop, the time flew by on the road. Soon the couple was pulling up in front of the tall white gate of their mini-mansion. In the middle of the gate were two beautiful golden angels with wide-open wings, as if they had just flown in and landed in that spot.

"These angels represent the real angels who are protecting this house," Rachel's husband had told her the first day she visited the house. "My mother always told me as a child that angels are always around me."

Just then the gate opened for them. Rachel drove in and parked in the driveway. She then opened her car door and jumped out.

Her husband noticed her long bare legs in the too-short skirt but decided to wait until later to speak to her about her wardrobe. Again. He would also remind her that she was a first lady and the church was watching her. Again.

He got out of the car, grabbed his bag from the back seat, then went and took his wife's hand in his. Together they entered the house, where Mattie was waiting for them.

"Hello, beautiful. I've missed you," he said to Mattie.

Rachel watched as her husband gave Mattie a kiss on the cheek and a big hug. She still couldn't understand why he treated the hired help like family. It didn't matter that Mattie had been with the family before he was even born. She was still a servant. Period.

Rachel's eyes met and held Mattie's over her husband's shoulder. She took her right hand and moved it across her throat, another warning to Mattie to keep her mouth shut, or she would take off her head.

Mattie quickly looked away.

"Where's my little princess?" her husband asked as he set Mattie loose.

"I just fed her and put her down for a nap. Go on up." Mattie gave him a little smile and glanced briefly at Rachel before scurrying away.

Just then the doorbell rang. "I'll get it," Mattie announced. She changed direction, walked to the front door, and opened it before finally taking her leave to the kitchen.

"Look who is here." Rachel's husband took long steps to meet the man who had entered the house, and the two exchanged man hugs. "It's so good to see you."

"Welcome back, little brother. You look well," Bobby said, smiling brightly, as he stepped back.

"It's great to be back, Bobby," Pastor Maurice Osbourne Jr. replied. "Thank you for being there for my wife when she went into premature labor. Man, I thought we had two more months to go and I would be back home before the birth."

Bobby winked, tugging on his earlobe. "Maurice, you know you can always count on me to look after the Osbourne ladies. I'm a very proud uncle."

Maurice beamed. "Speaking of which, I'm going up now to meet my daughter in person for the first time."

"Go on. I'll be here when you come back down," Bobby replied.

"Babe, are you coming?" Maurice asked Rachel.

"I'll be there in a minute, hon. Go and have a little private time with our baby."

Maurice kissed her on the cheek before he bolted up the stairs, taking the steps two at a time.

Both Rachel and Bobby watched him until he disappeared from their sight.

"That's one happy papa right there," Bobby muttered, his eyes now dark with hatred. "Always thinking he should have everything in life."

"One of his favorite Bible verses is Psalm thirty-seven, four. 'Delight thyself also in the Lord: and he shall give thee the desires of thine heart.' So I guess he does feel like he has it all."

"Look at you, quoting Bible verses and all." Bobby glanced up the stairs, then lightly slapped Rachel on the behind.

Rachel giggled and said, "You're forgetting that I'm a first lady, sir?"

"Oh, no, ma'am. After all, I'm *Reverend Ozzy*."

The two burst into laughter. Their deception was like a runaway train, headed off course and into an abyss.

Maurice tiptoed into the nursery. His heart raced in his chest as he approached the crib where his daughter lay. He stood looking down at the small baby, curled up in sleep, her little face turned to the side. An intense love he had never known before flooded his being as he gazed down at baby Gabby.

Almost robotically, he reached down and awkwardly lifted the baby into his arms, her face turned up toward his. "Hi, Gabby. This is Daddy," he whispered.

With the baby in the crook of his right arm, Maurice used his hand and gently traced the large white birthmark on baby Gabby's face. "Look at this beauty mark you have here. I'm going to make sure you grow up knowing how beautiful and loved you are."

As if she understood the kind and loving voice and what he had said, baby Gabby's eyes blinked a few times.

"Hey, you know your daddy is here." Maurice kissed her on the forehead. "You woke up because you heard your daddy's voice, didn't you?" He planted kisses all over the baby's face.

Maurice walked over to the nursery couch and lowered himself onto it, his daughter in his arms. Rocking the baby from side to side, he stared unseeingly ahead. His spirit was troubled. A man of faith who was led by the Holy Spirit, Maurice had learned to trust his instincts.

"Something is brewing, and I need to find out what," he muttered. "God, how I wish you were here, Father. I could use your advice right now."

Part Two

Chapter Fourteen

Maurice Osbourne Jr.

Four years earlier . . .

"I want to tell you something, son," Pastor Maurice Osbourne Sr. croaked as he lay propped up in his bed with at least six pillows behind his back, the sheet pulled up to his chin.

"Don't tire yourself, Daddy. We'll talk when you feel better. You just got home from the hospital." Maurice Osbourne Jr. sat down on the edge of the bed and took his father's leathery hand in his.

"No, this has waited long enough. I have to clear my conscience before the Lord calls me home." He began to cough violently, and his feeble body shook in response.

Maurice quickly got up and reached for the glass of water that Mattie had placed on the bedside table earlier. He guided it to his father's mouth so he could take a few sips of the water.

After he had settled down, the reverend dropped a bomb. "You have an older brother, Maurice."

Maurice froze, looking at his father like he was Frankenstein's monster. "Excuse me?"

"He's two years older than you."

Maurice reached over and felt his father's forehead to see if he was running a fever. "Maybe they released you too early from the hospital."

"Maurice, please stop and listen to me."

Maurice took a deep breath and settled back on the edge of the bed. "Daddy, you're not making any sense right now. I don't understand what you're saying."

"It happened about three years after your mother and I got married. I met a woman at a convention in Kingston, where I was preaching for a week. I don't know what it was and why I even succumbed to the devil, but I invited her back to the hotel one night. Before you know it, I slept with her and betrayed your mother. But, most importantly, I betrayed God.

"It was the first and only time I ever did anything like that. It was just one night, but that's all it took, I guess. A few months later she showed up here at my church one Sunday with her big stomach. I managed to take her back to the office to talk, and that's when she told me she was pregnant. I didn't believe her at first, because I had slept with her only once. But she was adamant that the child was mine."

Maurice didn't utter a word. His body was so still.

"I gave her some money I kept in the office and told her to go away and not to bother me again," Pastor Osbourne Sr. said, tears now running down the sides of his wrinkled face. "What was I supposed to do? I loved your mother, and I couldn't afford to lose her. I didn't want to bring shame to her and her family."

Maurice's mother, Elise Duke, was a wealthy socialite in Mandeville from a generation of doctors: her great-grandfather was a dentist, her grandfather was a cardiologist, and her father was a neurologist. At thirty years old, she met the handsome thirty-one-year-old associate pastor Maurice Osbourne when he visited her church as a guest speaker. It was love at first sight for both. With their parents' blessings, the two were married within a year of meeting and courting, and then they moved into the mini-mansion Elise's parents had given them as a gift.

"You know she wouldn't have been able to handle such scandal," Pastor Osbourne Sr. continued. "And I would have lost my church as well. I couldn't afford to lose everything that mattered to me because of one mistake I made."

Maurice finally spoke. "So you took the cowardly way out?" He took a deep breath. "Have you ever seen him?"

"Yes. Once. It was two years later when she showed up at church again with the boy. I took one look at him, and I knew he was definitely my son because the resemblance was so strong."

"Which means he resembles me as well," Maurice added. Everyone always commented that he was his father's mini, because they looked so much alike.

Pastor Osbourne Sr. nodded. "She left before service was finished. But my hands were tied, Maurice. Your mother had just given birth to you after trying for five years. We were happy and at a good place in our lives, and I just couldn't—"

"You just couldn't own up to your mistake and take responsibility for your action," Maurice snapped, jumping to his feet. "You abandoned your son, Pastor." He began pacing the carpeted floor, his brows knitted with anger.

"I was ashamed of myself for a long time, my son. I kept the secret for years from everyone, including your mother. She lost her battle with cancer a year ago, not knowing of my deception, and in some ways I'm happy I never hurt her."

Pastor Osbourne Sr. went on, "I have made peace with God, and I want to make peace with you and your brother before I leave this world."

"Do you even know where he is?" Maurice asked. "Do you even know if he wants anything to do with you?"

"I'm sure he doesn't. He probably hates me, and I don't blame him."

"Neither do I. God knows what kind of life he's had and is living."

"I'm hoping it wasn't too bad. I prayed for him every day and asked God to provide for him and protect him." Pastor Osbourne Sr. used the back of his hand to wipe his wet face. "Can you ever forgive me, son?"

Maurice turned and looked down at his father, the man he had loved and respected all his life. His father was his hero and could have done no wrong in his sight. But this? "I'm . . . I'm still in shock, Daddy. I mean, I never expected anything like this."

"I know, son. I'm a man that has fallen short, but I have taught you that forgiveness is for all. I know the Lord has forgiven me for my sins, and I'm hoping you will as well." Pastor Osbourne Sr. looked up at his son desperately. "I love you, Maurice. You know that."

Maurice felt the tears welling up in his eyes. His father had done wrong, but who was he to judge? He hadn't always been the perfect Christian, either. Mind you, he didn't have an illegitimate son, but as Jesus said in John 8:7, "So when they continued asking him, he lifted up himself, and said unto them, He that is without sin among you, let him first cast a stone at her."

Maurice walked over to the bed, reached down, and hugged his father. "I forgive you, Daddy. I wish none of this had happened, but we can't go back. We have to try to move forward, okay?"

Pastor Osbourne Sr. clung to his son for a long time, joy filling his soul. "You're an awesome man of God. I'm glad you're at the church."

Maurice had earned his bachelor's degree in theology at Bethel Bible College two years earlier, and one year after he'd been ordained, he had begun working as an associate pastor at the church. He had been getting ready to join a group of his former college classmates as a foreign missionary to Africa when his father had a stroke. He wanted to follow in his father's footsteps someday but thought he had enough time to fulfill his dream of spreading the gospel abroad. So he'd decided to put his plans on hold until his father made a full recovery. Now he had found out he had a brother, whom he didn't know, whom he had to find.

The following Sunday Maurice drove to Kingston and went to the church where his father had met Julie, his brother's mother. He knew it was a long shot, but that was all they had to go on. After twenty-six years, Julie and her son were probably living in another parish and maybe even in another country. But it was worth a try.

Maurice sat through the service, glancing around and studying faces, trying to spot the woman his father had described. Again, this was years later, and she wouldn't look the same. He even looked for a young man who resembled him and his father. But no luck.

After the service, Maurice went and introduced himself to the young pastor. He learned the pastor was fairly new to the church, having been there for only three years. He didn't bother to broach the subject of Julie and walked out of the church, disappointed.

"I guess this was just a wild-goose chase, after all," Maurice said aloud as he walked to his car, which he'd parked on the street, outside the church grounds.

"You said something, son?"

Maurice turned and saw a short elderly man leaning on a cane on the sidewalk beside his car. He was so consumed by his thoughts, he hadn't noticed the small man.

"Oh, just speaking to myself, sir," Maurice replied. "Sorry about that."

"Nothing to be sorry about, young man. I do that all the time. It's okay to speak to yourself, but when you start answering back, you have a problem." He began to laugh, showing large gaps in his mouth.

Maurice laughed as well. "Let's hope I don't get to that stage."

The man composed himself and raised his head higher to look up at Maurice, who towered over him. "They say everyone has a twin out there somewhere. I say you're the spitting image of Sister Julie's boy."

Maurice's heart began racing. "Really? I'm Maurice Osbourne, by the way." He reached out and shook the shaky right hand that the man offered.

"Elder Bott. Oh, dear Lord. Julie's boy's name is Robert Osbourne. But everyone calls him Bobby."

"Isn't that something? So who's Julie?" Maurice tried to play it calm. He didn't believe in coincidences. Julie was the name of the woman his father had had the one-night stand with, and she had a son that resembled him and had his last name. It had to be her.

"Julie was a member here for many years, but she passed away last Christmas. Poor lady had a heart attack and died in her sleep. God bless her soul."

Maurice's heart sank. Julie was dead. But what about her son, his brother? "Do you know where I can find her son?"

The man paused and gave him a curious look. "Do you know Julie? And why would you want to find Bobby?"

Maurice knew he had to tell the man something to get more information from him but not so much that he would reveal his father's secret. At least not yet. "To be honest, I learned recently that Julie's son and I may be related. I came here today from Mandeville to see if I could find them, because I knew Julie attended this church."

"Isn't that something? I knew it the minute I saw you." The man smiled, as if he was excited to be a part of a mystery story.

"So do you know where Bobby is?" Maurice stared at him, almost holding his breath.

"That boy doesn't come to church anymore since his mama passed. But I heard he works over at National," he said in reference to National Baking Co. Ltd.

"Thank you. I appreciate it very much."

"You're welcome. If you find Bobby, tell him Elder Bott says he's looking for him in church soon. Okay?"

"Okay, sir. Have a wonderful evening." Maurice opened his car door and got in. He quickly turned on the air conditioner, as the ripe Jamaican sun was out in full force. After reaching for his cell phone, he dialed his family's home number.

"Hello? Osbourne residence," Mattie answered.

"Hello, Mattie. It's me."

"Hi, Maurice. Where are you? I woke up this morning, and your father told me you had some business to take care of."

"Yes, I had to make a quick trip. How is Daddy doing?"

"Well, he ate a little breakfast, but he's still looking weak and pale."

"Is he up? Can I talk to him?"

"Hold on. I'll go up and tell him to take up the phone by his bed."

As Maurice waited for his father to come on the line, he wondered about Bobby. Did he know who his father was, and if so, would he be receptive to meeting the man who had abandoned him?

"Maurice? Did you find them?" His father's voice broke his thoughts.

"Hi, Daddy. Not really." He told his father about the conversation with Elder Bott.

"I'm sorry to hear that Julie passed away. I hope she found it in her heart to forgive me," Pastor Osbourne Sr. said. "So she gave him my last name?"

"I guess so. I didn't ask too many questions."

"Are you going to see Bobby?" Pastor Osbourne Sr. asked in an anxious voice.

"I was thinking I'll stay overnight and go to National tomorrow to see if he's working there."

"Sound like a good—" His father began to cough.

Maurice waited until he stopped. "You're not sounding too good, Daddy."

"I'm better now that you're close to finding Bobby."

"I'll be home tomorrow. Take it easy and get some rest, okay?" Maurice disconnected the call, started the car, and maneuvered his way into the light traffic on Red Hills Road. He drove to New Kingston and booked himself a room at the Pegasus Hotel for the night.

The next morning, after ordering room service, Maurice showered and dressed in the same white shirt and black pants he had had on the day before, minus his jacket. He had never planned on staying overnight in Kingston.

After checking out of the hotel, he drove down to Half Way Tree Road and parked across the street from National. With the engine still running, he watched for a while as men and women went in and out of the building and large vans loaded with products left to make deliveries.

Maurice looked intently at the faces of the men to see if any resembled his own. None did, and after a few minutes, he gave up. Then he shut off the car, hopped out, and clicked the door locks. After looking up and down the street, he waited until there was a break in the traffic, then quickly made his way across.

"Hello, sir," Maurice greeted the security guard sitting in a small booth at the front gate.

"Good morning. May I help you?" He was a large, burly man with a thick beard and small, beady eyes.

"Yes, I was wondering if Bobby Osbourne has arrived for work yet." Maurice smiled.

"Hold on a sec." The guard reached for a phone on his desk and punched a number. "Hey, Bobby there?" He listened for a few seconds. "Tell him someone is at the front gate for him."

Maurice rubbed his hands together nervously as he waited. He had a whole speech planned, but now that he was about to see Bobby, he completely forgot everything. So he prayed silently. *Dear Lord, please give Bobby a heart of understanding and compassion. I know what my father did was wrong, but I know you have forgiven him. Please help Bobby to do the same, so we can move forward, in Jesus's name.*

"Yo, Macky. Who wants me?"

Maurice looked up and saw a tall man walking toward them. The guide pointed to him, and the man turned his attention to Maurice Jr. In a few quick strides the man came to stand in front of him.

"Hello, Bobby. I'm Maurice—"

"Maurice Osbourne Jr. I know who you are."

Maurice was shocked. "So you know . . ."

"That you're my brother? Yes. I know." The smile that didn't reach his eyes seemed to stretch the long scar running down Bobby's right cheek. "I guess your father finally decided to tell you the truth, huh?"

Maurice nodded and said, "But how long have you known about him? You never contacted him."

Bobby tugged on his earlobe. "I've known for most of my life. My mother told me when I was fifteen years old who he was, but that he wanted nothing to do with me."

"I'm sorry. It was complicated, with him being married and a pastor."

"I came to his church for the first time when I was twenty years old. I just wanted to see what he looked like. It was there that I saw you as well. I walked away and vowed never to come back, but I did again on New Year's Sunday after my mother passed away. I heard a few members saying that your mother had also passed the year before."

"Yes. I'm sorry about your mother."

"Thank you. I'm sorry about your mother as well."

The two brothers stood in the sun and scoped out each other. There was that strong resemblance that Elder Bott and Pastor Osbourne Sr. had spoken of. But even though they were only two years apart in age, Bobby looked at least ten years older than Maurice, and the scar on his face seemed to add a few years.

Maurice wondered how hard life had been for Bobby. "He wants to see you."

Bobby tugged on his right ear again, and Maurice pondered if it had something to do with the scar or if maybe it was just a habit of his. "Does he?"

"Yes. He had a stroke last week and is in poor health. He wants to try to make amends."

Bobby stared out at the traffic for a while, deep in thought.

Maurice looked at him, praying inside that he would agree to see their father.

"I would like that," Bobby finally responded.

"Really? That's great, Bobby. He'll be so happy. I'm very happy." Maurice knew he was blubbering, but things were really turning out better than he had expected.

"We have to learn to let go of the past and move on. You know what I mean?" Bobby locked eyes with Maurice.

"Yes, I know what you mean, and I appreciate it. I hope you and I will also be able to get to know each other."

Bobby flashed that lopsided grin. "I would like that, little brother. Man, it feels good saying that. I was an only child, but now I have a brother."

"And a father who wants to get to know you."

"Yes, and a father. God is good."

"Speaking of God, Elder Bott said he's expecting you in church soon."

"Ah, so that's how you found me. I was just getting ready to ask you."

"Yes. I went back to the church where Daddy met Miss Julie. I ran into Elder Bott, and he saw the strong resemblance between us and mentioned it. One thing led to another, and here I am."

"That's just God right there," Bobby said. "He wants us to be connected, and I couldn't be happier."

"Let exchange numbers. I'll also give you our address, and I hope you can make it down to see Daddy soon."

"I'm off this Friday. I don't mind at all making the drive down to see the old man." Bobby took his cell phone out of his jeans pocket and programmed in the numbers Maurice gave him. He then hit the SEND button, and Maurice's cell phone began to ring. "Now you have mine as well."

"It's really nice to meet you, Bobby. And to see you harbor no ill will toward my father shows what an amazing man you are," Maurice remarked.

"Oh, I was angry for a long time. Don't get me wrong." Bobby frowned. "We had it real rough. So when I found out I had a father with financial means, and he refused to help so he could cover up his little secret, I was very mad. But I promised my mother before she passed away that I would forgive and let it go. That's why I came back to see Pastor after she passed."

"I'm glad you're willing to try to let us all move on from here."

Bobby nodded. "I won't lie that I'm over it all. I'm still working on it. But I'm more open-minded now to finally meet my father."

"So this Friday? I have a leader's meeting at the church in the morning, but I should be home at two o'clock."

"Yeah, my little pastor brother. Following in our father's footstep." Bobby used his shoulder to nudge Maurice's.

"I'm fulfilling my destiny, but I'm looking forward to going around the world as a foreign missionary as soon as Daddy gets better. There are millions of people who have never heard the gospel. I would like to introduce them to the true and living God."

"I see. Well, I have to go back and finish up my job before I get fired." Bobby pointed over his shoulder with his thumb toward the building. "Those breads won't bake themselves."

Maurice felt a little uncomfortable. Two brothers—the wealthy pastor and the baker. There was so much healing that needed to be done. "Thanks for talking to me, Bobby. I'm looking forward to seeing you on Friday."

"That's what's up." Bobby shook Maurice's hand before he strolled back through the gate toward the building.

Maurice made his way across the street to his Camry, used his key fob to click the doors open, then got in behind the steering wheel. His smile was as broad as the Causeway Bridge.

He quickly drove off and didn't see Bobby watching him from the side of the building, hatred and anger blazing in his eyes, his hands folded into fists at his sides.

Chapter Fifteen

Bobby pulled his beat-up pickup truck in front of the immense house that stretched toward the sky like a huge eagle. He had seen it before, of course. In fact, he had passed by many times since his mother finally revealed the identity of his father before she died.

He had lied to Maurice when he told him he had known about the reverend since he was fifteen years old. Had he known, he would have blown the good pastor's cover and forced him to step up to his responsibility a long time ago. But he had found out only a few days before his mother died.

"That's okay, though, Father," Bobby muttered under his breath as he looked at the house. "I have big plans for you and your little prince. You both owe me big-time, and I'm going to make sure you pay up in full."

Just then the gate opened, and Maurice was standing before him. He waved Bobby through, and Bobby drove the truck down the long driveway and parked behind Maurice's car.

Bobby got out to greet his brother. "What's up, man?"

"I'm glad you didn't change your mind, Bobby." Maurice exchanged a man hug with Bobby.

"Nah. I told you I want to meet the old man and bury all that mess from the past. It's time to move on."

"Come on. He's waiting for you upstairs."

Bobby followed Maurice into the house. He paused in the elegant foyer and looked up at the enormous crystal chandelier in the high vaulted ceiling. Then he glanced up at the long, elegant spiral stairway, covered with a rich burgundy and gold oriental carpet, that led to the second floor.

"This is a beautiful house," Bobby said to Maurice. "It must have been nice growing up here."

Maurice cleared his throat. "It was okay. Come on. Let's go up."

It was okay? He was raised in a freaking palace, and that's all he can say? Bobby pondered as he mounted the steps behind Maurice. *We lived in a run-down one-bedroom shack in the ghetto, with roaches and mice. But it's all good. Just wait and see.*

"Daddy, look who is here." Maurice walked over to the bed where Pastor Osbourne Sr., looking weak, lay. He turned to Bobby, who stood, uncertain, at the bedroom door. "Come in, Bobby."

Bobby entered the bedroom, one step at a time, his eyes locked on his father.

Pastor Osbourne Sr.'s eyes got teary as Bobby approached him. Not only did he see facial features similar to his own, but behind the haunted eyes, he also saw Bobby's pain. "I'm so sorry, Bobby." His voice sounded like he had sand in his throat. "If only I could do it over—"

"But you can't!" Bobby snapped.

Pastor Osbourne Sr. flinched, and Maurice stepped closer to his father, his eyes locked on Bobby.

Bobby took deep breaths, his chest rising and falling, as he tried to compose himself. "I'm sorry." He rubbed his hands down his face. "It's just that I spent my entire life wondering why you never wanted me. What did I do wrong for my own father to reject me?"

"I understand how you must feel. Please have a seat." Pastor Osbourne Sr. waved weakly at the La-Z-Boy chair by his bedside. "I'll try to explain everything."

Bobby took a seat in the chair, and Maurice perched himself on the edge of the bed beside his father. Apprehension filled his face as he looked at Bobby. Where was the man who told him a few days ago that he had forgiven their father and wanted to move on?

Pastor Osbourne Sr. began, "Bobby, I know—"

"Wait. Before you begin, I must apologize again." Bobby tried to do damage control. "I guess seeing you for the first time face-to-face brought back some of the anger I had as a child. But I can assure you, I have come a long way from that place, and that's why I'm here. I've forgiven you in my heart, and I want to do so in person."

Pastor Osbourne Sr. beamed. "My God is really good. I've prayed so much for Him to touch your heart, and He did. Glory be to His name."

"I'll go down and check with Mattie about when we'll be having dinner. You two need some time to speak in private." Maurice got to his feet and walked to the door. He paused and turned to look at Bobby. "Are we okay here?" His voice was calm, but his eyes held a warning.

"We're cool. I appreciate the time to hear what my father has to say. I've waited a long time for this." Bobby's eyes watered. "Thanks, man."

Maurice left, feeling a little more certain that Bobby was on the up and up.

That evening, Maurice lifted his feeble father out of bed and brought him downstairs to sit at the dining table. He wasn't too keen on doing so, but his father had insisted that he wanted to have a nice dinner at the table with his two boys.

Mattie had gone all out and had made a feast of jerk chicken, gungo peas and rice, steamed fish, fried plantains, and even a baked potato pudding. She was shocked when she learned the identity of their dinner guest, but quickly tried to make Bobby feel welcome.

The four of them enjoyed a delicious dinner as they laughed and conversed. Bobby told them about the wonderful life he had had with his mother in a nice area in uptown Kingston. While he admitted that he had dropped out of the University of Technology after his first semester, he noted that he had enrolled in a vocational program offered by the Human Employment and Resource Training, National Service Training Agency and had learned construction. He had had his own business for a while, but things had got slow, so he'd taken a full-time job at National. He also did construction projects on the weekends.

"You are such a hardworking man," Pastor Osbourne Sr. commented. "I'm proud of you, Bobby."

"Thank you, sir." Bobby blushed. "I believe in working for what I want."

"And we're going to help you any way we can, Bobby," Maurice told him. "In fact, we're doing an addition to the church, because our membership just keeps growing. With your experience in construction, I'm sure we can find some work for you. That's if you ever feel like relocating down here."

All three pairs of eyes were fixed on Bobby.

Bobby flashed that lopsided grin of his and tugged on his ear. "That's something I'll definitely think about. With my mother gone, I have no relatives in Kingston. Plus, it would be great to get to know my father and brother. And you too, Mattie."

By the time dinner was over, Pastor Osbourne Sr. had grown tired, and Bobby insisted on taking him back upstairs. He lifted his father in his arms and carried him upstairs, with Maurice following. The brothers then left Mattie to get their father ready for bed and returned downstairs.

They talked until the wee hours of the night, Bobby telling one lie after the other, and Maurice sharing as much of himself as he could with his brother, not knowing that this would later be used against him.

"Maurice! Maurice, open up!" Mattie pounded on Maurice's bedroom door early the next morning. "It's your father."

It took Maurice a few seconds for Mattie's voice to register before he bolted off the bed and ran to the door, wearing only his pajama bottoms. "What's wrong with Daddy?"

"He's not moving." Tears were pouring down Mattie's face, and her eyes were open wide with fright.

Maurice ran down the hallway, into his father's bedroom, and over to the bed. "Daddy?" He gently shook his father's shoulder, but it felt like a piece of a log. "Daddy, please open your eyes." He shook him again, but no response. Maurice knew there was no life left in his father. Still, he placed his fingers on Pastor Osbourne Sr.'s neck. But there was no pulse. He was dead.

"What's going on?" Bobby ran into the bedroom frantically. "I heard Mattie shouting and . . ." His voice tapered off as he moved toward the bed, where his father lay. "Why isn't he moving?" He looked at Maurice and noticed the small streams of tears flowing down his face. "Ah, man. Come on." Bobby's shoulders shook as he wept.

"Mattie, please call the coroner." Maurice sniffled loudly and pulled the sheet up to his father's neck, as if he were cold.

Bobby's crying tapered off, and he wiped his face with his hand. "I just met him, man. It's not fair."

Maurice patted him on the back and walked out of the bedroom.

Once the coroner confirmed that Pastor Maurice Osbourne Sr. was dead, he and his assistant took the body away. An autopsy later confirmed that the pastor had suffered another stroke as he slept.

It seemed as if the entire community was out for the pastor's funeral two weeks later. The church was packed from front to back. Bobby took a leave of absence from his job and was by Maurice's side all the way. Many people were curious about Bobby, and the only explanation Maurice gave was, "He's my brother."

This started the rumor mill, but the brothers paid it no mind. Some of the elders, mothers, and deacons demanded a full explanation of how their deceased pastor had an older son out of wedlock, but Maurice offered none.

"Let my father rest in peace," Maurice snapped one evening soon after the funeral, when Elder Davis came to the house, demanding some answers.

"Well, how old is he? Who is his mother?" the elder quizzed.

"That's none of your concern, sir. All you need to know is that my father was a good man. He served this community for many years, and he has gone home to find rest. He has done his time on earth and deserves to be remembered for all the good he did."

However, not all the leaders of the church agreed. They were even more upset by fact that Maurice had announced after the funeral that he was going to take over his father's church. A few of them had their eyes on the pulpit and wanted to be senior pastor.

But Maurice knew his parents had built that church from the ground up, and it had grown and flourished under their care from a measly thirty members to over two thousand and counting. It was also his father's dream that Maurice would one day take over as senior pastor of the church. Maurice felt he owed it to his parents to preserve their legacy.

"You're not ready to be senior pastor," one of the deacons told Maurice at a meeting that was held days to discuss the future of the church. "You just graduated from Bible school and have been an associate pastor for only a year now."

"I know I don't have as much experience as some of you in this room," Maurice admitted, "but I have the passion and desire to lead this church. I know I can do it."

"What about your plan to be a foreign missionary?" one of the mothers of the church asked. "In fact, you were about to go to Africa when your father got sick. Why not just go and preach the gospel to those that have yet to hear it?"

"I plan on doing both, actually," Maurice informed the group. "I'll pastor the church with two associate pastors. This will allow me to travel abroad as a missionary for a few months or weeks each year, as the pastors will be in charge while I'm away."

However, this decision was met with resentment. Maurice knew he had his work cut out for him.

Two weeks after they buried their father, the brothers were sitting in the backyard of their father's house, enjoying a beautiful, sunny afternoon.

"You remember that offer you made me if I ever wanted to relocate?" Bobby asked Maurice.

"Offer still stands, man. I have this big house to myself."

"You have everything to yourself, little brother. Don't you?"

Maurice looked over at Bobby, trying to read him. As expected, Maurice had inherited all his parents' money, most of which was his mother's and gone to his father after her death. This included the large trust fund Maurice had gotten after his grandparents died. The house was also a part of his inheritance.

"I have what my parents left me." Maurice locked eyes with Bobby. "Is that a problem?"

"No, no, no. No problem at all," Bobby replied, quickly backtracking, having realized that he had spoken his thoughts aloud. "I know you're a man who works hard, despite your money."

"That I do. I never take anything for granted."

"From what I hear, you're getting a fight down there," Bobby said in reference to the church.

Maurice shrugged. "That's expected, with my father gone. But I strongly believe my steps are ordered by the Lord and I'll prevail. I know in my heart this is what I'm supposed to do, and no one is going to stop me."

"Let me help you with that."

"Really? So you're moving down? That's great, Bobby. Daddy would like that."

"I'm sorry I didn't get more time with him. But I'll help with the construction that's going on and also keep an eye on things when you're off in the jungle, sharing the gospel and hiding from lions."

Maurice threw his head back and laughed out loud. He hadn't done that since his father died. "You're one funny guy. You know that?"

Bobby smiled. "I'll get an apartment and—"

"What do you mean, get an apartment? Why can't you live here?"

"This is a nice house, Maurice, but I like my own space. Don't worry. I'll be over here every day, eating some of that good food that Mattie keeps throwing down. This will be my home away from home. Okay?"

Maurice hesitated. "I guess that's all right. I still don't see why you can't stay here. Clearly, we have enough space, but we'll do it your way. I'll speak to the foreman next week and make sure you're added to the payroll. It's good to have you on board, Bobby."

"It's good to finally be on board, Maurice." Bobby tugged on his earlobe as he settled back into his chair, vengeance, and anger swimming in his gut. "Go and take your rightful place in that church, little brother. I've got your back."

And that was what Maurice set out to do. He never backed down, meeting over and over with the leaders and the members of the church and laying out his plan for the congregation's continued growth and success. Eventually, he got the support of his church family and the majority of the church's leadership, and he became senior pastor of Christian Deliverance Church of God.

Chapter Sixteen

A year later, Pastor Maurice Osbourne Jr. was in top form, ministering to his church as if he was born to preach.

"I know it gets hard sometimes, but never take your eyes off Jesus," Maurice shouted into the microphone. "Remember when you're lying on your back in the valley, at the lowest point in your life, the only thing you can do is look up! Look up to Jesus! I say look up!"

The church was in an uproar. People were on their feet, stomping and screaming. Some were in the aisles, dancing and weeping, and others had their hands in the air, praising and speaking in tongues. The Holy Spirit was in full force that Sunday morning at Christian Deliverance Church of God.

The handsome, charismatic young pastor—he was now twenty-six—slipped off his black pin-striped jacket and handed it to one of his assistants. A few young ladies began screaming, and it wasn't because they were in the spirit. At least not the Holy Spirit. It was their pastor's broad, muscled physique, now more conspicuous with his jacket off, that did the trick.

Sitting in the back row of the church, Rachel rolled her eyes at the women's shenanigans. Unlike them, she was calm, cool, and trying to be classy. No screaming and hollering to get the pastor's attention, well, not in the church, anyway. All that would be done in private when she finally roped in the rich young pastor.

"Keep your eyes on the Lord, my brothers and sisters. He'll see you through." The pastor's eyes scanned the church from front to back, his sincerity and passion for his message etched across his face. "Look at me. When my father passed away, many people didn't think I was fit to take over this church. But look at me now."

Hallelujahs and amens rang out, while a few deacons and elders looked down at their feet from guilt.

"Whatever God has in store for you must be for you. Don't ever forget your steps are ordered by the Lord. Glory."

After the service, Maurice slipped back into his jacket, wiped his sweaty face with his handkerchief, and drank a tall glass of water before making his way to the front of the church. Sandwiched between the two associate pastors, he stood by the doors and greeted his members with a handshake and a few words.

Rachel lingered there, waiting for most of the church-goers to leave. At one point, she looked around and realized that a few other ladies had the same idea. Her face twisted up. She glared at the women, her eyes shooting daggers.

After engaging in a standoff for a few minutes, Rachel sucked her teeth loudly, stood up, pulled down the hem of the formfitting bright red dress, and walked to the exit, to stand in front of Maurice.

"Good afternoon, Pastor. Great service today." Rachel's ruby-red lips parted in a seductive smile, and her eye-lashes fluttered over her catlike hazel eyes.

"Thank you, Sister Rachel." Maurice shook her right hand, amusement and curiosity shining in his eyes. Rachel had been attending church for a few months now, and she had been flirting with him ever since she first introduced herself.

"Ahem." One of the associate pastors cleared his throat, and Maurice quickly dropped Rachel's hand.

Rachel shot the associate pastor a nasty look before fixing the smile back on her face. *Old goat.* "Enjoy the rest of your evening, Pastor. I'll see you next week." With that, she sashayed away, her large behind rolling from left to right, her hips moving as if she were dancing.

Maurice and the associate pastors stared after her until she disappeared down the stairs.

"You have to stay away from that woman," said associate pastor Elder Davis, as if he, too, hadn't gotten an eye full of Rachel's assets. "I know trouble when I see it."

"I'm not in contact with her, Elder Davis. She's like any other sister in this church," Maurice replied, but he took another quick glance over his shoulder in the direction Rachel had gone.

"You're a wealthy, handsome young pastor," Pastor Bailey, the other associate pastor, commented, stating the obvious. "So all these women are vying to be your wife."

Maurice laughed out loud, but he was aware of all the attention he got from the ladies. He had been getting it from a very young age, before his parents passed away, largely due to their wealth and his rugged good looks. This had persisted when he became an associate pastor and had only intensified when he took over the church. He knew one day he would like to get married, but with his plans to be a foreign missionary and to devote himself to his church, it wouldn't be anytime soon.

"Don't worry, gentlemen. I'm married to the church for now." Maurice excused himself and made his way back to his office to review a few documents that the church's secretary had left for him before he headed home.

Approximately two hours later, he leaned back in his chair, yawned, and stretched his hands over his head.

Time had gotten away from him. "Okay, that's it. I'm hungry." His stomach rumbled, as if to confirm his statement. "Luckily, I'm not preaching tonight." Maurice grabbed his car keys and briefcase, then walked out of his office and pulled the door shut behind him.

Maurice made his way from the church to the parking lot, where his conservative but brand-new white Toyota Camry was parked. Even though he had inherited a lot of money after his parents died, he was a simple brother. So instead of a luxury car, which he could have easily afforded, he'd gone with something more modest.

Maurice pressed the key fob, and the car doors clicked open. He opened the front passenger door and threw his briefcase on the seat. As he turned to walk to the driver's side of the car, he bumped into a very soft feminine body.

Instinctively, Maurice reached out and grabbed her around the waist when she stumbled back. "Oh, I'm so sorry. I didn't see you."

"That's okay." Rachel looked up into his face and swiped her tongue across her glossy red lips. "You can bump into me anytime." She winked seductively.

Maurice shook his head and smiled. "Rachel, what am I going to do with you?"

"Marry me?"

Maurice threw his head back and laughed. He stopped suddenly when he realized he was the only one laughing. "Huh?" He took a few steps back to create some much-needed space between them.

Just then Rachel laughed out loud. "You should see your face. I'm just joking, Pastor." But she really wasn't. "As my pastor, I'd like your advice on a problem I'm having."

Maurice hesitated. "What problem is that?"

"We could have dinner, and I'll explain it to you."

"I don't think that's a good idea, Rachel."

"Why not? You have to eat sometime, and I'm hungry too. This way we kill two birds with one stone."

"People talk, and I don't want to start any rumors. Sorry."

"So you can't have dinner with a member of your church while she talks to you?" Rachel wasn't giving up. "Stop thinking about what people will say or do, and just live for you. That's what I do."

Maurice admitted inwardly that this trait was one of the things about Rachel that intrigued him. She didn't seem to care what anyone thought about her. He had never seen her before the day she stepped foot in his church about six months ago, and that had him curious.

"How about I speak with you at the church on Wednesday, before Bible studies? Say sixty thirty p.m.?"

Rachel paused, then said, "Sounds good to me. I'll see you Wednesday evening. Thank you, Pastor."

Maurice nodded and said, "And please remember to bring your Bible. The Lord has given me a Word to share, and we're going to have a wonderful time in the Holy Spirit."

Rachel bit her lips and nodded her head. "I'm looking forward to it . . . and to a lot of other things to come." With that said, she strolled out of the parking lot to the street, where her beat-up old Nissan Sunny was parked.

Maurice watched her for a few seconds, shook his head, and smiled before getting into his car. On the drive home, Rachel consumed his thoughts. Yes, he had sexy, beautiful women all around him. Some were more conservative in style and action and seemed more spiritual than Rachel. But, for some reason, none grabbed his attention like Rachel did. There was just something about her that intrigued him.

Later on that night, Maurice relaxed in his living room, watching the news. He had eaten his delicious dinner of oxtails and butter beans with rice and peas that Mattie had prepared, and he was stuffed and content. He heard the doorbell ring and wondered who it was, as he wasn't expecting anyone. He pulled himself to his feet.

"I'll get it," Mattie yelled from the hallway.

Maurice reclaimed his seat on the soft black leather couch and propped his legs on the leg rest.

Moments later his brother Bobby swaggered in and said, "What's up, little brother?"

Maurice's face lit up, and he stood again to hug to brother. "You tell me, Bobby. I didn't see you in church today."

Bobby took a seat on the matching couch across from his brother. "I had to finish a job out of town today, so I couldn't make it. You know how the construction business goes. You take it as you get it."

Maurice bobbed his head in understanding. "I'm glad you decided to move here."

"It was a good move," Bobby replied. "Here I am one year later. I started up my own little construction business again after completing the job at the church, have a nice little apartment in town, and get to eat all the delicious food that Mattie prepares at my little brother's house."

Maurice smirked. "Yeah, life is really good, isn't it?"

"Could get even better for you too."

"Really? How do I do that?" Maurice reached for the remote beside him on the couch and switched the television channel.

"More like who could do that? You think I don't see that sexy little thing coming to church every Sunday to see you. What's her name again? Rebecca?"

"Rachel. And please don't forget I'm a Christian and the pastor of that church."

"Hey, you have to get married sometime," Bobby replied. "Don't you, Pastor? Why not choose someone hot who likes church?"

Maurice chuckled lightly. "You really have a way with words. But for the record, I'm waiting on God to send me the right woman to be my wife. Until then, I'm doing fine just the way I am. Thank you very much."

Bobby held up both hands. "Okay. You can't say I wasn't looking out for you."

"Maybe I should introduce *you* to Rachel. In case you haven't noticed, you aren't married, either."

Bobby chuckled. "I'm not the marrying kind, Maurice. At least not yet. I'm waiting on the Lord too."

"Stop joking about the Lord, Bobby. That's why I want you to come to church more often and start attending Bible studies. I also think you and I should pray and study the Bible together. What do you say?"

Bobby jumped to his feet. "I say it's time for me to get my dinner, which Mattie left for me, and head home. I can't stay tonight."

"Bobby, come on."

Bobby turned to Maurice, the scar on his cheek stretching to accommodate his gigantic grin. "Maurice, you know I always come to church, except if I have a job that I have to finish. And I'll start coming to Bible studies when I can make it. How is that?"

"That sounds like a plan. Thank you."

"No, thank *you*. I appreciate you not giving up on me because I'm not as much a Christian as you."

"It's my duty as a child of God and a pastor. John fifteen, sixteen, says, 'Ye have not chosen me, but I have chosen you, and ordained you, that ye should go and bring forth fruit, and that your fruit should remain: that whatsoever ye shall ask of the Father in my name, he may give it you.' So I'll never give up on you, my brother."

"That's good to know, my brother. Listen, do you hear my stomach growling? I'm going to grab my dinner from the kitchen and head home. Good night."

"See you Wednesday night," Maurice yelled at his back. "And please bring your Bible."

Chapter Seventeen

Maurice looked up from the laptop on his desk when Rachel walked into his office Wednesday evening. "Hello, Rachel."

"Hi, Pastor. How are you?" Rachel reached for the door handle to close the door.

"Please leave the door open," Maurice stated. "Elder Davis is down the hall, in his office, but his door is closed. We have the privacy we need to talk."

Rachel went and lowered herself into the chair facing the pastor without waiting on an invitation.

Maurice shut down the laptop and closed it. Leaning back in his high-back chair, he turned his eyes on Rachel. "So what's going on? How can I help?"

"I just moved here from Spanish Town so I can make a fresh start. However, I've been unable to find a job, and the little money I brought with me is almost gone. Everyone here knows you, so I was wondering if you could maybe refer me to somebody. I know you don't know me well, but I'm a hard worker. After everything I've been through, I just need a break. You know?"

"A break from what? if you don't mind me asking. Why did you leave Spanish Town?"

This was the opening that Rachel was waiting for. "I didn't know my father, and neither did my mother. She was a prostitute and a drug addict, so most of the time she didn't know who she was sleeping with. One day after school, when I was twelve years old, I found her dead in the run-down apartment that we lived in. She died from a drug overdose."

Rachel continued, "I was placed in a girls' home but had to run away when I was seventeen years old, after I finished high school, because I was almost raped. I lived on the streets for a few years, running with a wild crowd, until I got a job working as a waitress in a restaurant when I was twenty years old. I worked there for five years before I decided to go to evening classes. I didn't want to end up like my mother. So I took three CXC exams last year—math, English, and principles of business—and passed them, with the hope of going to college one day soon."

Maurice was now leaning forward, his elbows resting on the desk, his sympathetic eyes on Rachel. "How did you end up here in Mandeville?"

"Some coworkers invited me on a boat ride to Treasure Beach. We drove through Mandeville, and I was interested in the little I saw. I came back here a month later by myself to get a feel for the place because I wanted to relocate. I really liked it, and here I am."

"I'm sorry for everything you've been through, but I so admire the way you took ahold of your life and turned it around for your good," Maurice told Rachel.

"God did that," Rachel replied. "One of my neighbors didn't stop harassing me to come to church until I finally agreed. I enjoyed the service and went back. Before you know it, I was there almost every Sunday. That's one of the reasons why I wanted to move from Spanish Town. I didn't want to fall back in the old crowd I used to run around with. I wanted a change. A new scenery."

"You are just amazing, Rachel. And I'll do what I can to help you in getting a job. I'll start asking around tomorrow, and I will also have my secretary speak to a few of our members here who are entrepreneurs. Let's trust God to continue making a way for you."

"Thank you, Pastor." Rachel's smile lit up the office. "I knew you were the right person to ask for some help."

"Let's get you a job first and then see how much I've helped. Do you have a copy of your résumé with you?"

Rachel reached in her handbag, pulled out the résumé, and handed it to him.

"Good." He opened the top drawer of his desk and tucked the résumé in it. "So, are we ready for Bible studies?"

"Ready as Freddy, sir."

They entered the sanctuary, laughing and talking, oblivious to the curious stares they received and the whispers around them.

The very next week Maurice's secretary, Sister June, called Rachel and asked her to come to the church to meet with Maurice.

"Rachel, thanks for coming by on such short notice," Maurice greeted her in his office. "I have some good news for you."

Rachel sat and looked at him anxiously. "You got a job for me?"

Maurice nodded. "We have two choices, actually. Do you know our associate pastors, Elder Davis and Pastor Bailey? They'll be in charge when I'm away on my missionary trip in Africa. We're looking for another assistant to work with Sister June here at the church. Our membership keeps growing, praise the Lord, and as such, we have a lot more to do."

He continued, "Brother Tyson, who owns the printing store in town, is looking for an assistant as well. I gave him a copy of your résumé, and he said he would love to speak to you about the position. So the choice is yours."

Rachel's eyes widened, as if she couldn't believe her good fortune. "I'm grateful for both opportunities, but I think I'm more interested in working at the church. The Lord has been so good to me that this would be another way for me to help do something in His house, for His people."

Maurice sucked it all up like sweetsop. "Of course, you'll have to have an interview with the associate pastors as well, but you already have my vote. I think you'll be a great addition to the Christian Deliverance Church of God staff."

But the two associate pastors didn't share Maurice's enthusiasm about the prospective employee.

"Definitely not." Elder Davis folded his arms across his round stomach as he looked over the top of his bifocals sitting on his broad nose.

"Not happening," Pastor Bailey spat. "That woman wants to work here only so she can get closer to you. You think I don't see what she's up to? You better open your eyes and see what's going on here, Pastor."

"What's going on here is a young lady who has turned her life around and needs a job, and we have one that she is qualified to do. Working here at the church will also help strengthen her walk in Christ. Isn't that what we do here, Pastors?"

It took some back-and-forth before the associate pastors reluctantly agreed that Rachel could have the job. Maurice didn't really need their approval, but as Rachel would be working mostly with them, especially when he was away, he wanted them on board.

Rachel started her new job the very next day.

Over the next few weeks Maurice watched as she won over the associate pastors and Sister June with her strong work ethic, charming personality, and her sense of humor. He, too, ended up spending a lot of time with her, and before long he was smitten by her.

"Do you like mannish water?" Maurice asked Rachel one evening after work. This was goat's head soup.

"I love it." Rachel licked her lips, as if she had actually tasted the soup. "I haven't had it since I moved here."

"We can change that. Mattie makes the best mannish water ever. You're welcome to come by the house and join us for dinner."

"Really? I would like that. Thank you."

"No problem," Maurice remarked. "You can follow me in your car, or you can ride with me, and I'll bring you back here later to retrieve your car."

"I'll just ride with you. My car has been acting up lately."

Maurice frowned. "I'll get someone to look at it tomorrow. We don't want you to break down at night, when you're alone."

The two chatted nonstop during the ride from the church to Maurice's house. Like most people, Rachel was in awe of the big, beautiful house.

"It's absolutely breathtaking," she told Maurice as he gave her a tour of the place.

"Thank you. Come on. Let's go around the back. Mattie will bring us the soup when it's ready."

Rachel and Maurice sat on lounge chairs, laughing and chatting nonstop. Maurice told her about his upcoming trip to Africa.

"So I'll be leaving in a couple weeks for four months. I'm excited to go, but a little nervous to leave the church for so long. But it's a great opportunity, and I'm lucky I get the chance to work with such great people."

"We'll miss you, but the church will be fine," Rachel informed him. "Go and do what's in your heart. They are the ones that are lucky to get a great pastor all wrapped up in one."

"Thanks. I'm going to treat not only the physical body but the spiritual one as well. All my patients will be hearing the gospel of Christ."

"You heal the soul, you heal the man. Isn't that—?"

"Well, well, well. What do we have here?" Bobby swaggered into the backyard, his lopsided grin on his face. "Am I interrupting?"

"Shut up, Bobby, and come and join us," Maurice responded.

"Hello, Bobby," Rachel greeted the newcomer. "You're in time for Mattie's mannish water."

"I wouldn't miss it for the world." Bobby found an empty chair and sat down. "So how's the job going at the church, Rachel? I stopped by last week to see my brother, but you were busy on the phone."

"Wonderful. I do enjoy working there. Thanks for asking."

"I'm sure you do." Bobby looked over at Maurice and winked.

"Bobby," Maurice warned.

"You know I'm not paying Bobby any mind, Pastor." Rachel playfully cut her eyes at Bobby, and Maurice laughed.

They enjoyed Mattie's mannish water that evening and a few more evenings after that. Rachel gradually became a regular at Maurice's house. They caught a movie here and there, dined out a few times, and even visited and prayed for the sick at the hospital together.

People were watching and talking, but at this point Maurice no longer cared. Whether he wanted to admit it or not, he was falling for the beautiful church assistant, and there was nothing he could do about it.

A few weeks later, Maurice left with a group of pastors organized by Bethel Bible College on a missionary trip to Africa for four months to spread the gospel in places that weren't previously accessible because of political barriers.

Though very busy, he called and checked up on Rachel every chance he got.

By the time he got back from Africa, he could no longer deny his feelings for Rachel, and the two became inseparable.

One evening, after they had just had dinner and were cuddling on the couch, Maurice pulled away and stood up. "I love you, Rachel Wyatt," he declared as he lowered himself to his knees on the carpeted floor of his living room.

"I love you too, Maurice. Very much." Rachel's eyes widened with excitement.

He took a little black box out of his pocket. "I think about you when you're not with me, and I don't want to continue living my life without you. Will you marry me, Rachel?" He opened the little box, and a huge diamond ring glittered under the light.

Rachel squealed and threw herself into Maurice's arms, knocking him over onto his back, with her on top of him.

The pastor laughed out loud. "Uh, is that a yes?"

"Yes, yes, yes." Rachel planted little kisses all over her fiancé's face.

That Sunday morning, with Rachel having moved on up from the back row to the front row, Maurice announced their engagement to the congregation. There was a loud uproar, with everyone talking loudly at the same time. A few disgruntled single ladies even stormed out of the church.

Most of the members were not receptive to an outsider coming in and claiming their pastor, especially one as "worldly" as Rachel. Some of the mothers and elders met with Maurice individually, but he refused to listen to anyone.

"Listen, baby," eighty-year-old Mother Zena said to Maurice one afternoon at the church. "I understand you're a young man with raging hormones."

"Mother!" Maurice stared at her pointedly. "Please watch what you're saying. I'm young, but I'm your senior pastor."

Mother Zena sucked her teeth and even rolled her eyes. "Young bud nuh know stamm," she said in patois. *A young bird didn't know about storms.* "Pastor, you're not aware of the danger that lies ahead."

"There is no storm or danger here, Mother Zena," Maurice informed her. "I'm just a man in love with a wonderful woman, whom I'm going to make my wife. That's all."

Mother Zena stormed out of his office as fast as her arthritic legs could go.

And there was much more to come for Maurice. "I'm following my heart," he told his associate pastors when they, too, met with him in his office at the church.

"Or are you following something else?" Pastor Bailey glanced down at his pastor's lap, his eyebrow rising and falling suggestively.

"Listen." Elder Davis leaned forward in his chair. He locked eyes with Maurice "You're a young man. We know you have . . . hmmm . . .well, certain needs."

"Elder!" Maurice jumped to his feet. "You may be my elder, but I'm your pastor, and I will be respected." He pounded his fists on his desk. "I'm marrying Rachel, and that's final."

Three months later, a little over a year since they'd met, Maurice and Rachel wed. The small wedding party at the church consisted of the bride and groom, Bobby, the associate pastors, sporting deep frowns, and a few other members.

The newlyweds honeymooned at Half Moon Hotel in Montego Bay.

Rachel Wyatt was now Mrs. Rachel Osbourne, the wife of the rich, handsome young pastor.

Chapter Eighteen

"Rachel, isn't that dress a little short and too tight for church?" Maurice stood at the bottom of the stairs, watching as his new bride descended. The little red dress hit her mid-thigh and was glued to her body like a second skin.

Rachel ignored her husband and strolled past him toward the front door, her red clutch tucked under her arm.

"Rachel?" His eyebrows met in a frown, and he had a look of disbelief on his face.

Rachel paused, sighed loudly, and turned around to face Maurice "My dress is okay, sir." She rolled her eyes and rested one hand on her hip in defiance.

"What's gotten into you?" Maurice closed the gap between them and stood facing her. "You are the first lady of the church. You have to conduct yourself accordingly."

"I'm a sexy young first lady who loves her body, and I'm not afraid to show it."

The pastor took a deep breath, willing himself to deal with the situation in an appropriate manner. He felt that little voice telling him he made a mistake rising up in his spirit, but he quickly dismissed it. This was his wife, he loved her, and he was going to make sure their marriage worked. *Till death do we part, right?*

"Your body is also the temple of the Lord. Or has that changed since you got married?"

Rachel heard the anger underlining her husband's words and realized that she had probably pushed him too far, too soon. "Babe, I think the dress is fine, but if it makes you feel better, I'll change. Okay?"

Maurice took a deep breath. It had been three months since they had got married, and he was beginning to notice changes in his wife that he didn't really care for. Rachel had always been a free spirit, and he had known that going in. It was one of the things that had attracted him to her. But she had never been this argumentative. After their honeymoon, Rachel had begun dressing more provocatively, her new look bordering on sleazy. Her makeup had become bolder, her hair wilder, and her behavior less modest.

The leaders at the church were getting concerned about this, as members were watching, and the public was talking. This first lady was the complete opposite of the late Mrs. Maurice Osbourne, who had been highly admired and liked by the community before she passed away.

"We're already running late. Just grab a shawl or something and cover yourself up." Maurice stormed out of the house and stomped over to the car in the driveway.

A minute later Rachel joined him. The silence in the car on the way to church was deafening. The rift between the pastor and his first lady was getting bigger and bigger, and the ink hadn't yet dried on their wedding certificate.

"What's that you wore to church today?" Bobby grabbed Rachel's forearm and shook it roughly. "Are you trying to get a divorce before we get what's ours?"

"Let go of me." Rachel pulled her arm away from Bobby, took a few steps back, glaring at him. "So I overdid it a little bit today. I'll do better, all right?"

"You make sure you do, Rachel," Bobby warned. He glanced out into the hallway to see if anyone was coming to join them in his brother's living room. "I've been waiting all my life for this, and you're not going to blow it for me. Understand?"

Rachel sucked her teeth. "Did you forget what's in this for me, too? We're partners, aren't we? Just relax and let me do what I do best. I'll placate my husband later." She swiped her tongue across her lips and winked at Bobby. "Pastor can't stay mad at his first lady when he sees her in the nude."

Bobby smirked and tugged on his earlobe. "Come here for a sec," he commanded.

Rachel peeped out into the empty hallway before she walked into Bobby's arms. They shared a hot, passionate kiss before quickly pulling apart. They were mindful that they were at Maurice's house and he was right upstairs.

They didn't see Mattie as she crept toward the kitchen.

"I have to run. See you later?" Bobby pinched Rachel's bottom, and she giggled. "We need to discuss that new development."

"Count on it. I have to visit a sick member at the hospital tonight." Rachel stuck out her tongue, as if she was about to throw up. "Woman is darn near ninety years old and refuses to die. What's her old behind waiting for? The Rapture?"

Bobby roared with laughter. "Watch your mouth now, First Lady. Go and pray for your member so she can receive her healing."

The two laughed until tears ran down their faces.

"Care to share the joke?" Maurice asked as he entered the living room, wearing a blue and white Adidas sweat suit that complimented his smooth, dark complexion and showed off his lean, muscular body.

"You know your brother is a mess, darling." Rachel used her fingers to wipe the tears from her face. She moved closer to Maurice and hugged him around the waist.

Maurice looped his arm around his wife's shoulders. "Yeah, that's Bobby for you. So what are you up to, man? Want to make a run with me to Deacon Mayne's house? I heard he's not doing too well."

"Nah." Bobby shook his head and rubbed his flat stomach. They had just had dinner. "I'm going to take my overstuffed behind home and get some rest. I have a big job to start tomorrow."

"That's cool. I hope everything goes well." Maurice looked down at Rachel. "Sweetheart?"

"Remember, I have to visit Mother Bentley at the hospital."

"Oh, yes. I forgot." Maurice leaned down and planted a light kiss on Rachel's lips. "See you later." He and Bobby left the house together. Rachel looked after them until they disappeared out the front door.

She then ran upstairs and quickly changed into one of her "granny" dresses, as she liked to call them. It was a simple white dress that fitted her loosely and stopped at her knees. She pulled her long hair back into a tight bun and applied only a thin layer of lip gloss to her lips. The look was completed with a pair of white pumps.

"Okay, First Lady," Rachel said to herself as she stood before the full-length mirror. "Let's get this crap over and done with. Bobby is waiting."

Rachel drove to the hospital, parked around the back, and turned off the engine. She sat in her car for a long time, trying to work up the nerve to enter the building. This was her first visit alone as the first lady of the church. She had made sure all her other visits to the hospital were with Maurice or other members from church.

Rachel didn't want to go in, because she knew she was expected to pray for Mother Bentley. While she could very well recite a few scriptures and mumbled some words, she didn't feel like playing the role right now. "Gosh, I can't wait for all this to be over," she said aloud. "I'm getting real tired of all this church rubbish."

Just then the cell phone in her hand rang. She looked at the caller ID and saw it was Bobby calling. She answered. "Hey."

"Finish praying already?"

Rachel sucked her teeth loudly. "I'm still in the parking lot."

Bobby snorted. "Just forget it and come on over. Who is going to tell Maurice? Mother Bentley? From what I heard, she's darn near comatose, anyway."

"You're right." Rachel started the car. "I'll see you in a bit."

"Make sure you come around the back and pull in the garage," Bobby reminded her. "You and your new BMW are becoming well known around here."

Rachel drove the car her husband had bought her as a wedding gift to the house where her brother-in-law lived. It was a two-story building, and Bobby rented the bottom floor from an elderly man who spent more time in bed than out of it.

She pulled into the two-car garage, which was all Bobby's because his landlord no longer drove, and turned off the engine. After exiting the car, she walked through the side door and entered the small, neat living room. Bobby was waiting for her in the middle of the room, buck naked.

"Well, hello again." Rachel reached up and undid her hair bun as she moved slowly toward Bobby. "Now, this is way better than a hospital visit." She turned her back to Bobby, and he lowered the zipper on her granny dress. The dress fell off her shoulders and puddled at her ankles.

In record time she was as naked as her lover. Bobby scooped her up in his arms, took her into the bedroom, and threw her on the full-size bed that came with the furnished apartment. The two made love as if their lives depended on it, with a sense of ferocity and familiarity. Something they had been doing for many, many years.

Moments later Bobby propped himself up on the pillows, with Rachel sandwiched between his legs, her head resting on his broad chest. "So tell me again what my brother said about his inheritance." Bobby pulled on a joint he had just lit, and blew the smoke up toward the ceiling.

Rachel related the conversation she had had with her husband a few days ago. "We were talking about his parents and grandparents when he said that his grandparents had left him an inheritance when they died. Then he dropped the bomb that his mother had also left a large sum for his heir." She paused for a moment. "I didn't want to probe too much and get him suspicious, so I asked, like, how much. He said a few million dollars."

Bobby whistled. "So if you have a baby with Maurice, then your child is entitled to that money."

"But you know I can't have kids, Bobby. You know I had my tubes tied after we had that miscarriage five years ago."

Rachel and Bobby had met six years ago at the Asylum Nightclub in New Kingston. Rachel had been hanging with her girls and rocking a micro minidress, with her assets on full display. Bobby had been on the prowl with his boys that night and had been dealing a little weed on the side. The two struck up a conversation and spent most of the night on the dance floor, gyrating against each other. That night Rachel went home with Bobby, and they became inseparable.

Three months after they began dating, Rachel got pregnant, but she miscarried in her first trimester. She took that as a sign that she wasn't supposed to have kids, or she would end up like her poor excuse for a mother, so she had a tubal ligation. Bobby agreed with the decision. He didn't want to be a father. After all, he had grown up not knowing who his father was. Now that decision was about to rob them of millions of dollars that they felt entitled to.

"I know," Bobby remarked and took another drag on the joint, "but my dear little brother doesn't."

Rachel raised herself up and looked at him. "What are you saying?"

"I'm saying you, my dear, are going to get pregnant"—he wiggled his index and middle fingers—"and have a child for your husband. We'll then get rid of Maurice, as we originally planned, then the little brat too. You as the surviving, grieving widow and mother of the heir will get all the riches."

"And then I'll marry you, my soulmate, and we'll live richly ever after." Rachel placed light kisses on Bobby's chest. "But we are back to the same problem. Where am I going to get a baby to fool Maurice that it's mine? Won't he know I wasn't pregnant? I say we stick with the plan and just whack my darling husband. I'll get everything he has, and we'll get the heck out of town for good."

Bobby shook his head and spat, "We're taking *everything* that belongs to me. And the money in that trust fund is mine." He pushed at Rachel, and she lifted herself off him. Bobby dropped the joint in an ashtray on the bedside table, jumped off the bed, and began to pace the floor. "He grew up in wealth, with parents who loved him, while I went hungry for days. My own father didn't want me. I never got a red cent from him. Everything went to the little prince."

Rachel watched him without uttering a word. Ever since Bobby's mother had told him who his father was before she died, his anger and vengeance toward his father and little brother had only grown.

Bobby carried on with his rant. "I came down here and watched them, planning on how I'm going to get what I was denied all my life. Then what do you know? Daddy dearest confessed his sins and sent little brother to find me. I mean, if that isn't God, then someone please tell me what it is. Then my father croaked the same night we met face-to-face. Can't you see this was just meant to be?"

Bobby paused and looked at Rachel. "I didn't have to kill the old man myself. God did it for me. You know why?" He answered his own question. "Because of what he did to me."

"You should have seen the look on that fool's face when I told him I stopped running with the wild crowd, went to evening classes, passed three CXC exams, and started going to church," Rachel interjected. She giggled and rolled over on her stomach, her big, bare bottom in the air.

Bobby chuckled and went to sit on the edge of the bed, facing her. "At least the story about your mother and the girls' home was true. I was surprised you shared that, because you never liked talking about it."

"You're right, but I figured it would earn me some sympathy points, and it did," Rachel told him. "I think that's when Maurice fell in love with such an awesome young lady."

They burst into laughter, high on their plan for revenge and wealth.

"Now you're my sister-in-law, and you are soon to be a wealthy widow." Bobby reached over and kissed her.

"And you said something about being a mother too?"

"Yes, about that. This is what we're going to do . . ."

Chapter Nineteen

"Darling, we'll get pregnant when the Lord says so." Maurice pulled his wife into his arms and cuddled with her on their bed. "We've been married for only ten months. Please give it some time."

Rachel sniffled in his shirt and nodded her head. "But I really want us to have a baby. I want to start a family with you."

"I want that too, sweetheart. Don't worry. God knows the desire of our hearts." Rachel's face was out of his sight, so he didn't see her rolling her eyes.

Rachel had just done a pregnancy test, and the result was negative. She was pretending to be devastated. "What if we consult with a doctor?" She raised her head and gave her husband that puppy dog look. "I was searching online, and there is an awesome ob-gyn at the Princess Margaret Hospital in St. Thomas. He got many reviews from mothers he helped have babies through artificial insemination and in vitro fertilization."

Maurice folded his lips and thought about it for a few seconds. "I don't really think we need to see a doctor. And why can't we find one here in Mandeville?"

"I don't want these inquisitive people in our business," Rachel replied. "You know everyone will be talking as soon as we leave that doctor's office."

"You're right. But I'm still—"

"Please, babes. For me? For our family?" Rachel reached up and kissed him with every ounce of skill she possessed.

Maurice moaned in response and returned his wife's kiss with a passion. "Okay, okay," he said when they broke the kiss. "I'll go with you for a consultation, but I'm not promising anything."

"Oh, thank you!" She planted kisses on his face. "I love you." Kisses on his nose. "You're the best husband ever." Kisses all over his face.

Maurice laughed, feeling good that he had made his wife happy. He loved that she wanted to start a family with him. He had grown up with a wonderful father and couldn't wait to be the same for his son or daughter. And a bonus was that ever since Rachel had told him a few months ago that she wanted them to try to have a baby, her whole attitude had changed. She was once again the Rachel he had fallen in love with—loving, caring, sexy, but modest and actively working at the church and by his side.

If she wanted a baby, Maurice was going to do everything he could to make that happen. His first lady deserved it.

So the next week Rachel, Maurice, and Bobby drove to St. Thomas to meet with Dr. Zandt. Maurice had shared with his brother his and Rachel's plan, and Bobby had insisted on driving them.

"I don't have any projects I'm working on right now, and both you and your wife have a lot on your minds. I'll drive you down," Bobby had told his brother. "I want to be an uncle, you know."

Maurice had gladly accepted, pleased that his brother had offered his assistance and supported their decision.

They arrived at the hospital around 11:00 a.m. Bobby parked in the parking lot at the front of the building, and the three of them made their way inside. They walked up to a receptionist's desk and asked for directions to Dr. Zandt's office.

"Go down the hall"—the young lady pointed over her shoulder—"and then take the second right on your left. Dr. Zandt is expecting you."

Maurice and Rachel took a few steps in the direction the receptionist had indicated, but Bobby didn't move. "I think I'll just stay here and keep this beautiful lady company until you guys come back." He winked at the receptionist, and she blushed and looked down at her desk.

Maurice shook his head in amusement, and Rachel subtly gave Bobby the beady eye. They then walked away and left Bobby at the receptionist's desk.

"Come in," a voice called out after Maurice knocked on the closed door.

Rachel and Maurice entered the office and came face-to-face with a small Asian man wearing a yellow and white suit, the pants clinging to his frame like spandex. He was standing behind his massive executive wooden desk and seemed to be a few inches short of the five-foot mark.

"Pastor and Mrs. Osbourne, welcome!" Dr. Zandt held out his hand and grasped Maurice's in a firm handshake. He then did the same with Rachel. "Please, have a seat." He waved to two chairs that were facing him, then re-claimed his seat behind the desk.

"So we are trying to get pregnant. Yes?" His smile looked more like a sneer, and Maurice disliked him immediately.

"Yes, we are," Rachel responded for the couple. "I did some research and learned that you're the right person to help us make this happen."

"You learned right, darling." Dr. Zandt snapped his neck from left to right and back. "Dr. Zandt is the best in the West. Hello." He and Rachel laughed at his humorless joke, while Maurice folded his lips.

Maurice's radar was on full alert. There was just something about Dr. Best in the West that didn't sit well with him. He wasn't sure what it was, but he would pray about it later and discern what the Holy Spirit was telling him.

"Babe?" Rachel nudged him in the side.

"Huh?" Maurice looked from her to Dr. Zandt and realized that he must have missed something that was said to him. "Sorry. What was that?"

"I said I would like to run some blood tests on both you and your wife to make sure you're in good health and also to assess if her uterus can support a pregnancy," Dr. Zandt said. "If everything comes back okay, then we have two ways to go, artificial insemination or IVF, which is in vitro fertilization. I would suggest we first try artificial insemination, which is the simpler of the two. If that doesn't work, then we can move on to IVF. But I have a feeling that won't be needed. Dr. Zandt can always tell. Hey!" He snapped his fingers.

I bet you can. "Please tell me some more about this artificial insemination." Maurice was now getting an attitude. His ego was taking a hit from the fact that he needed *assistance* in getting his wife pregnant.

Rachel, sensing the tension in the office, reached over and squeezed her husband's hand. He looked at her before turning his attention back to Dr. Zandt.

"Well, I'll do an intrauterine insemination, IUI, which is also called artificial insemination. You'll give me a sperm sample, which will be washed and prepared for the IUI procedure. I'll inject your sperm directly into your wife's uterus. This is more effective than regular intercourse. She would remain lying down for about a half hour or so, to be on the safe side. A week after that, we can do an ultrasound to see if the IUI was effective, or we can wait about fourteen days to do a pregnancy test to see if Mrs. Osbourne is pregnant. *And* I have a strong feeling she will be." He wiggled his index finger at Maurice.

The pastor felt a headache coming on. "You want me to . . . hmmm . . . to give a sperm sample? So I'll have to . . . to relieve myself in some container and save it?" His voice rose, and Dr. Zandt shrank back in his chair. "Is that what you're saying, Dr. Best in the West?"

"Honey." Rachel took Maurice's hand in hers. "Look at me." She waited until her husband's angry eyes met hers. "You promised to be open minded about this for me, for us."

Maurice practically yelled, "I'm a man, a real man. I can and will get my wife pregnant when it's the right time. We don't need Dr. Best in the West."

"Okay, fine." The tears began to leak down Rachel's pretty face. "I'm sorry I brought it up. I didn't mean to offend you, honey. I just want your baby so bad."

Now Maurice felt bad. Here his wife was doing everything for them so they could start their family, and he was letting his pride get in the way. He could at least try it once, even though he didn't like Dr. Best in the West. "Don't cry, darling. Come here." He pulled Rachel into his arms. "Maybe we could try it and see what happens. Okay?"

"Really?" Rachel wrapped her hands around his neck and hugged him tightly.

"That's wonderful." Dr. Zandt clapped his hands. "I'll go over my price, then I'll examine both of you. Little baby Osbourne, here we come for you!"

Rachel giggled, while Maurice gave him an annoying look.

After going over his high price for the procedure, Dr. Zandt had his nurse come in and escort Maurice to the examination room. There, she drew his blood, then asked him to step outside so Dr. Zandt could examine Rachel.

"So are we good?" Rachel asked Dr. Zandt when they were alone in the office.

"As I told Bobby, you bring me a healthy young woman and I'll make sure she gets pregnant with your husband's sperm."

"For the money that we're paying you, you better make this happen." Rachel's serious eyes met his. "There can be no mistake here, Dr. Zandt. We're paying you a lot of money to make sure this woman gets pregnant."

"I'm a doctor, not a magician, Mrs. Osbourne. Do your part and choose the right woman, and I'll do mine and make sure she conceives. I need the money, and you need a baby. Let's make it happen."

Rachel stared at him for a while. It was Bobby who had done the research on Dr. Zandt and had met with him about the procedure. In talking with the doctor, Bobby had realized that he spent a lot of time talking about money, and so he had taken a chance on recruiting him into their scheme. Dr. Zandt had been happy to join the team for the right price.

"We've already started to look for the right girl for the job," Rachel told him. "We'll let you know when we have chosen someone."

"Try Port Antonio," Dr. Zandt suggested. "I was there this weekend to meet my man, and there were some cute young ladies walking around. Of course, you know I'm batting for the other team, but a man can always look, right?"

Rachel smiled. "That sounds perfect. It's far away enough from Mandeville for Bobby and me to put our plan in motion. We'll go down this weekend to scout out the place and see what we can find."

"I'll be here waiting. Don't forget the money when you're coming." Dr. Zandt showed his little yellow teeth, which looked like fangs. Dollar signs were almost visible in his beady little eyes.

Back at home that night, Rachel made love to her husband like the world was coming to an end. If Maurice even wanted to abort the artificial insemination procedure, he was rendered too weak to carry through with it. His mind was consumed with pleasing his wife and giving her what she wanted at any cost—their baby.

That weekend Rachel and Bobby, aka Reverend and First Lady Ozzy, were in Port Antonio searching for the perfect naïve girl so that they could put their plan into action. And as fate would have it, someone recommended Mrs. Moon's place when they asked about somewhere to stay for a few days. And over the next several weeks, the couple stayed with Mrs. Moon whenever they were in town "doing the Lord's work." They went out of their way to befriend her, and their efforts succeeded.

Part Three

Chapter Twenty

Back to the present day . . .

"So we start tonight," Bobby whispered in Rachel's ear as they left church that Sunday afternoon and walked to their cars in the parking lot. "You got the powder?"

"Safe and sound at the house," Rachel mumbled under her breath. "Will you relax? I got this, babe."

"Don't do too much all at once," Bobby warned. "It has to be slow and—"

"What are you two plotting behind my back?" Maurice walked up to them with baby Gabby in his arms.

Bobby and Rachel stared at him in shock.

"What . . . what . . . what do you mean?" Rachel swallowed the lump in her throat. "No one is plotting, darling."

Maurice's face broke out in a grin. "I'm just teasing you." He used one hand and touched his wife's cheek. "You, I'm not worried about. But that brother of mine? He's another story."

"Hey!" Bobby frowned, as if his feelings were hurt.

Maurice laughed out loud, and Rachel joined in, happy that he was only joking.

"Bobby, look. Even Gabby agrees with me." Maurice placed little kisses all over the smiling baby's face. "You know Daddy's right, don't you, laughing sweetie pie?" he said in a baby-like voice. "Yes, he is, Gabby."

Bobby and Rachel looked on, fake smiles plastered on their faces.

"Gabby is smiling at her uncle because she loves him." Bobby walked closer and tickled the baby's tummy. "I love you too, Gabby."

Rachel felt like throwing up, but she put on her "Mommy" face and peered down at her supposed daughter with false adoration. "That's Mommy's little girl."

"You know my daughter will soon start talking and walking, though?" Pride filled Maurice's voice.

"She's only eight weeks old, Maurice," Bobby pointed out.

"The best eight weeks of my life." Maurice gave Gabby more kisses. "Time is going by so fast, my little princess. Every day with you is a gift from God."

Some members greeted them as they walked to their vehicles; a few stopped to play with the baby.

"I have to run," Bobby finally announced. "I need to get a head start on my drive to Kingston."

"I thought you were coming back to the house for dinner first?" Maurice replied, rocking the baby in his arms.

"Nah. I want to get in early and get some rest for that meeting in the morning."

"All right, man. We'll see you when you get back." Maurice raised one of Gabby's little hands. "Say bye to Uncle Bobby, Gabby."

"Bye, Gabby." Bobby leaned over and kissed the baby on her cheek. "I'll bring back something nice for you. Rachel, take care." He patted his brother on the back. "We'll talk soon, man."

"Drive safe and good luck on getting that contract tomorrow," Maurice said. "My wife and I will be praying for you."

"Yes, we will," Rachel added. "God go with you, Bobby."

Bobby nodded and strolled over to his truck.

"Okay, let's go home and see what Mattie made for dinner, Gabby." Maurice went over to the car, opened it, and placed the baby in her car seat in the back. He then held the front passenger door as his wife got in, before he went around to the driver's seat.

On the drive home, Maurice chatted nonstop about the plans he had for their daughter and the upcoming activities for their church. "I'm just in awe of God's grace toward me," he noted. "I'm a very happy man."

Rachel made an effort to listen, but her mind was already running ahead to what she had to do that night.

Soon after they arrived home, Mattie served dinner. All throughout the meal, Rachel made conversation, smiled when necessary, and laughed on cue.

Luckily for her, Maurice wasn't planning on attending family training hour that night. So after they put Gabby to bed, the couple went into their private sitting area and spooned on the couch as they watched a program on the sixty-inch flat-screen plasma television.

"You're quiet, darling." Maurice ran his hand through his wife's hair. "Are you okay?"

"I'm fine, hon." Rachel bent her head back, lifting her face and offering her lips.

Maurice obliged and planted a big kiss on her lips.

"I'm just relaxed." Rachel snuggled back into him. "I feel for some coffee before bed. Can I make you some too?"

"Sure. Thank you." Maurice leaned back so Rachel could get up off the couch, then focused his attention back on the television.

Rachel walked to the door that connected their private sitting area and the nursery, glanced back over her shoulder, then quickly made her way into the smaller room. She moved over to the baby's crib. Leaning over, she gently reached in and felt under the mattress, careful not to wake Gabby. Her fingers found the package she had hidden there, and she grabbed it.

On tiptoe she left the nursery and walked out into the hallway, then made her way to the staircase. She swiftly descended the stairs and headed to the kitchen. Once in the kitchen, Rachel noticed that Mattie had brewed a fresh pot of Blue Mountain coffee. "Saved me the trouble," she muttered under her breath.

Rachel looked over her shoulder to make sure she was alone. She poured Maurice's coffee into his WORLD'S GREATEST DAD cup. She opened the package she had retrieved and sprinkled some of the powder in the cup. She took a tablespoon and stirred the coffee until the powder dissolved.

"I should probably add a little bit more, just to be sure." She added some more powder and stirred. "This should fix your business."

She poured a cup of coffee for herself, put both cups on a tray, and took it upstairs to the sitting area.

"Here you go." Rachel handed Maurice his spiked coffee after he sat up on the couch. She lowered herself down beside him and sipped some of her coffee.

Maurice brought the cup to his lips. Rachel anxiously watched him over the rim of her cup. Then he paused and said, "Lord, please bless the food I eat and drink always. Amen."

Rachel shook her head.

Her husband looked over at her and smiled. "I know I'm a little weird. But my parents taught me to pray over everything before I eat or drink." He drank some of the coffee. "See? It even tastes better because it's blessed." He leaned over and kissed Rachel on the cheek.

Rachel tried to smile but grimaced instead, her heart beating fast in her chest. The hand holding her coffee began to tremble so she placed the cup on the coffee table.

Maurice had just brought the cup to his mouth for another sip of coffee when the baby suddenly wailed from the nursery. He whipped his head around toward the sound of his daughter's voice, tilting the coffee cup in the process and spilling hot coffee on his leg.

"Gosh!" Maurice leaped to his feet, and the cup of coffee fell from his hand to the carpeted floor. He rubbed the wet spot on his shorts. "The baby is crying," he said and practically ran into the nursery.

Rachel heard him say, "Hey, princess. Daddy is here." She looked down at the wet carpet and the coffee cup on the floor. She folded her fists and swore under her breath. *But at least he drank some. Is it enough to do the deed?*

"Here's your mama." Maurice came back with Gabby over his shoulder. The crying had stopped, and the baby was purring her way back to sleep.

"I'll clean this up." Rachel bent down and picked up the coffee cup, trying to avoid holding the baby. She also grabbed her own cup. "I'll take these down to the kitchen and get some paper towels." Before Maurice could say a word, she fled from the room.

In the kitchen Rachel almost threw the used cups into the kitchen sink. She inhaled deeply and exhaled loudly through her mouth. "He should have drunk the entire thing," she hissed through her teeth. "Gosh!" She felt like she wanted to punch something. Or even someone. Maybe her annoying husband?

Rachel took more deep breaths to calm herself. Maurice had drunk some of the coffee, so maybe, just maybe, that would do the trick. She grabbed some paper towels and went back upstairs.

"She's out again," Maurice said when she came back into the room, Gabby still in his arms. "I'm not sure why she screamed out like that. She's not hungry or wet. Isn't that strange?"

Rachel knelt down and dabbed at the wet spot on the carpet with the paper towel. "You know how babies are. I'm glad she went back to sleep."

"Darling, please leave that. I'll use the carpet cleaner and take care of it in the morning." Maurice took a few steps toward the nursery. "I'm going to put down the baby and be right back."

As they got ready for bed, Rachel eyed her husband to see if he was looking or acting any differently. But Maurice knelt by his bed as usual and said his night's prayer. After that he went and lay down on his side of the bed.

"I'm so tired." Rachel yawned. She turned off the light and joined him on the bed. Her head inches away from his, she draped her hand over her husband's waist.

Maurice pulled her closer and kissed her on the lips. "Good night, sweetheart."

Minutes later Rachel heard his light snoring and knew he had fallen asleep. However, she was wide awake. What was she going to tell Bobby? The reason he had gone to Kingston was that when his brother died that night, he wouldn't be anywhere nearby.

Bobby's going to be so pissed, Rachel thought and rolled over on her other side, her back facing Maurice. *But I can try again. Maybe as soon as tomorrow at breakfast.*

Maurice was jolted out of his sleep by a cramping pain in his abdomen. It felt as if his intestines were tangled up and were trying to hang him internally. Groaning, he pressed his hand to his stomach. He moaned as he tried to raise himself up into a sitting position. It took a lot of effort for him to lower one foot to the floor, then the other.

Once he was upright, he was overcome by the sensation of the room spinning around and around like a merry-go-round. He closed his eyes, cold sweat now covering his face from the excruciating pain in his stomach and the whirling of the room.

"Rachel," he said, his voice a decibel above a whisper. He reached out and touched his wife's shoulder. "Sweetheart." But Rachel didn't stir.

Maurice folded his lips and forced himself to stand. He staggered across the room and was about to fall when he grabbed onto the dresser. His head felt like it was about to explode. He waited a few seconds and then took a few more shaky steps toward the bathroom. With no more strength to hold up his body, he crumpled to the floor, knocking over figurines and perfume bottles on the dresser.

Still his wife slept.

Maurice twisted in agony before rolling himself into a ball on the floor. He was nauseated now, and bile filled his mouth. He knew he needed to get to the bathroom, but he felt so weak. His body was now wet with perspiration from head to toe.

"Lord, I need you now." He bit his lip and crawled a few inches, fire exploding in his belly, the house leaning on its side. "The Lord is my shepherd . . ." He crawled some more, mumbling the psalm, and finally made his way into the bathroom.

It was with great difficulty that Maurice pulled himself to his knees, leaned his pounding head over the toilet, and emptied the contents of his stomach. He threw up until he dry heaved. He was so weak when he finished that he stretched out on his back on the bathroom floor, begging God for relief.

"Help me, Lord. Help . . . help me." With his eyes closed, Maurice bit his lip and curled into a ball again as he continued to pray. He knew he needed to get to the hospital, but he had no strength to shout to his wife or move from where he lay and retrieve his phone. So he suffered in agony and waited.

Bang! Bang! Bang! "Pastor Maurice!"

Maurice opened his eyes. He could have sworn he heard someone calling his name.

"Mrs. Osbourne! Pastor Maurice!"

Maurice's breathing sped up. It was Mattie's voice. "Mattie? I'm in here," he muttered.

"Hello? Is everything okay in there?" The banging on the door continued for a few more seconds; then the pastor heard voices.

Thank God Mattie has awakened Rachel, he thought. *Thank you, Lord.*

Wearing her nightgown, Mattie rushed into the bathroom and fell down on her knees beside her boss, whom she loved like a son. "Pastor Maurice!"

Rachel followed behind Mattie. "Baby! Oh, Lord, what happened?" Rachel said, hysterical. "Why are you on the floor? Oh, Lord! Oh, Lord!"

Mattie got up and glared at her before hurrying back into the master bedroom. She picked up the telephone on the bedside table and called 119, Jamaica's emergency number. "Yes," she said when the operator answered. "We need an ambulance right now." She gave the address, hung up the phone, and hurried back into the bathroom.

Rachel stood over her husband, crying, asking over and over what happened, but not making a move to help him.

Mattie grabbed a towel off the towel rack. She wet it in the sink, knelt down again beside Maurice, and wiped his face with it. "Hang tight, dear. The ambulance is on its way."

Maurice mumbled a thank-you before he whimpered.

The wail of an ambulance siren could be heard about ten minutes later. Its volume grew as it neared the house.

"Can you please go and let them in?" Mattie looked up at Rachel. She was now sitting on the floor, with Maurice's head on her lap, while Rachel was still on her feet.

Rachel, who had stopped crying a minute after she'd started, stared down at her like she was speaking French.

"Mrs. Osbourne, please go and open the door," Mattie snapped.

"Yes, sure." Rachel ran from the bathroom to let the emergency medical technicians in the house.

Moments later two men burst into the bathroom with a stretcher and a medical kit. One of them knelt down beside the pastor.

"Sir, where are you feeling pain?" he asked.

Maurice touched his stomach and groaned.

"And he threw up," Mattie added, Maurice's head still in her lap. "I flushed the toilet."

"Thank you, ma'am," replied the other EMT. "We are going to take it from here. Please stand up and step back so we can help him."

"We need to make sure his lungs are clear," the kneeling EMT said to his colleague.

Once the EMTs has conducted their assessment and determined it was safe to move Maurice, they worked swiftly to transport him to the ambulance. Maurice kept his eyes closed as they lifted him onto the stretcher and placed an oxygen mask over his face. He moaned as they carried him out of the bathroom, through the bedroom, and down the stairs.

With the ambulance lights flashing and the siren screaming urgently, the ride to the Mandeville hospital was a fast one. After parking in front of the emergency room, the EMTs unloaded their patient.

"Pastor Osbourne?" The attending nurse was shocked to see him on the stretcher. Maurice was on clergy duty at the hospital and was a constant presence there. Soon word that he had fallen ill spread like the flu virus around the hospital wards.

In the examining room, the doctor on call checked Maurice's vital signs—his pulse, breathing rate, temperature, and blood pressure. He was connected to airway and oxygen support.

"Take some blood for testing," the doctor instructed the nurse. "And then we'll take him for a chest X-ray."

"That won't be necessary," Maurice told him in a feeble voice, breathing heavily through his mouth. "It's something I ate. I know the symptoms."

"We need to be sure. What—"

"Trust me, I had it once in Africa. I just need something strong for the pain."

The doctor hesitated. "Well, your vitals are good. We'll try that, and I'll give you some fluids, because you mentioned that you'd vomited. But if the pain doesn't ease up, we'll need more tests to figure out what's going on."

Maurice nodded. And even though he was still in a lot of pain, surprisingly, it had eased up a little bit.

He was given some strong pain medication and hooked up to an IV to get fluids. Within minutes the abdominal cramping began to slowly go away. His breathing wasn't as shallow, and the nausea wasn't as bad as before.

"How are we doing?" The doctor looked down at him intently. "Is the pain getting better?"

Maurice gave him a thumbs-up. His eyes were closed.

"I think it was a good thing you vomited. It seems as if you got most of it out of your system."

Maurice tried to open his eyes, but the medication had kicked in. "Sleepy," he mumbled. His head dropped to one side, and he fell into a deep sleep.

Late the next morning, Maurice awoke in a private room and slowly opened his eyes. Hovering over his bed was his worried wife.

"Hi, baby. How are you feeling?" Rachel asked, scanning his face.

Maurice smiled. "I'm actually feeling much better, darling." He yawned and stretched his arms over his head. His stomach felt sore, but he felt no excruciating pain. "I'm not sure what I ate last night that messed up my stomach so bad. But to God be the glory. Satan is defeated. Hallelujah!"

"Hallelujah." Rachel's smile conveyed that she was perhaps constipated rather than relieved.

The rat poison hadn't done the trick it was intended for.

Chapter Twenty-one

"What do you mean, he's not dead?" Bobby screamed into his cell phone. "You were supposed to spike his coffee with the rat poison!"

"I did!" Rachel peered over her shoulder where she stood in the backyard to see if that inquisitive Mattie was lurking nearby. Her husband was upstairs, resting after his overnight stay at the hospital. "I put a lot in his coffee, and he drank some. Then that hideous little baby suddenly screamed out, and he jumped up to check on her, spilling the rest on the floor."

She continued, "He tried to wake me up later that night, when the poison started to work on him, but I pretended to be asleep. He fell down on his way to the bathroom but managed to make his way in there. I just knew he was going to die in there. But who do you think began pounding on the bedroom door and refused to leave? That fast, dry-headed, wrinkled little old woman. I swear, I could have strangled her behind." She proceeded to tell him everything that had happened after she was forced to open the bedroom door and let Mattie in.

Bobby's breath came through the phone seemingly with the force of a river that had overrun its banks. Then he remained silent for a few seconds, trying to process what Rachel had just told him. "So Mattie saved him. It's almost like she knew he was dying. But how could she?"

"I don't know, but before I left for the hospital this morning, I heard her telling someone on the phone that the Holy Spirit woke her up and told her Pastor Maurice was in trouble and she must go to him now."

"Holy Spirit? I think that woman is drinking mad-puss piss."

Rachel giggled. "You're crazy. You know that?"

"Did they do any blood tests at the hospital?"

"I asked Maurice, and he said he told them not to bother," Rachel reported. "He said he knew that it was just an upset stomach, even though it was so painful. At one point he felt like he was going to die."

"It's good that he didn't get any tests. Although he didn't drink the entire coffee. Plus, he threw up. At least we don't have to worry about that."

"So when do I try again? I want to try this again right away." Rachel lowered her voice, even though she was alone in the backyard. "This time I'm going to put all that's left in his drink, and I'm going to make sure we're not interrupted."

"No, we can't do that," Bobby informed her. "We have to wait awhile before we make another move. If he dies or ends up in the hospital again so soon, it will be suspicious."

"You're right. So how long do we wait?"

"A month or two, maybe even a little longer. And we have to find another way to take him out. It's not wise to try the rat poison again. So get rid of what's left now."

"Okay. I hid it under the mattress in one of the guest rooms. I'll go get it."

"I'll be back tonight. I wasted a trip for nothing." Bobby was getting pissed off again. "Now I'm going to have to wait months before I can get my money."

"*Our* money."

"Of course, baby. We're equal partners in this. You know I love you, girl."

Rachel's bright smile could almost be felt through the phone. "I love you too, partner. Anyway, let me run. See you tomorrow?"

"Can't wait."

They clicked off, and Rachel hurried inside the house. She practically dashed up the stairs and into the guest bedroom where she had hidden the rat poison, then closed the door behind her. She went over to the bed and felt under the mattress, in the exact spot where she had put the poison, but her hand found nothing. Puzzled, Rachel pulled out her hand. She could have sworn this was where she had hidden the package. She put her hand back under the mattress and searched once more, but there was nothing there.

"Where is it? I have to find it." Rachel was getting more desperate by the second. If someone else had found that rat poison after her husband was hospitalized for a "severe upset stomach," she would be in some serious trouble. She pushed the mattress off the bed and stared down in dismay at the naked box spring. The rat poison was gone.

Rachel fell to her knees and looked under the bed, but nothing was there, either. She searched in the closet and the dresser drawers but found nothing. "So this isn't where I put it," Rachel mumbled, her eyes scanning the room, as if they could pick up where the poison was. But she knew she had placed the rat poison under this mattress, in this room, and now it wasn't there. This wasn't good.

She left the guest room, and instead of going into the master bedroom to check on her husband, she went down the stairs and headed to the kitchen. As she approached, she heard sounds coming from there. It had to be Mattie.

It was. "Hello, Mattie," she greeted the aged housekeeper. "What are you cooking?"

Mattie added a little butter to the big pot of rich yellow chicken foot soup on the stove, thyme and scallions swimming at the top. "I'm making some soup for Pastor Maurice. This will help his stomach."

"It certainly smells good. I can't wait to get some."

Mattie nodded and continued to tend to her pot while Rachel peered at her, trying to get a read on her.

"Is there something else you needed, ma'am?' Mattie asked respectfully.

"Oh, no. I . . . uh . . . I just want to thank you again for waking me up last night and coming to Maurice's aid. I can't believe I slept so dead. God knows what would have happened to him if you hadn't come."

"I do as my Lord bid. And today I give Him all the glory that Pastor Maurice is alive and that he'll be back to his old self in no time. That's the power of the God that *I* serve."

"Right. I'm very happy he's alive too. What would Gabby and I do without him?"

"Uh-huh," Mattie grunted, her lips fused together in a tight, straight line. A few seconds later she added, "First Corinthians fifteen, fifty-seven, says, 'But thanks be to God, which giveth us the victory through our Lord Jesus Christ.' Pastor Maurice is blessed and highly favored. Plus, he has his parents looking down on him from above. He'll not be defeated by the devil at no cost!"

Rachel hesitated, unsure of what to say. To her ears, it almost seemed as if Mattie had issued her a warning. What did the old hog know? "Well, I'll just run upstairs to check on my husband and daughter. Call us when dinner is ready." She strolled away.

"Mrs. Osbourne?"

The sound of Mattie's voice caused Rachel to pause at the door. She turned around and made eye contact with Mattie.

"If yu pit inna di sky, it fall inna yuh y'ye," Mattie said in patois. *If you spit into the sky, it falls into your eye.* "What you do to or wish for others could eventually be the cause of your own downfall."

Rachel held Mattie's gaze for a moment before she turned on her heel and strode out to the veranda. She took the cell phone out of her pocket and dialed the familiar number.

"She knows," she said when Bobby answered. "Mattie knows, and she took the rest of stuff I hid under the mattress."

Bobby fired off a few expletives. "Did she say something to you?"

"She said some mumbo jumbo about people spitting in the sky," Rachel responded. "I don't even know what she's talking about. You know she's always saying those proverbs rubbish. But it's the way she looked at me. Her eyes were telling me something. I could feel it, Bobby."

Bobby breathed loudly into the phone and said, "I'm not going to allow that old goat to ruin this for us. If we have to take her out, too, then so be it. Don't say anything unless she says something. Although I have a feeling she won't. She's watching to see what happens next, and that is why we have to lay low for a while."

"Got it. We wait."

"Yes, we wait. So go be a good wife and keep my little brother happy until we kill him. I'll see you tomorrow." He hung up the phone.

Rachel stayed on the veranda for a few minutes, deep in thought. Everything was going according to plan—except for the failed attempt to poison her husband last night, and now the missing rat poison, which she was sure Mattie had taken. Now she had to wait months before they could make another move. This wasn't sitting well with her, but she had to go with what Bobby said.

She walked back inside the house, went upstairs, and entered the master bedroom, where Maurice was lying on the bed, with Gabby resting in the crook of his arm.

"Look at my two babies." She went over to the bed and kissed Maurice, then planted little kisses all over Gabby's face.

"She's banned from lying on Daddy's stomach for a while," Maurice replied.

"Come here, you." Rachel scooped up Gabby in her arms. "Look how big Mommy's baby is getting." She kissed Gabby again on the side where the white birthmark was.

"And more beautiful each day," Maurice said. "I love her so much."

"So, how are you feeling?" Rachel asked him, rocking Gabby in her arms.

"My stomach feels a little sore, and occasionally, I get this nauseated feeling, but I'm on the mend. Still trying to figure out what caused it. The curry goat I had for dinner or the coffee I drank before bed? I mean, I've been eating curry goat all my life, and coffee I drink every day."

"It's probably the curry," Rachel told him. "You just had a bad reaction to it. I'm going to tell Mattie to lay off the curry for a while."

"All right. I'm probably going to miss Bible studies Wednesday night, but I plan on preaching Sunday."

"I'll go Wednesday night, sweetheart. At least one of us will be there."

"Thanks, babe. Now, where is my other favorite girl with my chicken foot soup?" he said in reference to Mattie. "She saved my life last night, and now she's getting me back on my feet. What would I do without Mattie?"

"What would I do without you?" Mattie asked in response as she entered the bedroom through the open door, a tray containing a big bowl of soup in her hands. A tantalizing aroma filled the bedroom. "Now, sit up and try some of this. It should help with the queasy feeling."

Rachel watched as her husband propped himself up on the bed with a pillow behind his back. Mattie then placed the tray on his lap and fed him a spoonful of soup, like she had when he was a kid.

She sees him as a son, Rachel pondered. *So she'll do anything to keep him safe. We definitely have to get rid of her too.*

As if she had read Rachel's mind, Mattie glanced up and locked eyes with her. Rachel's glare was meant as a threat, and Mattie's as a promise.

Chapter Twenty-two

"Are you ready?" Rachel whispered, her eyes staring straight ahead at her husband at the podium, his hands lifted in praise, his eyes closed in reverence. It was Sunday night, and instead of conducting the usual FTH meeting, Maurice had decided to make it a praise and worship service. The church was almost filled to capacity, as it had been earlier that day for the morning's worship.

"Everything is set." Bobby was standing beside Rachel in the front row, bobbing his head slowly to the soulful song being played by the organist. "Just make sure you do your part."

"Praise the Lord," Rachel said loudly and raised her right hand in the air. "He's worthy to be praised."

"Amen, First Lady," a church sister said behind Rachel. "Worthy is the lamb."

"Look at him," Bobby remarked as he looked at his younger brother. "Singing and clapping and he don't even realize it's his last night on earth."

"At least he's getting ready to meet his Maker." Rachel dipped to the right, then to the left, then did a little skip, as if she was feeling the Holy Spirit.

"Don't even think about speaking in tongues," Bobby warned her. "But you're doing well, First Lady. Keep it up."

Rachel wanted to laugh out loud but bit her lip. She knew eyes were on her at all times, including her husband's. He was now smiling down at her as he swayed to the music. She smiled back at him, and he winked at her. "It has been six months, and nothing can go wrong this time. I'm tired of this crap."

"Don't worry. Everything is everything," Bobby responded. "You knew why we had to wait until now. It's time."

The two continued to clap, rock, sing, and worship while they finalized under their breath their destructive plan for later that night.

It was after 11:00 p.m. when Rachel and Maurice got home from church.

"Let me go and get a peek at my princess," Maurice said as he moved toward the nursery and Rachel headed to the master bedroom.

Moments later Maurice entered the bedroom. "Gabby is sleeping like the little angel that she is," he said in a raised voice so that his wife, who was standing at the sink in the bathroom, might hear him. "Now, tonight was what I call a Holy Ghost service. Don't you agree, darling?" Maurice began unbuttoning his shirt.

"It sure was." Rachel pulled her hair back in a ponytail and splashed some water on her face.

"I'm so full of the spirit right now." Maurice's voice was filled with excitement as he changed into his pajamas. "I don't know if I'm going to sleep anytime soon."

"I was thinking the same thing." Rachel walked into the room and over to the dresser. She took up a canister of Purelene Natural Cocoa Butter Cream, opened it, and applied some to her face. "I'll make some coffee. We can go and sit on the veranda and unwind for a while."

"Make that mint tea, sweetheart. I'm already too hyped up for any caffeine."

"Okay. I think I'll have the same." Rachel moved toward to door. "See you downstairs," she added over her shoulder before she left the room.

Maurice changed into pajama pants and a T-shirt, humming, "What a mighty God we serve," and nodding his head to the tune. He then went into the bathroom and washed his face, sporting a grin as big as the Caribbean Sea. Once he was done, he left the bedroom and went downstairs to join his wife.

He sat down across from her on the chaise longue on the veranda. "Thanks, hon," he said when she handed him a cup of mint tea. He took a sip, sighed contentedly, and rested back on the chaise. Rachel had turned off the veranda light, creating an even more relaxing ambiance.

"You know it's almost that time to start planning our annual rally." He looked over at his wife. "I want to continue with the theme of praise and prayer. I want my members to know the power of 'P and P.' They need to know that when praises go up, blessings come down. Thank you, Lord. There is deliverance in praise and prayer."

"Yup." Rachel took a sip of her tea, staring straight ahead.

"Satan trembles when you cover yourself with prayer and praise. Hallelujah." Maurice took a few more sips of his tea, his eyes sparkling like a newly waxed hardwood floor. "I just want God to bless—"

"Babe, I'll be right back. I need to use the bathroom." Rachel got up, put her cup on the glass table between them, then hurried inside.

Maurice kept on talking to his God and drinking his tea. After draining the last drop, he leaned forward and put the empty cup beside his wife's almost full cup. He crossed his legs and looked out at the leaves on the big East Indian mango tree in the front yard as they slow danced to the cool light Mandeville breeze. The full moon and the twinkling stars that decorated the heavens shone down on Mattie's enchanted exotic flowers that decorated both sides of the driveway. It was a beautiful sight to behold.

As Maurice reflected on his blessings with a heart full of thanksgiving, Bobby, dressed in black from head to toe, peeked out at him from his hiding place in the thick shrubs surrounding the front gate. He lifted the big M16 rifle, drew a bead on Maurice's head, and steadied his grip. "Unless you're Jesus, let me see you survive this bullet to your head." With his left eye closed and the right one blazing with hatred and anger, he rested his finger on the trigger. "Say hello to Daddy Dearest for me, little brother."

"Get down on the floor now!" said a loud voice in Maurice's ear.

Maurice jumped as if struck, then looked around him, his mouth agape. "Huh?" It was as if someone had shouted in his ear, but he was alone, because Rachel was still inside the house. Puzzled, he pondered this for a few seconds, before understanding hit him in the gut like a sledgehammer.

Maurice threw himself down onto the veranda tiles two seconds before the wall behind his chaise longue exploded from two shots fired in rapid succession. Bells began ringing in his ears. It was as of an 8.0 magnitude earthquake had just hit Jamaica. Shocked, he froze there on the tile, unable to move.

Suddenly a loud scream came from upstairs, echoed in the house, and then boomeranged out into the neighborhood. This caused Maurice to spring into action. He quickly crawled on his belly like a crab through the open front door. He had just pushed the front door shut when Mattie came hurrying down the stairs, yelling and screaming at the top of her lungs.

"Pastor Maurice, are you okay?" Mattie fell to her knees beside him on the floor.

"Go . . . go call the police," he told her. Maurice's chest was rising and falling dramatically, and his heart was racing in his chest.

Mattie got up and rushed over to the telephone to make the call, tears running down her face.

Within minutes, the wailing of sirens filled the air as police cars drew near to the house.

Maurice pulled himself to his feet and quickly grabbed onto Mattie when his rubber legs felt like they were going to buckle under him.

"Come sit down." Mattie guided him into the living room and over to the couch just as bright red and blue lights shone through the glass windows. "I'll let the police in."

Maurice watched as Mattie came back into the living room moments later with two police officers who looked like Mutt and Jeff: one was very tall, and the other very short.

"I'm Officer Carty, and this is my partner, Officer Peters," the tall man said as he peered down at Maurice, who was still sitting on the couch. "We heard that you were shot at?"

Maurice nodded, and Mattie whimpered, rocking from one leg to the other as she stood there.

"There are four other officers outside, scouring the area," the short man, Officer Peters, informed them. "We're going to take a look outside, and then we'll be back to take your statement."

Rachel came dashing down the stairs as the officers turned to leave the living room. She ran over to her husband and threw her arms around him, as if trying to protect him. "Maurice! Are you all right?"

The officers paused to stare at her, then exchanged a look before they left the room to do their investigation.

"What happened?" Rachel asked. "I heard a loud sound, but I didn't know what it was, and so I didn't think much of it, until I heard sirens, then saw the police cars pulling up."

"Someone tried to kill him," Mattie informed her. "Again."

Maurice and Rachel stared at Mattie.

Maurice asked, "What do you mean—"

"Thank God you're okay, darling." Rachel pulled her husband's face to hers and planted kisses all over it. "Who would try to shoot you?"

"I thought you didn't know what the sound was that you heard," Mattie muttered, loud enough for Rachel to hear.

Rachel ignored her as she comforted her husband, whispering to him in hushed tones.

A few minutes later Officers Carty and Peters returned to the living room.

"We found one of the bullets that was fired," Officer Carty announced as he walked over Maurice and Rachel. "I think there is another still lodged in the wall. An officer is removing it and will bring both of them back to the station for testing. Maybe we'll get lucky with some forensics."

"Just so you know, the shooter is long gone," Officer Peters noted. "But we still have officers canvassing the area and speaking to your neighbors. A few calls came in to the emergency line about the shots that were fired. I'm hoping someone saw something."

"So tell us what happened, Pastor." Officer Carty had his pen on a page of his notebook, ready to start writing.

Maurice recounted what had happened while the officers took notes.

"Let me see if I got this right," Officer Peters said. "A voice screamed in your ear to get down on the floor, but you were alone on the veranda?" His eyes narrowed before he looked at Maurice as if he was as crazy as a drunken roach in a rum bottle.

"Whose voice was it?" Officer Carty inquired. "A ghost's?"

The officers chuckled lightly but stopped abruptly when Maurice stood to his full height, his eyebrows almost touching, a look of fury spread across his face. "Let me tell you something, Officers," he said, pointing his finger at them. "If you're going to try to insult *my* God in *my* house, please leave."

"Okay, okay." Officer Peters held up a hand. "We're sorry about that. We meant no disrespect. It's just that I've never heard anything like that before."

"Like what?" Maurice muttered through his teeth. "Like I was sitting down when the Lord told me to get down on the floor seconds before the place where my head had been exploded from gunshots? Who do you think that was if it wasn't the Lord?"

Mattie glared at them. "Do you think this is a joke?"

"No, ma'am. Someone did try to kill Pastor, and we're going to find out who it was." Officer Carty's expression got very serious. "This is attempted murder and is no joke."

Officer Peters turned his attention on Rachel, who had been silent all this time. "So, Mrs. Osbourne, where were you when your husband was shot at?"

"I . . . I was upstairs, using the bathroom," Rachel responded, shifting from one leg to the other. "I heard the shots but didn't know what they were at first."

"Why didn't you use the half bathroom that is right over there?" He nodded in the direction of the bathroom across the hall from the living room.

"Because I wanted to use the one upstairs," Rachel snapped. "What does it matter which bathroom I used?"

"Luckily, you went inside before the shooting happened, darling." Maurice moved closer to her and wrapped an arm around her waist.

"So you were on the veranda with your husband earlier, right? We saw the two cups." Officer Carty jotted something down in his notebook.

"Yes, I was," Rachel admitted, tears gathering in her eyes. "But I had to use the bathroom, so I came inside. Thank you, Lord, for sparing my life and that of my husband."

Mattie coughed loudly into her hand, and everyone turned to look at her. "Yes, thank you, Lord, for your protection."

"Hmm. Ma'am, why don't I take your statement outside while my partner finishes up with Pastor and his wife?" Officer Carty said to Mattie. He walked toward the door, leaving her to follow him.

Later that night, after the police had left and Mattie and Rachel had gone to bed, Maurice sat on the chair in the nursery, with Gabby in his arms. The baby had woken up crying during the commotion but then had fallen back asleep. However, he just needed to hold her as he thought back on how close he had come to death.

"How do I say thank you, Lord?" The tears now flowed freely down his face. "I've tried so hard to help others and be kind to everyone, yet someone tried to kill me." He rocked the baby gently. "But I'm leaning on your words as you promised in Psalm one-thirty-eight, seven. 'Though I walk in the midst of trouble, thou wilt revive me: thou shalt stretch forth thine hand against the wrath of mine enemies, and thy right hand shall save me.'"

Chapter Twenty-three

"Ahhh!" Bobby kicked the couch in his living room and yelled out in pain. F-bombs bounced off the walls as he cursed up a storm. "Why can't he just die?"

"Because God is protecting him from us," Rachel answered, attempting some humor, but her eyes were serious. There was just something about what had happened two nights ago that freaked her out a little bit.

"I had him in my line of fire." Bobby's eyes met Rachel's and held her gaze. "And just as I pulled the trigger, the man dropped to the floor. Can you believe that?"

"He said a voice told him to get down on the floor." Rachel wasn't joking this time. "You must admit it's a little freaky."

Bobby sucked his teeth loudly. "Please don't buy into that voice rubbish. He's just lucky." He fired off a few more curse words.

"He spent most of the day yesterday locked in the guest room, praying and praising God for saving his life," Rachel said of her husband. "The only time he came out was to check on his precious Gabby."

"Let him pray as much as he wants," Bobby replied. "He's going to need more than that. Trust me."

"Mattie hinted that she thought I was involved," Rachel told him. "She spoke to the cops alone outside, and I'm not sure what she told them."

"She can't say anything that can really hurt you, because she has no proof." Bobby walked into the kitchen, and Rachel followed him. He opened the refrigerator and took out two Dragon Stouts. Using the can opener that was on top of the kitchen counter, he opened both bottles and handed one to Rachel.

"So where do we go from here?" Rachel put the bottle to her mouth and took a big gulp. "Do we just cut our losses and let it go?"

"Are you crazy? Let it go? Let *my* money go?" Bobby glared at her. "Are you getting cold feet on me now?"

"No, no, no." Rachel shook her head. "You know I'm riding with you to the end, baby. I'm just saying the police promised they were going to find the person who tried to kill Maurice the other night. That's why I didn't come over here yesterday. We have to be careful because there is an investigation going on."

Bobby nodded in agreement and drank some of his beer. "Yes, we may have to wait a few more months before we go at him again. If that old goat told them about the whole stomach virus thing, then this happened, they're definitely not going to drop this now."

"So, I have to continue playing the loving wife and mother." It was Rachel's turn to let loose some curse words. "I thought I would be a rich widow by now, but we can't seem to kill one little man. Are you kidding me?"

"The third time is a charm." A nasty snarl appeared on Bobby's scarred face. "Next time I'm going to gut him like a fish, face-to-face. Let his God whisper to him while my butcher knife is lodge in his gut."

"Yuck." Rachel put her beer on the kitchen counter, leaned over, and gave Bobby a passionate kiss. "I love it when you talk like that." She bit him on his bottom lip and tasted a little blood.

Bobby placed his beer beside hers. He then lifted her up and slammed her down on the counter, her bottom narrowly missing the beer bottles.

Rachel giggled as she tore at his shirt, the sexual tension between having reached a peak. The two mated like wild animals, turned on at the thought of Maurice's blood running like the Red Sea.

Almost an hour later Rachel left through the back door of Bobby's apartment. Her hair was combed back and flowing down her back. Her swollen lips were painted ruby red, and her sexy but conservative light green summer dress was perfectly in place.

She walked a few feet to where her car was parked under some trees. She pressed the key fob to open the car doors, got in, closed her door, and started the car, then drove off in absolute bliss.

Rachel was so caught up in the afterglow of her afternoon rendezvous with her brother-in-law that she failed to see the plain black Honda Accord with dark tinted windows parked down the street from Bobby's apartment. Inside Officers Carty and Peters watched her intently until she drove away.

"Sweetheart, look who is here," Maurice said when Rachel walked into the living room minutes later. He nodded to the short, heavyset man that was seated across from him on the couch. "This is Minister Sonny, Mattie's son."

Instantly Rachel's good vibe was cut. Maurice had told her that Mattie had a son who lived in St. Ann, but she had never met him before. This was his first time visiting since she and Maurice had got married. He had never even made it to their wedding, so what was he doing here now? "Hello, Mr. Sonny," she said as she walked over to the men. "It's a pleasure to finally meet you." She put out her right hand, her white teeth sparkling.

Minister Sonny stood up and stared pointedly at Rachel, leaving her hand hanging. His small, beady eyes seemed to be looking into her soul. "Glory!" He spun around in a circle like a whirlwind and began speaking in tongues.

Rachel's hand fell to her side.

Soon Minister Sonny was running around the living room, praying in an unknown language, hopping from one leg to the other. He was very flexible for someone his size. "Evil, evil, evil. Satan, I rebuke you in the name of Jesus! No weapon, Lord. I say no weapon!"

"Hallelujah!" Maurice lifted his hands in the air. "No weapon, Lord."

Mattie appeared out of nowhere and joined in with the two men, shouting praises one second and rebuking "the devil and his followers" the next.

Rachel closed her eyes, as if in reverence, and mumbled some curse words under her breath, disguising them as praises.

"I'm under the rock, the rock that's higher than I," Mattie sang as she bent and dipped, her wide flared skirt fanning around her legs, like she was dancing to a folk song.

Maurice joined in with Mattie, and the two began to get down.

Rachel took a peek out of one eye and quickly closed it again, swaying from left to right to the off-key song that her husband and Mattie were singing.

"Go tell my enemies, I am under the rock." Minister Sonny shouted in Rachel's ear, and she gave a yap and opened her eyes. He then placed his hand on Rachel's forehead, smearing holy oil all over it.

Rachel angrily jumped back from him. "What the . . ." She caught herself. "What . . . what are you doing?" The oil ran down her face and dripped onto her dress.

Mattie and Maurice stopped singing, as if someone had hit the PAUSE button. They stared at Rachel.

But Minister Sonny was still working. He ran over to Maurice and began anointing him with the holy oil. "Protect him, Lord," he repeated over and over. "Deliver him from those who despise him and want to bring him harm."

Just then Gabby's cry filtered down into the living room. That was Rachel's cue to get out of Dodge. "I'll get her." She sprinted up the stairs like a Olympic gold medalist in the hundred-meter dash.

Rachel angrily entered the baby's room and slammed the door behind her. She reached into her handbag and took out her handkerchief and wiped at her oily face. "That fat, ugly disgusting pig. I could just—"

"Wahhh." Gabby took her crying to another level, demanding some attention.

"What?" Rachel snapped, and the baby began to cry even louder. "Okay, okay," she said in a lower voice.

Gabby was lying in her crib, tears running down her cheeks as she cried. Rachel knew she had to tend to Gabby herself, because she had said she would. Plus, Mattie was downstairs, busy auditioning for a folk dance music video.

"What's the matter?" She lifted Gabby into her arms, and the baby's crying tapered off. She looked into Rachel's face with her beautiful bright eyes, the birthmark surrounding the left one. "You know, you would be a pretty girl if you didn't have this ugly thing on your face."

The baby smiled.

"Gosh, what's that awful smell?" Her face screwed up, Rachel went to change Gabby. "I told Mattie to stop giving you that cornmeal porridge like you're grown, but would she listen to me? No." Still pissed off at Minister Sonny for plastering oil all over her face, she cursed at poor little Gabby, as if she was the one who had done it.

"Now you're all done." Rachel put Gabby on the floor and reached for her cell phone. She quickly dialed a number.

"Do you know what that little Humpty Dumpty did?" she screamed when Bobby answered. "I'm going to kill his . . ." She let loose a string of curse words like she was singing a hymn. "Then those two idiots have the nerve to be looking at me like I shouldn't have said anything. Those . . ." Curse words and F-bombs ricocheted off the walls. Her chest rising and falling, Rachel paused to catch her breath.

"Are you finished now?" Bobby asked.

"I'll be finished when I get out of here!"

"Rachel, calm down. What are you talking about?"

Rachel told Bobby all about Minister Sonny and the spectacle that he, Mattie, and Maurice carried on. "Singing and dancing like darn fools."

"You do know you handled this wrong, right?" Bobby's voice was hard. "What's wrong if you had joined in with them and taken a little oil to the face?"

Rachel scoffed.

"Now you've put even more suspicion on yourself."

"He's already suspicious. Talking about 'evil' and 'enemies.' I'm sure his nosy mother already told him all sorts of things about me."

"That's why you have to step up your game and play to their tune for now," Bobby replied. "Where are you now?"

"Upstairs, in the baby's room. I had to pacify and change that little . . . Gabby." Rachel turned around, but she was the only one in the room. "I keep forgetting that little girl is crawling around like a reptile. I have to go, Bobby."

"I was going to tell you to do that. Go downstairs and clear the air, especially with your husband. Now."

"I'm—" she began, but she got a dial tone. Bobby had hung up on her.

Rachel took a few deep breaths to try to calm her nerves. She rushed out into the hallway to see Gabby at the top of the stairs on all fours, as if she were getting ready to crawl down the staircase.

"What the . . . ?" Rachel snapped under her breath as she ran over to pick the baby up. She quickly glanced downstairs but neither saw nor heard anyone. "Thank God," she muttered as she walked back into the nursery. "Can you imagine what would have happened if you had fallen down those stairs on my watch?"

She put Gabby in her crib and went into the master bathroom. She showered, changed into another white maxi dress, and reapplied her bright red lipstick. Then she took Gabby out of the crib and rested her over her shoulder. Then she grabbed her cell phone and made her way downstairs.

The living room was empty when Rachel got there. Just then she heard laughter coming from the backyard and headed that way.

"He's so cute, Sonny." she heard Mattie say as she stepped outside. Mattie had a furry little dog in her lap, one that Rachel was seeing for the first time. He could fit in the palm of her hand. "Hello, Tuff," Mattie said,

"I like the name you gave him, Mattie." Maurice laughed. "Sonny, you certainly know what our little girl wants. She's going to crawl behind him all over the house."

"I knew Gabby would love him. Consider this an early first birthday present for her."

"Yup, she'll be one year old soon." Maurice beamed. "And will be walking around with Tuff."

"Mama, remember my dog, Santro, I had as a child?" Minister Sonny asked his mother.

"How could I forget?" Mattie responded. "He followed you everywhere. Once he even went with you to school, like he was a student too."

Maurice, Mattie, and Minister Sonny roared with laughter. No one saw Rachel as she stood watching them with the baby.

"Hello," Rachel said as she took a few steps closer to where they sat, and all three turned to look at her.

"Hi." Maurice looked at her with apprehension as he stood up. "Are you okay?"

"Yes, I am. Thanks, darling." Rachel went to stand by her husband, and he took Gabby out of her arms. "Listen, Minister Sonny, I'm sorry for overreacting. It's just . . . Hey!" Rachel jumped back a step.

Tuff, Gabby's new Bolognese dog, was at Rachel's feet and was growling and baring his little teeth.

"Someone please get this dog." Rachel shot Mattie a stern look as she moved a little closer to Maurice. *Before I snap his little neck.* Just then Tuff latched onto her dress. "Get away!" Rachel pulled on her dress, trying to get the dog to let it go. "Let go right now!"

Maurice handed Gabby to Mattie and knelt down beside the little dog. "Okay, let go, Tuff." Instantly, Tuff released the dress and lowered his head, as if he were ashamed.

Mattie and Minister Sonny hollered. Rachel stood with her face screwed up. She just knew Mattie had let that dog go intentionally.

"Say hi to Tuff, Gabby." Maurice now had the dog in his arms as he walked over to where Mattie sat with Gabby.

Tuff playfully licked Gabby's face, and she wiggled and smiled.

Rachel's nostrils flared in anger, and she snorted. She opened her mouth to chastise the dog but felt the adults staring at her. So she took a deep breath and plastered a fake smile on her face. "I guess Tuff and I started off on the wrong foot, huh?"

"He started off on the right foot with Gabby, Pastor Maurice, and me." Mattie smirked.

Rachel shot her a nasty look, but Mattie met her stare this time with one of her own. *You act like you're bad only when Maurice is around*, Rachel thought. *I'll get your behind when he leaves to go to some godforsaken place again. Well, if we haven't killed him by then.*

"Ms. Rachel." Minister Sonny's voice brought Rachel's attention to him. "I once heard that a dog could sense the depth of a person's soul. Do you believe that?"

"She has none," Mattie muttered, loud enough for Rachel and the two men to hear.

Rachel looked down at Maurice, who had reclaimed his seat, but he said nothing, just stared straight ahead.

"Why don't you ask your mama? She'd know." The first lady turned on her heel and stormed back into the house. She was tired of playing nice, and she would let Bobby know it. But one thing bothered Rachel: her husband hadn't come to her defense when Mattie insulted her. Was he onto her?

She quickly removed her cell phone from a pocket, pressed a button, and put the phone to her ear. "We have to act soon," she whispered when Bobby answered her call. "I think he's onto me."

Chapter Twenty-four

Isabella Pigmore

"Bella, it's me." Mrs. Moon knocked on Bella's bedroom door.

"And me," Sophia added. "I drove down this morning to see you, and we're not going away until we talk to you."

Inside the room Bella was lying on her back on the bed. She sighed loudly and glanced at the door. She knew Sophia meant what she'd said. "Come in." She watched as Mrs. Moon and Sophia opened the door and entered.

"Sweetheart, I know you're hurting right now, but you can't stay locked up in this room," Mrs. Moon said as she sat on the edge of the bed, beside Bella.

"She's right, Bella." Sophia stood there, looking down at her. "It has been a month. You have to continue with your life until we find your daughter."

Tears welled up in Bella's eyes at the mention of her daughter. She had spent the past four weeks, ever since her baby was taken, being depressed, locking herself in her room for the most part, and crying herself to sleep, sleep plagued by nightmares.

"How do I go on after this?" Bella asked in a small voice.

"By going to college, like you promised your mother," Sophia replied.

"I don't have enough money for college," Bella told them. "Plus, I'm not in the frame of mind to study right now."

"That's why you need to go to school," Sophia responded. "It will take your mind off everything, at least for a while. Start by taking a few classes. You can pay for those once you get a job and with the money you have saved up."

"And I don't need any more money from you for rent," Mrs. Moon added. "You're a part of this family now."

"I heard Dr. Denny is looking for a receptionist." Sophia's eyes twinkled. "I even went and put in a word for you a while ago. You know, I used to work there part-time when I lived here."

Bella couldn't help the little smile that crept up on her. "Mama once told me that she always tried to be good to other people's children so God would allow others to be good to hers. She said the blessings of the parents would fall on the children. I never believed it, because of everything I was going through. But now I'm wondering if she was right. Thank you both for everything."

"You're welcome." Mrs. Moon patted Bella's arm.

"Thank me by taking this job and starting college. Deal?" Sophia held out a hand to Bella.

Bella looked at it for a few seconds and then shook it.

Bella kept her promise. A few days later, she took the receptionist job at Dr. Denny's medical office. It entailed answering the phone, making and rescheduling appointments, and aiding the medical assistant as required. The pay wasn't that great, but it was much better than what she'd earned at Mertella's grocery store and would help pay for college.

Within four months of working full-time, doing a lot of overtime, and not having to pay rent, Bella had enough money saved to register for evening classes at CASE. Her coursework helped tremendously in terms of shifting her focus to something other than the Ozzys and her daughter. Her grades were okay but were below her standard in high school of mostly As, at least before her mother died.

The days ran into weeks, and the weeks into months, and before long Bella had completed her first year as a student at the College of Agriculture, Science and Education, where she was working on her associate's degree in business studies.

"So how was the final exam?" Mrs. Moon asked Bella one Thursday evening, after Bella entered the living room, where Mrs. Moon sat watching television.

"It was all right. I did the best I could." Bella sat down on the couch beside Mrs. Moon, tiny beads of sweat sprinkled all over her perfectly made-up, sad face. She had started using her Avon again when she got her new job.

"That's all you can do, baby. Your best." Mrs. Moon reached for Bella's hand and sandwiched it between her own hands. Her love for the young woman was transparent in her eyes. "She's okay, you know?"

Bella knew whom she was referring to, and tears sprang up in her eyes. "She's now fifteen months old. If she's still alive."

"Don't you dare think like that, Bella." Mrs. Moon's voice was stern. "Your daughter is happy and well. I know because I can feel it deep down in my soul, and my God is not dead."

Bella turned her head and locked eyes with the woman who reminded her so much of her mother. "What could I have done without you? You have been there for me since I met you."

"And God is doing the same for your daughter. He has placed someone in her life that's protecting her from those two evil people. Please believe that, sweetheart."

"I'll believe it when I see it, Mrs. Moon. Seeing is believing, right?"

"I'm certainly not saying no to that. But as children of God, we also believe without seeing. Hebrews eleven, one, says, 'Now faith is the substance of things hoped for, the evidence of things not seen.' I have faith that your little girl is happy and doing well. And I have faith that God is going to reunite you with her soon."

Bella reached over and hugged Mrs. Moon. "Thank you," she whispered. "I really needed to hear that." She rested back against the couch. "I love her so much, and yet I've never seen her. Isn't that crazy?"

"No, it's not. You carried her for nine months and gave her life. There's a bond between mother and child that cannot be broken by time or distance. It's that love why you scour the internet every day, trying to find a lead on the Ozzys. It's that love why you call that telephone number every day, knowing you'll never get an answer. It's a mother's love for her child."

Over the past year Bella had spent countless hours looking for any sign of the Ozzys online. Taking Sophia's advice, she had even created a Facebook account under a fictitious name, one without a profile picture, and had been scanning the timelines of anyone with the name Ozzy in Jamaica. So far, she had had no luck.

"I'll never stop loving her," Bella told Mrs. Moon. "Nor will I stop looking for her."

"And I'll never stop praying for both of you, and I know my prayers will be answered in Jesus's name. Just continue working on your schooling and doing your job. Let God do the rest."

Just then the telephone rang on the little table by Bella. She picked it up nad answered. "Hello?"

"Hey, Bella. How are you?" Sophia was her usual chirpy self.

"Okay, I guess." Bella, on the other hand, sounded stressed.

"How was your final exam?"

"Okay, I guess."

"Listen, I have a great idea, and I won't take no for an answer," Sophia said. "You need a little break from Port Antonio. So how about you come and spend this weekend with me?"

"Sophia, I'm not so sure. I mean—"

"Oh, come on, Bella. You'll love Mandeville. It's very nice here." Sophia had relocated to Mandeville a few months ago to take an assistant principal position at Mandeville High School. She had been inviting Bella to come and visit her, but Bella always refused.

"Tell Dr. Denny that you're taking Monday off. You haven't had a day off since you started to work there," Sophia remarked. "So you'll leave tomorrow evening and return on Monday. Please, Bella, you need this getaway."

"Okay. I guess I can—"

"Great! I'll text you the information on where to get off the bus. I'll be there waiting for you. We're going to have such a fun time." Sophia quickly hung up, as if she feared Bella would change her mind.

Bella moved the receiver from her ear and looked at it. She heard Mrs. Moon giggling and glanced over at her. "You knew she was going to call, didn't you? Both of you planned this." Bella gave her a little smile.

"She called earlier with the suggestion, and I agreed with her. You'll like Mandeville." Mrs. Moon had visited her daughter shortly after she moved to Mandeville, and talked constantly about the cool weather and the places she had visited.

Bella nodded her head. "A little break may be what I need. In fact, I'm going to ask Dr. Denny for Tuesday as well and come back that evening for work on Wednesday."

"Sounds wonderful, Bella. Now, go pack, because you'll have to catch the bus right after work. I don't want you traveling by yourself too late at night."

The next day, after work, Bella boarded the bus for Mandeville. Not only had Dr. Denny given her Monday and Tuesday off, but she had also given Bella permission to leave work early.

Bella had *accepted*, but as the bus ate up the road, she began to feel a little on edge. The closer she got to Mandeville, the more the feeling intensified. It wasn't the usual depressing feeling she'd had over the past few months, ever since the Ozzys had tricked her and taken her daughter. It was something else. Almost like a sense of anxiety. *But what am I anxious about?* Bella thought. *It's probably because I haven't seen Sophia in a while, and I've never been to Mandeville.*

But the feeling didn't go away, not even after Bella got off the bus and found Sophia waiting for her.

"You made it." Sophia hugged Bella affectionately.

Bella returned the hug. She knew Sophia had grown to love her like a sister, and the feeling was mutual. That was why Sophia had made it her mission to help Bella find the bogus pastor and his wife who had stolen Bella's daughter. Bella was family now, and hurting Bella was hurting Sophia too. It was very personal.

"I found a Raquel Ozzy on Facebook the other day," Sophia told Bella as she drove them back to her house.

"What?" Bella turned so fast in her seat that she almost got whiplash. "Was it her?"

"At first, I thought it was, and that she had lied about her first name and where she lived. This woman lives in Hanover and posts something about her church's concert and that her husband was a pastor. I inboxed her, pretending I needed more information about the concert and her church. I found out she's fifty-five years old and her profile picture is that of her daughter, who is currently residing in the United States."

Bella shook her head in disappointment. "Another false lead. For a minute I was hoping you'd say it's her. I've been getting this weird feeling today, as if something is about to happen."

"Maybe it is, Bella. Maybe God is saying enough is enough. You've stayed away from your daughter too long, and He's going to connect you with her. Let's not lose hope, okay?"

Bella nodded her head.

"In fact, on Sunday we're going to a church that a teacher has been inviting me to since I moved down here. She says Pastor Osbourne of Christian Deliverance Church of God is a strong man of God. I think we should go and ask him to pray for you and your daughter. What do you say?"

"I'll take all the help I can get," Bella replied.

"Alrighty. I have lots of cool stuff planned for us to do this weekend. Bella, I think you're in for some surprises."

"Now, give me that old-time religion! Give me that old-time religion!" Voices were singing, hands were clapping, feet were stomping, bodies were jiggling, drums were beating, cymbals were knocking, and the guitars were jamming. Christian Deliverance Church of God was on fire for God.

"Now, this is what I call church," Sophia yelled in Bella's ear. "Mama used to sing this song all the time when I was growing up."

"Mine too," Bella said loudly, shaking her head to the beat. The energy coming from the church was infectious and hard to resist.

Sophia peeked inside the church from where they stood at the entrance. "It's crowded in there. I don't see an empty seat anywhere."

"Good morning, my sisters." An usher appeared in front of them, wearing white from head to toe, with a bunch of programs in her hand. "Sorry we're just getting to you. We're extremely full this morning."

"We can see that," Sophia replied. "Sounds good in there."

"Yes, it is. I'm afraid we only have one or two seats at the back."

"That's fine," Sophia told her.

"Please follow me." She took a few steps down the aisle, with Bella and Sophia behind her. Then she stopped two rows from the back. "There are two empty seats in the middle. You ladies are going to experience something really awesome today."

Bella and Sophia made their way to the middle of the row. They nodded and smiled at the people on either side of them before they joined in with the clapping and singing.

After a few more lively choruses, praising, and dancing, the moderator walked up to the podium and lifted his hand. The worship team singing tapered off, and the musicians stopped playing. However, it took a few more minutes before the church settled down; people were worshiping, skipping, shouting, and speaking in tongues.

"I can feel the presence of the Holy Spirit in our midst this morning. Hallelujah! Thank you, Lord."

"I'm enjoying the service, Sophia," Bella said as she gently dabbed her face with her handkerchief, careful not to ruin her makeup. "Thanks for bringing me."

"Oh, I'm glad I came too." Sophia was still rocking her shoulders, as if the music hadn't stopped. "I think this is going to be my church from now on."

"I'll definitely be coming back when I visit you again."

"I wonder if that's Pastor Osbourne." Sophia was looking toward the front of the church.

Bella followed her gaze and saw a tall man wearing a black pinstripe suit enter the church from a side door. He walked to the front seat, where a woman was standing, her arm around the waist of a child who was standing on the seat beside her. His back was turned to her.

"That must be his wife, and the little girl, his daughter," Sophia whispered, leaning her head to the side to see over the big hat of the lady standing in front of her.

But even though Bella couldn't see the woman's face, there was something familiar about the long, straight black hair that flowed down her back. Bella's heart skipped a beat like a misplayed drum.

"I guess we'll meet them after church, when we go to speak to the pastor," Sophia continued. "We're still . . . Bella, what's wrong?"

Just then the man turned around and said something to the lady in the row behind him. He flashed that cheeky, lopsided grin as he tugged on his earlobe. He had a long scar running down his right cheek.

"Reverend Ozzy," Bella muttered, tears leaking out of her eyes.

"What?" Sophia looked at Bella, then at the front of the church. "*That's* Reverend Ozzy?" Her eyes were wide as porridge bowls. "Is the woman her?"

Bella's body began convulsing, as if she was having a seizure. She grabbed Sophia's hand, and her nails dug into her skin. "I . . . I have to . . . to . . . get air." She breathed loudly through her mouth.

"Excuse me please." The four people made way as Sophia took Bella's arm and practically dragged her out of the bench. They rushed past the two ushers standing by the front door, down the stairs, and into the church-yard.

Bella bent over with her hands on her knees, inhaling and exhaling, snot, tears, and makeup running down her face. "We found them," she chanted over and over.

Sophia's face was wet with tears as well. For a little over a year, they had searched for Reverend and Mrs. Ozzy, and now here they were. "Yes, we found the rascals." Sophia's eyes flashed with anger. "And I think we've also found your daughter."

"My daughter." Bella stood straight and looked up into the beautiful clear blue sky. "Thank you, Lord."

Sophia pulled Bella in for a much-needed hug and whispered in her ear, "As Mama would say, 'Lang run, shaat ketch.' *Long run, short catch.* We catch them now, Bella. This time they're not running anywhere."

Part Four

Chapter Twenty-five

Time is longer than rope . . .

"We have to call the police." Bella turned in her seat to face Sophia as they sat in Sophia's car. She was now more composed and really pissed. "We have to report those frauds for what they did to me."

Sophia was gazing out the car window, looking up at the church, deep in thought. "Yes, we will. Don't worry. I'm just trying to figure out what's going on here. I'm sure my co-worker told me Pastor Maurice Osbourne Jr. is the senior pastor here. But you just saw Reverend Ozzy. So that means he lied about his name, and he is actually Pastor Osbourne."

"They lied about their names, the name of the church, and where they live." Bella glanced at the church. "They lied about a lot of things, and I fell for it. I'm so stupid." She pounded her hand on the dashboard. "I just wanted to help them, Sophia." Tears welled up in her eyes again. "And I wanted to prove Papa wrong. You know he said I would never have kids, because no man would want my ugly behind? I wanted to stick it to him, but it backfired on me. He's probably laughing at me in his grave."

"Bella, your father was a jackass. Okay? I told you that already. And it didn't backfire on you. It didn't go the way you wanted, but you still have a daughter. I think that's her we saw beside the Jezebel. You'll now get a chance to be in her life."

"They're going to say I agreed to give her to them when she was born. Plus, she's his daughter too." Bella hung her head.

"Well, they were the ones who broke the agreement. Did they allow you to be in her life like they said they would?"

Bella shook her head.

"Okay, then. Did they give you the money for college like they had agreed?"

Again, Bella shook her head.

"And the apartment and car?"

"No."

"Okay, then," Sophia said. "Then as far as I'm concerned, any agreement between you and them is null and void. That's *your* daughter. As for Reverend Ozzy or Osbourne, or whatever his name is, he better get ready to pay child support and hold his corners."

"Do you want to call the police now or wait until after church?" Bella asked.

"I would like to embarrass them in front of all their church members, so everyone can see them for the scumbags that they are, but we have to remember your daughter," Sophia replied. "We have to determine the best way to deal with this. Maybe we should find out where they live and go see them there. We'll then confront them and call the police. What do you think?"

Bella thought for a while. She kept glancing back and forth between Sophia's face and the church, nibbling on her bottom lip. "All right. That's probably better. Let's do it."

"Fasten your seat belt." Sophia started the car. "We'll ask around until someone tells us where they live." She drove out of the church's parking lot and out onto the street.

They didn't see Bobby hiding around the side of the church, watching them until the car disappeared down the road.

"We have a problem," Bobby whispered to Rachel, his body seemed to be vibrating from the fury coming from inside him.

"What's going on?"

"Bella found us."

Rachel turned to stare at him. She then spun around, looking over her shoulder, scanning the faces behind her.

"Turn around," Bobby snapped. "She's not back there. She just left."

Rachel did as she was told. "So that's why you ran out of here so fast."

"Yes. I turned to greet the idiot behind me and just happened to glance toward the back of the church. I wasn't too sure at first, but when I looked back again and saw her and a lady rushing out of here, I decided to make sure. It was her, all right."

Rachel muttered expletives. She looked up at the pulpit, and her eyes met those of her husband's, where he sat in his tall chair, watching her and Bobby as Elder Davis delivered the Word. It was Maurice who was supposed to preach, but before they left the house that morning, he called the associate pastor and asked him to do so.

Rachel looked away and said under her breath, "He's onto to us, you know?"

"Yeah, I know. And now that Bella is here, we have to take him out tonight or tomorrow. She can't get to him before we do."

"Okay. Especially now that the Penguin is gone," she said of Minister Sonny. "It's time to move."

Minister Sonny visited for twenty long weeks, stating that he needed the long overdue vacation, plus he had to make up time with his mother. He even preached at church a few times as if he was vying for an associate pastor position. With him following Maurice around like how Tuff did with Gabby, Rachel and Bobby's assassination plan went as cold as a microwave dinner in the freezer. But Minister Sonny left for home yesterday, so it was time for the plan to thaw out.

"He stayed that long because he's suspicious of us too," Bobby informed her. "That's why he was shadowing that fool so much. Our hands were tied unless we were going to kill him too."

"We couldn't do that. The police—"

"I can barely concentrate on what the preacher is saying," a church member complained behind them, loud enough for Rachel and Bobby to hear.

"All this susu susu in the Lord's house," another added. "It's a crying shame."

Rachel was about to spin around, but Bobby squeezed her thigh. "Ignore them and chill out. No more talking until we meet later to finalize things."

"There is a young girl coming this way. Let's ask her." Bella nodded at the young girl walking toward where Sophia's car was parked by the road. She seemed to be around thirteen or fourteen years old. Bella and Sophia got out the car.

"Hello there," Sophia said when the girl reached them. "How are you?"

"Fine. Thanks." She paused in front of them.

"Say, do you happen to know where Reverend Ozzy live?"

"Who?"

"Sorry. I meant Pastor Osbourne," Sophia added quickly, as if she had misspoken.

"Oh, Pastor Osbourne. That's my pastor, but I didn't go to church today. He lives in a big house not too far from here," she said without hesitation. No questions asked, as Bella and Sophia had hoped.

"My grandmother and Ms. Mattie are good friends," she continued. "But anyhow, when you go over that little hill"—she pointed to her right—"keep going until you come upon the big houses. That's where the rich folks live. You know what I mean?" Her eyebrows were rising and falling suggestively.

Bella nodded and Sophia smiled.

"But, anyhow, Pastor's house has a tall, big, wide gate like this." She opened her arms wide. "And it has two golden angels on it. They are so beautiful, like angels in heaven. You know what I mean?"

Both Bella and Sophia nodded.

"But, anyhow, you can't miss it. Look for the angels and you find the shepherd." She chuckled at her attempt at humor. "Got it?"

"We got it," Bella and Sophia said together.

"Thank you so much," Bella told her. "We appreciate your help."

"You're welcome." The young girl bobbed her head.

Bella and Sophia sported big grins as they watched her stroll away.

"So we find the golden angels and we find the devils." Sophia looked at Bella. "You ready to go see your daughter?"

Bella choked up and couldn't speak, so she nodded her head.

"Okay. Let's go 'angel' hunting."

They got in the car and drove off in the direction the young lady had indicated. Bella and Sophia found the house without any problem, thanks to the two golden angels.

"I have to admit, they are beautiful," Sophia said of the golden angels on the gate. "They really know how to fool people, don't they?"

"They certainly do. They fooled me and so many others." Bella stared at the impressive house.

"At least your daughter is growing up in a mansion," Sophia remarked. "It looks very nice from outside."

"It's not the house that makes the child, Sophia," Bella told her. "It's the home. Trust me I know. Sometimes you don't know the evil that's hidden behind those impressive looking walls. If the Ozzys are what we know them to be, then my poor little baby is probably living in hell like I did after Mama died." She sniffed loudly.

"Or maybe not." Sophia patted Bella's hand. "The girl said a Ms. Mattie live here too. I don't know who that is, maybe the housekeeper? But certainly Mattie wouldn't stand by and see them abusing a baby and not do anything about it?"

"If Mattie is working for them, then she's just like them."

Sophia shuddered at the thought. "That all comes to an end soon. Thank God." She drove off a little down the road from the house and parked between two cars, in front of a neighbor's house. "We'll wait here for them to come home."

The two ladies passed the time refining their plan to expose the Ozzys and get Bella's daughter. All this time glancing in the rear view and side mirrors at every vehicle that headed their way.

"This white Camry is slowing down in front of the home," Sophia said two hours after they took up their surveillance. She bent her neck to the left, then right, to ease the crick in it.

Bella sat up straighter in her seat, looking through the side mirror. "It looks like it's them, but we can't see inside."

"It's tinted and we're too far down."

They watched as the gate opened, separating the two golden angels on either side of it. Then, the car pulled through and it then closed again.

"Let's give them a few minutes before we go," Sophia said. Just then Sophia's cell phone rang. She picked it up and looked at the caller ID. "It's Mama. Let me quickly tell her that we found your daughter, okay?"

"Okay."

As Sophia brought Mrs. Moon up to date on what's going on, Bella anxiously wrung her hands together. "Sophia." She touched Sophia's leg as she looked through the side mirror. "Look."

Sophia glanced in the rear view mirror. "Mama, I have to go." She quickly pressed the End button.

Bella and Sophia watched as the gate opened up again and a black pickup truck pulled in, before it closed again. Its windows were also too dark for them to see who was inside.

"Now who was that?" Bella looked at Sophia.

"That's a good question. Maybe someone coming to dinner?"

"There goes our plan," Bella said with disappointment. "What do we do now?"

"We come back later," Sophia replied. "We'll go back to my house, change out of these heels, and get something to eat. Then we come back."

Bella took another glance at the towering house as Sophia drove away. Her daughter was trapped in there with those monsters. *I'm coming back for you, sweetheart. I failed you once but not again. I'll be back.*

Chapter Twenty-six

"Sophia?" Bella peered down at Sophia who was sprawled out of the long brown velvet couch, snoring lightly. "Sophia, I'm ready to go back now." She gently shook Sophia's shoulder, but she didn't budge from her deep sleep.

Bella nibbled on her bottom lip as she thought. She could wait until tomorrow and let Sophia rest tonight. But tomorrow Sophia had to work. If she woke up Sophia now, then she would feel guilty because it was obvious how tired she was.

Bella paced the living room as she contemplated how to get back over to Reverend Ozzy/Maurice's house. She moved over to the window, looking out as dusk settled in. She watched as a car pulled up in front of Sophia's neighbor house.

"Mama, the taxi is here," shouted a teenage boy who was standing outside with two other boys.

Bella eyes widened before she grabbed her handbag off the other empty couch and rushed to the front door. She pulled the door closed behind her and ran out to the gate. She got there just as Sophia's neighbor got to her gate.

"Hello, Mrs. Green," she greeted the lady. Sophia had introduced them that morning when they ran into her as they were leaving for church.

"Hello, Bella. Is everything okay?"

"Yes, ma'am. I was just thinking of getting a taxi be-cause I need to take care of something when I saw this one pull up for you. Do you mind sharing? He could drop you off first, then take me where I'm going."

"No problem. Come on." Mrs. Green got in the back of the taxi on one side, Bella on the other.

The driver dropped off Mrs. Green at her ailing sister's house. "So where are we going now?"

Bella told him, grateful that she had memorized the address from earlier that morning. Minutes later she got out in front of Maurice's house. She paid the driver and walked up to the gate. Butterflies began fluttering in Bella's stomach, but determination was etched across her face.

"You can do this," she told herself as she pressed the buzzer on the wall beside the gate post. Bella waited a few seconds, then pressed it again. But the gate remained closed. "So you think you can ignore me, huh?" Bella put her finger on the buzzer and kept it there, clearly now pissed off. "You hid from me for almost two years, but not anymore." Her finger remained on the buzzer.

"Hey! Lay off the buzzer," said the very handsome, tall man who walked out to stand in front of Bella on the other side of the gate. "You need to press it only once and wait."

Bella lifted her head to look up at him. "I'm tired of waiting," she replied. "I'm here to see Reverend Ozzy, I mean Pastor Osbourne, and I want to see him right now."

"Well, you saw him." The man opened his arms as if to say, "Here am I."

"Please don't joke with me. Tell Pastor Osbourne or his wife to get out here immediately, or I'm going to call the police." Bella opened her handbag and fished out her cell phone. She held up in his face. "The clock is ticking, pal."

Maurice's eyes twinkled with amusement as he peered down at the exquisite but irate young woman before him. "The clock is going to tick for a very long time, because

I am Pastor Osbourne, and this is my house. Now, how may I help you?"

Bella stared at him in confusion. "You are Pastor Osbourne?"

The man nodded and said, "That's me. Pastor Maurice Osbourne Jr. Again, how may I help you?"

"But . . . but I don't understand." *Don't believe him. He's lying to protect them,* she thought.

Just then a little dog raced down the driveway and ran up to the gate, sniffing and wagging its tail. Following right behind him was a little girl who walked unaided, her steps wobbly.

"Oh, dear Lord," Bella muttered as the little girl who came to stand beside the man. She noticed the white birthmark on the left side of the child's face. It was just like hers. With her hand covering her mouth, she gazed at her daughter for the first time, a small river now poured down her face.

"I'm so sorry," Bella whispered over and over, deep sobs shaking her body. Then she wept even harder.

Maurice stood frozen, unsure of what was going on and what to do. Then he quickly opened the gate and rushed over to Bella. "Are you okay?"

But Gabby wobbled over to the weeping woman and wrapped one tiny hand around her mother's leg.

Bella peered down at Gabby through teary eyes. She fell to her knees and came almost face-to-face with the child she had given birth to fifteen months ago.

Maurice stepped closer. "Hmmm . . . Gabby?"

"Hello, Gabby." Bella smiled through her tears. "I'm so glad that I finally get to meet you."

Gabby smiled as if she understood, and Tuff ran around Bella, wagging his tail in greeting.

Bella reached out and pulled Gabby in for a big hug.

"Okay, please let her go." Maurice reached down for Gabby, but Bella held on to her.

"Do you help them beat on her?" Bella asked, her tears dripping on Gabby. "Do you call her ugly? Slap her? Kick her?"

"What? Of course not!"

"Do you call her a freak because she has this mark on her face? It's not her fault, you know? It's mine."

"That's it. Please let her go." Maurice reached down again and scooped up Gabby into his arms. "Who are you? What's going on here?"

Bella stood to her feet, wiping her wet face with her hands. "Why don't you stop lying and tell those two criminals who sent you to come out and face me? If they think I'm going away, they make a sad mistake."

Just then Mattie stepped out of the house. She walked through the open gate and stood beside her boss. "Pastor Maurice, is everything all right out here?"

"Mattie, please take Gabby back inside. I'll be there as soon as I figure out what's going on here." Maurice placed Gabby in Mattie's arms.

Mattie took one more puzzled look at the young woman before she walked back to the house with Gabby, Tuff right on her heels.

"I have a strong feeling we need to talk," Maurice said to Bella. "Please come and sit with me on the veranda."

Bella hesitated then followed him through the gate, before it closed behind them. As she walked up to the veranda, she noticed that the truck that they had seen going through the gate earlier that day wasn't in the driveway, just the white Camry. *Probably hidden in there*, she thought when she saw the three-car attached garage. *Fool me once, shame on you. Fool me twice, shame on me.*

"Please have a seat." Maurice pointed to the veranda chair, and Bella sat down. He then sat down across from her. "I don't know what's going on here. Can you please start by telling me who you are and what you're doing here?"

"I'm Bella, and I'm here to see Reverend Ozzy and his wife, Rachel. I thought he was really Pastor Osbourne, since it turns out he lied when he told me he was Reverend Ozzy. But if you're Pastor Osbourne, then I guess he's really Reverend Ozzy."

"Huh?"

"It's a long, complicated story."

"I have all the time in the world. As I told you already, I'm Pastor Osbourne, and Rachel is *my* wife. I don't know a Reverend Ozzy. So why don't you start from the beginning and tell me why you thought I was lying about who I am and how you know my wife."

"So you're really not working for them? They're not hiding in there?" Bella pointed to the door.

"The only people inside are Gabby and Mattie. Oh, and Tuff. My wife went to visit one of our sick church members earlier."

Bella stared at him as if she was trying to sort through what he had said. "So you're really Pastor Osbourne," she said when she saw the sincerity in his eyes. "And you really don't know what's going on here?"

Maurice shook his head, a tight feeling in his gut.

"It all started when I met Reverend and Mrs. Ozzy in Port Antonio," Bella began.

Moments later Maurice bent his head between his legs as he sucked air into his lungs. He had just got sucker punched with the truth of his wife and brother's deception. He knew immediately that the man with the "lopsided grin, who was always tugging his earlobe and had a long scar on his cheek" and who masqueraded as Reverend Ozzy was, with a doubt, his older brother.

"It was them all along," he whispered. "My 'stomach poisoning' and the shots fired at me that night. My wife and brother have been trying to kill me all this time."

"Your brother? Reverend Ozzy is your brother?"

"Yes, and he isn't a pastor. His name is Bobby, and he's my half brother."

"Wow. I guess Gabby and I were part of the plan too. But why?"

"They want the money." Everything was now falling into place. "Mine and Gabby's. They wanted to make sure they got it all."

"Good God. They were planning on killing my daughter too?"

"So . . . so . . . so you're really saying Rachel isn't Gabby's mother?"

"No." Bella stared down on him with sympathy. She was realizing that he too was just a victim like her. "I'm Gabby's mother."

Unable to stop them, the tears trickled down Maurice's face. He grabbed his gut because his intestines felt like they were in knots. There was a pain so deep inside, he wished he could reach into his gut and pulled it out. "But it can't be," he said to Bella. "I was there when she had the artificial insemination done."

"Were you there for Gabby's birth?"

Maurice raised his head and looked at Bella. "No, I was away in Africa on a missionary assignment. She went in premature labor two months before I came back home." He felt like he was grasping at straws, but that was better than the truth. "I'm not saying you didn't have a child, but it's not Gabby. It can't be."

"May I use your bathroom please?"

"It's right inside. The first door on the left." He whimpered loudly like a wounded animal as he looked out into the garden. "Why, Lord? Why is this happening to me?"

"I'm sorry they used you like they did me," Bella said when she returned and stood in front of him.

Maurice looked up and clasped his hand over his mouth to stifle the scream that rose up. "Lord have mercy," he finally managed to say, his eyes bugging out of his head. Bella stood before him make-up free, the white milk birthmark covering the left side of her face as it did Gabby's. "You're Gabby's mother."

"Yes. So you see, it's my fault why she's probably ugly to you."

"She's not ugly." He stood up and walked to her. "And neither are you."

"So you don't beat on her?" Bella turned pleading, teary eyes to him.

"I would never do that. I love Gabby and have been taking great care of her."

"Mrs. Moon said God would send someone to take care of her. I'm glad He sent you." Bella smiled up at him. "Thank you so much."

Maurice nodded and said, "You don't have to thank me for looking after my daughter. It's my responsibility to do so."

"But you're not Gabby's father," Bella told him. "Reverend Ozzy . . . I mean Bobby is."

Maurice staggered back as if drunk. He heard Bella calling his name, but her voice was muffled. The veranda began to spin, the house swaying from left to right. His legs felt like cooked spaghetti. He heard a loud scream before his body crumbled to the ground.

"Pastor Maurice." Mattie waved the smelling salt under Maurice's nose.

Maurice sniffed, shaking his head from side to side, as he came to. "Mattie?" He looked up into Mattie's concerned face, lying on his back on the floor.

"You scared the living daylights out of me," Mattie told him. "I almost called the ambulance when this young lady screamed and I came and saw you on the ground."

Maurice turned his head to the side and saw Bella kneeling there. So it wasn't a dream, after all. Rachel wasn't Gabby's mother, and he wasn't her father.

"They are going to pay for what they did," Maurice said to Bella as he pulled himself up into a sitting position. His head felt like a baked potato. "Don't worry. God is not dead. You'll see. Mattie?"

"Yes, Maurice?"

"Please give Officers Carty and Peters a call for me. Tell them I would like them to meet someone."

"Yes, sir." Mattie gingerly rose to her feet. "Are you sure you're okay? Is someone going to tell me what's going on?" She glanced down at Bella. "Why does this young lady look so much like Gabby?"

"I'll fill you in later. Please make that call for me. Okay?"

"Okay." Mattie hurried inside to make the call.

"They're finally going to get theirs, aren't they?" Bella stared at Maurice with expectation.

"Job 4:8-9 says 'Even as I have seen, they that plow iniquity, and sow wickedness, reap the same. By the blast of God they perish, and by the breath of his nostrils are they consumed.'"

Bella nodded and looked away, a little smile tugging at the corners of her mouth. "Sounds good to me."

"I'm so angry with myself," Maurice remarked. "Why didn't I see what was going on all this time? I could clearly see that Rachel didn't bond with Gabby. And as for my brother, his jealousy was so apparent at times. For someone to be so smart, I'm really stupid. And I call myself a man of God. Please."

"Come on. Get up off the floor." Bella stood up.

Maurice held on to the table and pulled himself up. He quickly sat down as his head still didn't feel right. "I bet this plan went into motion after I tracked down my brother," he continued. "I was just a mark for my wife, and I fell into her trap."

"Maybe because you were in love with her," Bella said. "I've never been in love, but I heard it can make you blind to the obvious."

But Maurice shook his head. "No, I wasn't in love with her. I thought so at first, but after a while I realized it for what it was—lust. But I had made a commitment and was determined to make my marriage work, ignoring the Holy Spirit all this time. And it almost cost me my life and that of my daugh . . ."

"You're the only father she knows, you know?" Bella reached over and touched his hand. "Please don't stop loving Gabby now. I'm begging you."

"I would never do that." Maurice placed his other hand over Bella's "I'm still her father and I'll always be." Tears welled up in his eyes. "Gabby is my little princess."

"She's adorable. I'm glad you saw that despite this." Bella touched her birthmark. "I wish my father could have done the same for me, but he didn't. Thank God Gabby didn't go through what I did."

"Then your father was an idiot." Maurice reached over and touched Bella's face where the birthmark was. "Gabby is as beautiful as her mother."

Bella's eyes met his before she looked away, blushing. "Thank you."

"Ahem."

They looked up at Mattie watching them from the doorway. "The officers are waiting for you at the station. But first Gabby wants her father to come and put her to bed."

Maurice stood to his feet. "And her mother too." He stretched out a hand to Bella, and she took hold of it as she got to her feet.

"Say what again?" Mattie looked from one to the other.

"It's a long story." Maurice patted her on the shoulder as they passed by to enter the house. "I'll tell you in a little while."

"Lord, you know I think I'm getting too old for all this soap opera," Mattie said, loud enough for Maurice and Bella to hear as they went up the stairs, hand in hand. "And I have a strong feeling there's a whole lot more to come."

Chapter Twenty-seven

Later that night Rachel and Bobby entered Maurice's quiet house. It was in darkness except for the dim light coming from Gabby's bedside lamp. The pastor didn't like her sleeping in the dark. "I think they're sleeping," Rachel whispered.

"Good," Bobby answered. "You go in and keep him distracted while I go take care of that old hog. We can't afford for her to ruin this again. It's now or never."

They both tiptoed up the stairs. Rachel went to the right toward the master bedroom. As she passed by Gabby's bedroom, the door wide opened, she pulled it closed before going in to see her husband.

Meanwhile Bobby went to the left, toward Mattie's bedroom which was facing the street in the front. As he approached the door, he realized it was partially opened. He hesitated before he slowly pushed the door back and crept into the room. It was semi-dark with beams of light from the streetlight outside coming in through the glass pane window and the sheer curtains.

He moved slowly over to the bed, pulling out the big butcher knife that was hidden under his loose shirt. But the bed was empty except for a note in the middle. Puzzled, Bobby walked over to Mattie's bathroom and looked in. It was empty too.

He went back over to the bed and picked up the note. Not wanting to turn on the light he edged closer to the window and read it using the streetlight. *Pastor Maurice,*

I'll try to be back from Mother Brown in the morning before you and Gabby wake up. But if not, please don't burn down my kitchen trying to make breakfast. I'll be back to do that. Mattie.

Bobby almost wet himself with joy. Nosy Mattie wasn't there to hear the voice to save her boss again. That's one less killing for him. Chuckling lightly, he left the room and headed over to his little brother's.

Bobby entered to stand beside Rachel. She stood looking down at Maurice as he slept in the partially dark room with only the moonlight filtering in.

"He doesn't even know that he's about to die," Rachel whispered. "I wish it wasn't so but there's too much on the line now."

"Getting scared?" Bobby whispered back in her. "We have to do it before Bella gets to him. If not, he'll figure out you tried to poison him and I tried to shoot him. We're looking at prison for a long time, baby."

Rachel said, "You took care of Mattie?"

"Guess what? She's spending the night at Mother Brown's."

Rachel frowned. "I don't think she has done that before."

"Who cares," Bobby said in her ear. "She's not here and a burglar is about to break in and kill the pastor and his daughter. We'll come in and find the bodies and call the police. Got it?"

"Step over to the corner while I wake him up." Rachel turned on the bedside lamp; the forty-five-watt bulb cast an eerie glow in the room. Then she reached down and shook her husband's shoulder. "Babe?"

Maurice opened his eyes, rolled over onto his back, and yawned. "Hey. You're just getting in?"

Rachel didn't answer but sat down on the bed beside him. "You know, for some strange reason, a small part of me is going to miss you."

Maurice looked puzzled. "Excuse me? What are you—"

"Enough with all this chatting," Bobby spat as he walked over to the bed, the big butcher knife in his hand.

"Bobby, what's going on?" Maurice sat up with his head against the headboard. "What's with the knife? Rachel?"

Rachel stood up with a smirk on her face. "You're about to die. That's what's going on. It took so many freaking years but finally I'm about to become a very rich woman."

"And me a very rich man." Bobby bent over and slapped Maurice hard across the face. "I wanted to do that since the first time I saw your little rich, spoiled, disgusting face. But then I thought about it and decided to take what I was deprived of all my life—your money that our father left you."

"You're crazy, you know that?" Maurice tasted blood in his mouth.

"I'm crazy or you're stupid? My girlfriend seduced and married you, tricked you into believing she gave birth to your daughter, and you didn't even know it. The rich humanitarian travelling to Africa to help suffering, poor people. The popular pastor with thousands of members. But as dumb as a jackass's behind."

Rachel giggled. "You certainly have a way with words, darling."

"You think you're going to get away with this?" Maurice glared at them.

"Who's going to talk, dear husband?" Rachel moved closer to him. "Mattie escaped her own death because she's luckily spending the night with Mother Black."

"Mother Brown," Bobby corrected.

"Black, Brown, who cares? And that little ugly thing sleeping in the next room will have her throat slit from ear to ear." Rachel used her hand to demonstrate, wiping it across her own throat, a nasty grin on her face.

"You sicken me." Maurice hissed through his teeth. "Both of you."

"Oh, you just hurt my feelings, little brother." Bobby raised his hand with the knife. "And for that you're about to die. Say hello to Daddy Dearest for me."

Just then Rachel moved down to the end of the bed and grabbed Maurice's legs. "Do it now, baby."

But Maurice reached up and grabbed Bobby's hand that held the knife. He was pushing up and Bobby was pushing down. Both very strong men, the veins in their necks standing at attention, strength verses strength.

Rachel let go of Maurice's legs and walked back up to the head of the bed as the men struggled for the knife. "Enough!" She slapped Maurice so hard across the face, his head snapped back and he let go of the knife.

This was the opportunity that Bobby was waiting for; he positioned the knife directly over his brother's heart. "Now you die."

Just then the room was flooded with a bright light. "Police! Drop the knife!"

Both Rachel and Bobby spun around to face Officers Carty and Peters who had entered the bedroom with their guns drawn.

"You set us up?" Bobby asked Maurice over his shoulder. "How?" But in his gut he knew. Bella had gotten there before they did.

"Who is stupid now, Bobby?" Maurice asked. "If you had checked my daughter's room you would have realized it was empty just like Mattie's."

"I said to drop the knife," Officer Carty yelled.

"It's not what you think, officers. We were just playing with my brother."

"Don't let us have to shoot you, man," Officer Peters said, ignoring the rubbish that just gushed from Bobby's mouth. "Do you see that little red light by the telephone?

That's a tape recorder. Now step away from Pastor and drop the knife."

Bobby stared at the men for a few seconds wishing he had planned to shoot his brother instead of gutting him. He would have his gun and a better chance of taking out these two cops. But a knife wasn't a fair match against two guns. So he dropped the knife and raised his hands in the air.

"Mrs. Osbourne, please step away from the window," Officer Carty said with his gun now on Rachel, while Officer Peters ran over to cuff Bobby's hands behind his back.

While everyone's attention was on Bobby, Rachel used the time to edge closer to the window. "No, I'm not going to prison." Rachel shook her head.

"Sweetheart, we'll get a good lawyer," Bobby informed her.

Bella then appeared in the doorway. Bobby stared at her like he was seeing Bob Marley and Rachel gasped loudly.

"All these years of deception, betrayal, heartache, pain, and nightmares, and for what?" Bella stepped further into the room, tears streaking down her face.

"Good God, she's as ugly as her daughter." Rachel exclaimed, looking at the birthmark on Bella's face with horror. "You fooled us."

"So much for her being perfect." Bobby shook his head as if he was disappointed in himself for selecting Bella as the surrogate mother. "Mystery now solved."

"She's perfect." Maurice got up off the bed and walked over to Bella, placing his hand around her shoulder. "She's a beautiful woman, inside and out, made in the image of Christ."

Rachel rolled her eyes and Bobby snorted.

"I loved and respected you, Mrs. Ozzy . . . I mean Rachel." Bella was still crying softly, the wound in her heart still deep and fresh. "I thought you loved and cared for me too. That's why I wanted to help you."

"Idiot," Rachel spat. "You were a means to an end, and you're lucky we didn't see your hideous face before we selected you."

It was almost as if Bella had received an antidote for the venom spewing from Rachel's mouth. Her words landed and bounced off Bella with no impact like a hard rain on asphalt. "What end? You just got caught and are about to spend the rest of your life in prison. I get to spend mine with my beautiful daughter."

"Oh, I'm not going to prison, you ugly heifer." Rachel took another step closer to the window.

Bella walked up until she was almost in Rachel's face. "You should take a look in the mirror sometimes, *Rachel*." A loud sound rang out in the room when her right hand connected with Rachel's face. "That's for deceiving me."

Rachel's mouth popped wide open, her hand on her cheek. "Why, you little—"

Slap! Rachel's head snapped back from the impact.

"And that's for stealing my baby." Bella raised her hand in the air again.

"Okay, that's enough, ma'am," Officer Carty remarked.

Rubbing her hands together to ease the sting, Bella strolled over to Bobby, her face etched in anger.

Bobby stood tall looking down on Bella with his hands handcuffed behind his back, a smirk on his face. "You think I'm scared of you?"

Bella landed a kick in Bobby's groin.

He doubled over in pain, screaming at the top of his lungs, and firing off expletives in rapid succession. "You little b—"

"Say it." Bella raised her leg and pulled it back in position. "I dare you."

"Okay, ma'am. That's enough." Officer Peters gently rested his hand on Bella's shoulder. "We'll take it from here."

Bella glared at Bobby with disdain, then at Rachel, who was standing by the window, rubbing her cheek. She then marched out of the room with her head held high.

"Mrs. Osbourne, let's go." Officer Carty took a few steps toward Rachel. "Please don't make this harder on yourself."

"Stay back!" Rachel's eyes were dancing wildly in her head. "I'm supposed to travel the world as a rich woman, not be locked up like a caged dog."

"Rachel, it over," Maurice told her. "Please don't do anything stupid."

Officer Carty took a few more steps and said, "Mrs. Osbourne . . ."

Suddenly Rachel ran and threw herself at the glass window. Her haunting scream echoed in the room and then reverberated in the night as she fell to the ground below.

Officer Carty and Maurice bolted out of the bedroom.

"You aren't going anywhere, Bobby." Officer Peters leveled the gun at Bobby when he moved toward the door.

Outside Maurice and Officer Carty looked down at Rachel as she lay on the ground, unmoving, her limbs twisted and her head at an unusual angle.

Officer Carty knelt down and pressed his fingers to Rachel's neck. No pulse. "She broke her neck," he said softly. "She's dead."

Maurice knelt down beside his wife and took her hand in his. "I'm so sorry you felt you had to do this." The floodgates opened up, and tears streamed down his face. "May God have mercy on your soul."

"Rachel." Bobby yelled from the broken window up-stairs, looking down at the body of his girlfriend on the ground below. "Baby, get up. Come on, darling."

But Rachel wasn't getting up ever again.

Chapter Twenty-eight

It had been eight months since that fatal night when Bobby tried to murder Maurice and his wife Rachel jumped to her death. For weeks everything was like a circus—*The Jamaica Gleaner*, *The Star*, and *The Jamaica Observer* all had the story on the front page of their newspapers. One titled it "The Foursome: The Pastor, His Wife, Her Brother-in-law Lover, and the Baby Momma."

Reporters and television crew camped outside their house for days, all wanting an exclusive interview with Maurice and Bella.

But Maurice couldn't have gotten through that hard time without Bella who stayed by his side. At first Bella wanted to return to Port Antonio with Gabby but knew it would be hard for her to leave the only father she knew. Also, Gabby had just recently met her and didn't know her well enough. So, Maurice and Bella talked about it. .

"Stay here," Maurice had told you. "Gabby needs you."

"But what will people think?" Bella had asked him. "They are going to gossip about us even more now."

"We know in our hearts we are doing the right thing, but most importantly God knows, and that's what counts." Maurice replied. "Also, Mattie lives here and I'm sure Sophia will be around a lot."

" I could stay with Sophia."

"Sure, if that makes you more comfortable. But people are going to talk anyway as long as you're in town and coming around to see Gabby. We can't worry about them. Let's do what's best for Gabby."

That was enough for Bella. She missed the first fifteen months of her daughter's life and wanted to get to know her. So Bella stayed.

With Mattie and Minister Sonny taking charge, a beautiful funeral was planned for Rachel Osbourne. It was like the entire community came out to help Maurice lay his wife to rest. Most came in support of their pastor, and others came just to watch and gossip.

"His poor father is rolling over in his grave," eighty-two-year-old Sister Means told her buddy, Sister Chunks. They were sitting in the second row of Rachel's funeral service behind Maurice who had Bella by his side, holding Gabby in her arms. "It's like this *Old and Wild* soap opera that my granddaughter watches every day."

"You mean the *Young and Restless*."

"Same difference. Pure drama." Sister Means sucked her teeth loudly and crossed her arms across her ample bosom as she glared at the back of Maurice's head, not concerned that he was overhearing their conversation.

"I knew that boy was too young to be no pastor. What a something in our little community, huh? Pastor baby is not his but his brother. While his wife is really his brother's woman and not really the mother of the baby that pastor thought was his."

"Mind you bite your tongue with that tongue twister," said Sisters Means. "Now the baby momma is sitting on the front row with her baby beside pastor while the baby daddy is in jail."

"Lord, take the cake and two slices of pie with it." Sister Chunks waved the paper fan across her face, cutting her eyes at Maurice and Bella's backs.

"All I know is that I'm not coming back to this theater they're calling a church," Sister Means said loud enough for her pastor to hear. But Maurice kept his head straight, ignoring them and all the others who were whispering and pointing.

"Shucks, if I didn't know any better I would think its Pantomime. Pure puppet show in this church. Everyone needs Jesus, starting with the so-called pastor."

But not everyone shared Sisters Means and Chunks opinion. Many of the church members, including the elders, mothers, and associate pastors decided to stand by Maurice after he called a meeting and explained Rachel and Bobby's deception to the leaders of the church.

Some could have said, "I told you so," but they kept quiet and promised to hold down the fort while their pastor got through this hard time in his life.

To understand a lot of what had transpired, Maurice knew he needed answers and only one person could give them to him—Bobby. So he decided to pay his brother a visit.

"I'm surprise to see you, little brother," Bobby said when he entered the visiting room of the Richmond Farm Correctional Centre, where he was imprisoned.

"Have a seat, Bobby." Maurice's face was stern. "I need to talk to you."

"So now you want to talk, huh?" Bobby sat on the bench across from his brother with a smirk on his face. The long scar seeming more pronounced than ever as he tugged on his earlobe. "You waited until you knew I would probably spend the rest of my life in here. Didn't you?"

"For once you did the right thing," Maurice told him. "You saved all of us the heartache of reliving everything you and Rachel had done." He was referring to the deal that Bobby took to avoid a trial. He had pled guilty to two attempted murders, possession of an illegal weapon, and kidnapping of a child. He was sentenced to twenty-five years to life in prison, with the possibility of parole.

"Don't call her name!" Bobby jumped to his feet and the guard took a few steps toward him. "We're cool, man." Bobby waved at him and sat back down.

"I can see why it's hard for you to hear her name." Maurice glared at him. "She was a broken woman and you used her for your own selfish reason. It cost her, her life."

The scar on Bobby' face jumped, his nostrils opening and closing. "Rachel knew what she was getting into. She agreed with the plan because she knew we would be rich. It was a chance she was willing to take."

Maurice looked at him with disgust. "But you knew she was mainly doing it for you. If you had called it off, she would have agreed and would probably be alive today. You're an evil man, Bobby."

"Thanks for the compliment." Bobby leaned back with a smirk on his face. "You know where I messed up? I should have killed that marked beast after she had the baby. As a matter of fact, we should have forgotten about the whole baby thing and just killed you after Rachel married you. But she wanted that money in the trust fund for your heir too."

"What did I ever do to you for you to hate me so much, Bobby?"

"What you did to me?" Bobby leaned forward and locked eyes with his brother. "You lived the life I was supposed to have! Then our father left all his money to you. What about me?" He pounded his hand on the table and the guard shot him a warning look.

"I never knew about you until Daddy told me, and I came to find you right away. Plus, he passed away the same night he finally met you. I invited you to come and live at the house with me, you refused. I offered to give you money to build up your construction business, but you didn't want that. Do you know whose money I inherited, Bobby? It was *my* mother's, not our father's. So you weren't entitled to anything. You wanted too much, and now you have nothing!"

Bobby gave Maurice a death stare, as if that would finally do the trick in killing him.

"You know what? Despite everything you've done. I don't hate you," Maurice told Bobby. "I do get angry at times when I think about the deception, especially letting me think Gabby was mine and Rachel's when she was actually yours and Bella. But with God by my side, I'll be fine. Bella and I are going to raise Gabby to be a beautiful, smart woman of God."

"'Bella and I.' It seems like you've fallen for the ugly beast, little brother. First it was baby Godzilla, now Mother Godzilla. What are you building up? A zoo?" Bobby threw his head back and roared with laughter.

Maurice shook his head and looked at him with sympathy. "You're pathetic. I'm getting out of here." He stood to his feet.

"So how does it feel to be raising my daughter, little brother?" Bobby smiled broadly.

"It feels pretty good actually, Bobby. Gabby is still my blood. She's my niece and I love her, and I know she loves me too."

The smile fell from Bobby's face.

"Oh, I'm sure you also heard what had happened to your crooked friend, Dr. Zandt." Maurice leaned over to stare at Bobby. "His license to practice medicine has been suspended for five years. Also, he's on probation for ten years and was fined five million dollars. Of course, I wanted him to be suspended indefinitely, barred from ever practicing medicine again, but the board found that he did not commit any malpractice."

He continued, "According to them, he carried out a successful AI and then delivered a healthy baby. He was wrong for taking part in this scheme for money, but it's not enough to take away his license forever. Can you believe that? He should be in here with you."

"He's greedy, but he's actually a good doctor," Bobby replied.

"Well, if he ever does anything like this again it may not turn out too good for him," Maurice remarked. "I'm going now. I don't know if and when I'll visit again, but I'm here if I can help you with anything," Maurice said. "I'm not going to just turn my back on you. After all, you're my brother."

"I can't figure you out." Bobby frowned at him. "After everything, you'd help me?"

Maurice nodded his head and said, "It's not me, Bobby." He met his brother's eyes and held it. "It's the God in me." He took a few steps away, then turned back to his brother. "I'll also be praying for you. Your body may be locked away in prison, but your soul doesn't have to be trapped in hell. You too can find redemption." This time he turned and walked away to the exit door.

"Yo. Little brother," Bobby yelled at his back.

Maurice paused with his hand on the door handle and sighed loudly. He turned partway and then glanced back at Bobby. "Just have to get one last shot in, right?"

"Yes, I do." Bobby stood up and stared at him for a few seconds. He opened his mouth and closed it. He opened it again but hesitated.

"Goodbye, Bobby." Maurice pulled the door open.

"Gabby is your daughter," Bobby shouted.

Maurice let go of the door and turned around as if in slow motion. It was like a silent wind had passed over the room and froze everything. On shaky legs, he walked back to Bobby and lowered himself onto the bench. "What did you just say?"

Bobby sat back down also and repeated, "Gabby is your daughter. She's not mine."

Tears leaked from Maurice's eyes, and he quickly wiped them away. "You're just trying to hurt me all over again, aren't you?"

For the first time Bobby seemed sincere. "Go and get a DNA test if you don't believe me. We lied to Bella about Gabby's father, and to you about Gabby's mother."

"But how did you and Rachel pull that off?"

"Dr. Zandt." Bobby leaned back on the bench. "You know what they say. 'When money talks . . .'"

Chapter Twenty-nine

The truth, the whole truth, and nothing but the truth . . .

"Thank you for doing this for us, baby." Rachel kissed Maurice's lips. "I know you don't want to . . . you know."

"No, I'm not thrilled at giving that doctor my sperm sample. As a matter of fact, I think he's enjoying this too much." Maurice frowned.

"He does seem to have a little sugar in his tank." Rachel giggled. "Well, once we're pregnant, we don't need to see Dr. Zandt again. There goes his crush on you."

"That man needs Jesus."

"Do you . . . hmmm . . . need help with the sample."

"I think I'll manage," Maurice replied. "Okay, out you go."

Rachel gave another quick kiss before she left the hospital room. Dr. Zandt was waiting for her in the corridor.

"Pastor Stud Muffin all set?" Dr. Zandt's eyes twinkled with amusement.

"I would get ahold of myself if I was you. Keep focus here."

"All right." Dr. Zandt held up a hand. "Can't I admire a fine specimen of a man?"

Rachel sucked her teeth and cut her eyes at him. "Where's Bella?"

"She's in the room, ready for Bobby's, or should I say Reverend Ozzy's, sperm to be injected into her body."

A nasty look flashed across Rachel's face. "But she'll be impregnated by my darling husband instead."

"I hope you two know what you're doing," Dr. Zandt said. "But it's not my problem."

"No, it's not," Rachel snapped. "We're paying you a lot of money to do this. And as Bobby warned, you better keep your mouth shut or else."

Dr. Zandt said, "No need for threats. I already agreed to do it, didn't I? Bella has passed all the tests and is ready to go. Your husband is healthy with a strong sperm count. I see no reason why they can't conceive. Now please get into the room and undress."

Rachel shot him another threatening look before she entered the hospital room.

Bobby was sitting on a chair waiting for her, and asked, "Little brother all set?"

"Yup, he didn't even need my help. I have a feeling Maurice has some experience with masturbation."

The two shared a healthy laugh. Rachel then took off her clothes, pulled on the flimsy blue hospital gown and got on the little bed. "You need to go and be with Bella. My darling husband will be here soon to be with me for my intrauterine insemination with his sperms. Ewww."

Bobby smirked. "And I'll go keep little Bella calm. After all, the little virgin is about to be impregnated with my child. Yuck."

Rachel chuckled and nestled back on the bed, content. Things were looking good. Her eyes closed, she imagined all that she would do with the money she would inherit from her dead husband and supposedly dead child. Money, money, money.

Twenty-five minutes later there was a knock on the door. "Come in." Maurice entered with Dr. Zandt right behind him.

"Hi, sweetheart." Maurice walked over to his wife and looked down on her. "Nervous?"

Rachel nodded, her face etched in concern. "I really want us to start our family. I don't know what I'll do if this fails."

"We'll trust God," Maurice told her. "Everything must be done according to God's will." He pulled the chair closer to the bed. "I'm here—"

"Sweetheart, don't be mad, but I don't want you to stay."

"What do you mean?" Maurice looked at her, puzzled. "I want to be here with you while you have this done."

Rachel gave him a sweet smile. "I know, and I love you for it. But this is a little . . . embarrassing. Like it was for you when you . . ."

"Okay. I get it," Maurice said. "I'll be right back in when it's done." He leaned over, kissed his wife gently.

"You can wait in the waiting room," Dr. Zandt told him. "I'll come and get you when we're done here."

"Thank you." Maurice left the room.

"Let's get this done." Rachel jumped off the bed, slipped off the hospital gown, and got dressed in a matter of seconds. "After you."

Dr. Zandt opened the door a crack and peeked out, looking up and down the corridor. "All clear." He pulled the door wide opened and walked out with Rachel behind him.

The two went the opposite direction from the waiting room where Maurice was waiting, and walked into another hospital room a few feet away.

"Hello, Bella," Rachel greeted the nervous young lady lying on the bed. "Dr. Zandt and I were just going over a few things."

"Is everything okay?" Bella's eyes were wide in her face.

"Everything is fine," Dr. Zandt replied. "The sperm sample has been washed, and we're ready to go."

"My wife and I are so happy that you're going to be doing this for us," Bobby said from where he sat in the chair by her bed. May God bless you, Bella."

Bella beamed. "I know in my heart this is the right thing to do. My child will have great parents and I'll get to be in his or her life. We'll all be happy."

"Yes, we will dear." Rachel patted her hand. "We all deserve to be happy."

"I couldn't agree more." There was determination in Bella's eyes.

"Now that we have settled that, shall we begin?" Dr. Zandt moved closer to the bed as he pulled on a pair of blue latex gloves.

"Uh . . . is Reverend Ozzy staying?" Bella shyly looked down at her legs.

"Not if you don't want him to," Rachel answered.

"Reverend Ozzy, why don't you wait in my office?" Dr. Zandt gave him a pointed look. "We'll come and get you when we're done here."

Bobby stood up and exited the room. Rachel sat in the chair he was in.

"Okay, Bella. This won't take too long." Dr. Zandt smiled at Bella.

True to his words the procedure was over in a short time as Dr. Zandt had promised.

Rachel and Dr. Zandt left the room after Bella said she wanted to take a nap while she waited the forty minutes before she could move.

Rachel hurried to Dr. Zandt's office where Bobby was waiting. She waited thirty minutes before she headed to the waiting room where Maurice sat watching a small television and sipping a D&G ginger beer.

"Hey, I thought Dr. Zandt was coming to get me so I could sit and wait with you?" Maurice got up and walked to his wife. "Are you okay?" He pulled her into his arms for a tight hug.

"I'm fine." Rachel pulled back and smiled at him. "We'll know in two weeks if we're pregnant. Let's go home." She quickly hurried him out of the hospital and out into the parking lot, glancing over her shoulder along the way. She left Bobby to take Bella back to the apartment in town with some excuse for her absence.

Two weeks later Dr. Zandt confirmed that Bella was pregnant. The next day he told Rachel that she was not. Rachel cried uncontrollably.

"We'll keep trying the natural way, darling," Maurice comforted his wife. "I strongly believe that God is going to let us have a child when it's time."

Over the next few days Rachel cheered up and appeared accepting of the fact that the artificial insemination didn't work. During this time Maurice got a call from a group of pastors to join a team going to Africa again in a few months.

"I can't go," he told Rachel. "You need me here now."

"I'm fine." Rachel held out her hands wide to her sides. "I was disappointed that I didn't get pregnant but God knows best, right?"

So reluctantly Maurice agreed to go on another trip to Africa. Exactly two months to the day of Bella's pregnancy Rachel rushed into Maurice's home office as he sat behind his desk going over some paperwork for church before he left for his missionary trip.

"I'm pregnant!" She threw herself into his arms, waving a piece of paper in her hand.

Maurice was stunned into silence

"Darling, you heard me? We're pregnant." Rachel peered at his face.

"How?" Maurice asked. "I mean when? How did you find out? Why didn't you tell me you thought you were pregnant?"

"I suspected I was but didn't want to get your hopes up. So I made an appointment with Dr. Zandt because he knows our history and Bobby took me to see him three days ago. He did a urine test and also a blood test. The urine test was positive, but I wanted to wait until the blood test results came back. He called me earlier with the results, and I asked him to fax a copy to me at the church."

"So that's why you ran out of here so fast earlier." Maurice took a look at the blood test results, and his eyes watered with each word he read. "It says here that you're about one month along. We're pregnant!" He lifted his wife into the air. "Didn't I tell you we would conceive naturally when God says so?"

"Okay, put me down." Rachel giggled. "This baby is already making me feel nauseous."

Maurice lowered her to her feet. "You know what that mean, right? I can't leave for my trip tomorrow."

"Oh yes, you can, and you will," Rachel informed him. "I'm just a month pregnant and you'll be gone for only six months. So you'll be back in time to rush me to the hospital and be there for our child's birth."

"But what if something happens and I'm not here?" Maurice was concerned. "I need to be here with you."

"I have Mattie and your brother here. I'll be fine," Rachel insisted. "I want you to do this now because after the baby is born you won't be going on another trip for a longgggg time." She kissed him passionately. "Go do what you're passionate about and come back so we can spend the rest of our lives with our baby. Okay?"

Maurice reluctantly agreed. "I'm going to call as often as I can. And I think I may be able to get a video chat here and there also."

So Maurice left for Africa to be back in six months. He called as often as he promised and Rachel updated him on her supposedly pregnancy and emailed him tons of pictures of her prosthetic belly.

"My God, your stomach is getting so big," he told Rachel one night when he called.

"I'm five months along but it feels like nine," Rachel replied. She began wearing the prosthetic belly when she was expected to be far along, fooling Mattie and everyone at the church. She only took it off for Bobby and when she went to sleep, careful to lock her bedroom door from nosy Mattie.

A week before Maurice was scheduled to come back home to Jamaica he got an urgent call from his brother. He and Rachel were attending the Faith Temple New Testament Church of God annual rally in St. Thomas, representing Christian Deliverance Church of God, when his wife went into premature labor.

"Thank God we're in St. Thomas," Bobby said to Maurice "I rushed her to the hospital and Dr. Zandt is taking care of her."

"Thank you, Lord," Maurice replied. "I'm glad she's with Dr. Zandt because I know she's more comfortable with him. Please call me back as soon as possible and let me know how they're doing." Maurice's worry transmitted through the telephone. "The baby is two months early. I'll be here praying that everything goes well."

Later in the wee hours of the morning as he and Rachel lay on the bed in the hotel, with Bella's baby on the other bed beside them, Bobby called back to let Pastor Maurice know that he was the father of a beautiful baby girl.

"Is she okay?" He was worried that his daughter may have some medical complications after being born early.

"No she doesn't. In fact, even Dr. Zandt said if he didn't know better he couldn't tell she's a preemie. He wants Rachel and the baby to stay in the hospital for two days or so before we can go home."

So Rachel and Bobby spent two days at the hotel before they left for Mandeville with the baby. Rachel was angry and upset with the baby's ugly birthmark but had no choice but to take her home. Her husband would be there soon and his daughter should be waiting for him.

Chapter Thirty

"I can't believe that I'm really Gabby's father." Maurice searched Bobby's face for a sign that he was lying.

"I'm still not sure why I told you because I promised myself I wouldn't, but it is what it is," Bobby replied.

Tears trickled down Maurice's face as he stared at Bobby. The guards, a few inmates, and their visitors turned to look at him, but Maurice didn't care. "Gabby is really mine?"

Bobby rolled his eyes in annoyance. "Didn't I just tell you that she is? I love money and God knows I wanted every cent you had but not at the expense of becoming a father. I would rather slit my wrists."

Maurice wiped his face with the back of his hand. "My little princess. I just knew we had a bond that goes beyond her being my niece. But Bella was so sure that she wasn't mine."

"Bella believed what we wanted her to believe. Same for you too."

"Thank you for telling me, Bobby." Maurice smiled. "I do believe you're telling the truth, but I think I'll still go ahead and get that DNA test to put this to bed once and for all."

"Knock yourself out," Bobby replied. "You'll see that this time I'm telling the truth."

Maurice rushed home to share the news with Bella. She was floored.

"So you're really Gabby's father?" Bella was smiling through her tears.

"That's what he said, and I believe him. But tomorrow we'll go and get tested to be sure. Not that it makes a difference to me," Maurice quickly added. "Gabby's my daughter, and I love her."

"I know you do," Bella told him. "I agree that we should do this for Gabby's sake. I want to put this all behind us and move on from here."

They got the DNA test done the very next day.

Ten days later Maurice walked into the living room where Bella and Mattie were watching television, a letter in his hand. "The results are here," he announced and two anxious pairs of eyes turned to him.

"Go ahead. Open it." Bella got up off the couch and slowly moved closer to him, fear dancing in her eyes.

"Pastor Maurice, I can't take all this suspense and all." Mattie stood up.

Maurice's hands shook as he ripped the letter open and took out the piece of paper in it. Drops of tears leaked from his eyes.

Bella gasped loudly, her eyes too filled with tears. "I'm so—"

Mattie said at the same time, "Bobby is a lying, low-down, dirty—"

"It says 99.9% that I'm Gabby's father," Maurice told them.

"What?" Bella and Mattie spoke together again like two identical-twin parrots.

"Yes!" Maurice pumped his fists into the air as he danced around the living room.

Bella and Mattie laughed out loud, happiness resonating around the room.

"We're Gabby's parents," Maurice stated the now obvious to Bella as he came to stand before her.

"Thank God," Bella replied. "I was so . . ."

Maurice leaned forward and kissed away the rest of her words with jubilation and a touch of passion.

Bella's eyes bugged as she stood frozen, unsure of how to respond to her first kiss with the very handsome pastor. Her daughter's real father.

Mattie's eyes twinkled with amusement as she looked on. "It's about time he get himself a good woman," she mumbled under her breath. "Thank you, Father Jesus."

"I'm so . . . so . . . so sorry," Maurice said after he broke the kiss and stepped away from Bella. "I'm not sure why I did that."

"I am." Mattie smiled mysteriously when they both turned to look at her, only then remembering that she too was still in the room. "But I'll let you two figure it out. See ya." She walked away with a little pep in her steps, humming a song.

"Bella, please forgive me."

"There is nothing to forgive." Bella looked away and consciously raised a hand and touched her face where the birthmark was hidden under her makeup. "You were just caught up in the moment. That's okay. I know a man like you would never be interested in someone like me."

"That's not true at all. Why would you say that?"

Bella gave him a sad smile and said, "You saw me without all this," she made a circular motion with her hand in front of her made up face. "You know how ugly I am. Please don't patronize me. Isn't the face a reflection of the soul?"

Maurice moved closer until they were a few inches apart, and Bella hung her head down.

"Bella, please look at me." Maurice waited until Bella glanced at him, her eyes blinking like a malfunctioning taillight. "Is Gabby ugly?" he asked her.

"Of course not." Bella sounded offended. "My daughter is very beautiful. She's precious. She's perfect. She's . . ." She paused and gradually a smile worked its way on to her face.

"So are you." Maurice returned the smile. "I think *you* are a very beautiful woman, Bella. Just like our daughter."

"Thank you." Bella fled to her room but could not flee her growing feelings for her baby's daddy. It started after Maurice asked her not to return to Port Antonio and to stay with Gabby after everything went down with Rachel and Bobby. As the days ran into weeks, her feelings for Maurice grew. This was new to Bella. Here she was almost twenty-three-years old with an almost two-year-old daughter, but she had never been kissed or had sexual relations with a man.

"He'd never want someone like me," Bella often told herself. "He goes for the Rachel type—tall, slim, beautiful, sexy, and flawless. As Papa would say, I'm a werewolf." Bella's self-esteem had hit rock bottom again, even with her face beautifully made up. Avon just wasn't doing the trick anymore.

The one person who always brought a smile to Bella's face was Gabby. She took to Bella like disposed chewing gum to a shoe bottom.

"Hey!" Bella said when a small splash of water hit her in the face.

Gabby laughed and splashed her mother again with water from the almost full bathtub.

"Oh, I'm going to get you now." Bella laughed from where she was kneeling beside the bathtub, she reached for Gabby and began to tickle her sides and tummy.

"No," Gabby said in her little baby voice, giggling and wiggling, twisting this way and that way, kicking her little legs, sending water everywhere.

By the time the "tickling game" was over, Bella's hair was wet and limp, her clothes soaked, and water was running down her naked face, the makeup all washed away.

"All right, we need to get you dried off, sweetheart." Bella stood up, with Gabby in her arms. "As a matter of fact, we both need to get dried off." She placed little kisses all over Gabby's wet face. "Next, it's a bedtime story, and then Daddy and I will tuck you into bed. Okay?"

Looking up into her mother's face, Gabby reached up and gently touched the left side with the birthmark, as if she understood the bond they shared through it.

Tears shimmered in Bella's eyes. She leaned over and kissed Gabby on hers in return.

Bella didn't see Maurice slowly backing away from the bathroom door, a smile on his face and tears leaking from his eyes.

"We have to talk about me returning to Port Antonio," Bella said to Maurice as she entered his home office about four months after the kiss. "I can't live in your house forever."

Maurice looked up from his desk at Bella. "Why not? It's a very big house. Don't you like it here?"

"Of course I like it here, but I'm not your responsibility."

"But Gabby is your responsibility too." Maurice was using their daughter because he didn't want Bella to go. "She needs her mother."

"I'll always be here for Gabby. I'll come to visit often and take her to spend time with me and Mrs. Moon. I'm not abandoning my daughter. I'm going to see if I can get a job, so I can start living independently."

"You can get a job here, Bella." Maurice got up and walked over to her. "I'll contact a few people for you. This way you can still work and be here with me and Gabby. I meant with Gabby," he added quickly. "Be here with our daughter. She has grown so attached to you over the past year. It will break her heart if you leave."

Bella nibbled on her bottom lip. She didn't want to leave, but she wouldn't stay around the charismatic pastor anymore. She had to go, at least for a while. "I'll be back in a few weeks and then I'll let you know what I decide to do. And as I said before, I'll never leave Gabby."

"You think running away will stop what's going on between us?" Maurice addressed the thousand-pound gorilla in the room.

Bella cleared her throat and replied, "I don't know what you're talking about."

Maurice smiled and said, "I told myself that too. In fact, I'm still questioning my judgment where women are concerned. After all, I married my brother's girlfriend and didn't even know it. I deserve to be by myself. I'm a fool."

"No, no, no. You loved her. That's why you didn't see her for who she was."

"I lusted after her. There's a difference, you know." Maurice walked over to the opened window. "She was different from the other women who were trying so hard to get my attention. She was feisty and alluring. Just exciting to talk to and be around, well, at first. I wanted to be with her." He looked down at the green manicured grass in his backyard. "As a pastor, I knew I had to marry her to be with her. So I did. It was a little over a year after meeting her. I quickly realized that I loved her, but I wasn't in love with her. Especially with her changing attitude and behavior, but I was determined to make my marriage work."

Bella remained silent and let him speak. She knew it was important for him to get this off his chest.

"I saw the red flags," Maurice continued. "The harsh way she treated Gabby, especially when she thought I wasn't around. Her nasty attitude to Mattie and some of the pastors and church members. I even walked in on her and Bobby a few times, looking as if they were in deep conversation, probably planning my murder. Mattie saw through her, even Minister Sonny saw her for what she was. Heck, even Tuff saw what I didn't want to see. But I chose to ignore it." He turned around and looked at Bella. "But you know where I failed the most?"

Bella shook her head.

Maurice strolled back over to her. "I ignored the voice of the Lord. He was right there all along speaking to me and warning me, but I didn't listen. And it nearly cost me my life and my daughter's."

"Uh, you did listen sometimes," Bella told him. "You listened to me when I told you what had happened. It helped saved your life. Plus, Rachel was a very beautiful and sexy woman. I'm nothing like her."

"I agree."

Bella's head snapped back as if slapped.

"Rachel's heart was filled with evil, yours is of compassionate and kindness. So much so that you decided to selflessly become a surrogate mother for a woman you grew to love and thought loved you in return." Maurice gently tapped her on the nose. "Rachel would do whatever it took to get what she wanted, while you give so much of yourself without expecting a thing in return. You're a phenomenal woman, Bella."

Bella blushed and glanced down at her feet.

"I don't know what this is." Maurice pointed his index finger from himself to Bella and back. "But I'm not in a hurry to get involved with any woman at this time. Let's focus on what's best for Gabby and get you a job if you decide to stay here. In fact, maybe you should finish your associate degree at the Northern Caribbean University that's right here in Mandeville. Maybe even go on to your bachelor's degree if you want. What do you say?"

Bella sighed loudly. "I would like to finish college as I promised Mama. I guess I could work and finish up my associate degree. I'll think about moving on from here when the time comes."

Maurice clapped his hands excitedly. "That's awesome, Bella. I also have to work on mending bridges in the hearts of my church members who are questioning my leadership and dedication to the Lord."

"No more trips to Africa?" Bella asked him. Maurice had told her of his love of being a foreign missionary and the awesome experience he had spreading the word of God to hundreds of people in Africa before Gabby was born.

"Maybe in a few years when Gabby is older and only for a few months. For now, I have a lot to focus on here at home."

Bella replied, "As you said we'll keep our focus on Gabby. I don't have any experience with men and all this . . . stuff."

Maurice grinned at her. "Okay. We'll work on your resume on Monday and I'll give it to a few of my colleagues. We'll also drive down to the college and start working on transferring your credits from CASE."

Three weeks later Bella got a part-time job as a registration clerk at the Mandeville Hospital and began evening classes at Northern Caribbean University.

"Isn't it funny how the two of you keep sneaking glances at each other?" Mattie smiled sweetly at Bella and Maurice one evening at dinner as they all sat around the dining table.

"It's very funny indeed." Mrs. Moon's eyes twinkled mischievously, looking back and forth between Bella and Maurice. Sophia had gone and got her the day before for a visit. This was her second time visiting with Bella since she began living in Mandeville. She first came to meet Gabby after Rachel died and stayed for a few days. She and Mattie developed a good friendship, and she simply adored Gabby and, in her own words, "the dashing, handsome young pastor."

"Both of you are nothing but troublemakers," Maurice replied. "You keep it up."

Laughter rang out around the table, Gabby's the loudest.

Once things settled down, Mrs. Moon glanced over at Maurice and asked, "Are you ready for church on Sunday?"

"As ready as I'll ever be," Maurice replied. "Mentally, I'm ready to get back in the pulpit. I was born to preach, and I can't let one setback by the devil keep me from what the Lord wants me to do." This would be Maurice's first time preaching since Rachel had died and Bobby had gone to prison, a little over a year ago.

"God will give you the words to share with everyone," Bella told him. "Just go with what's in your heart." She shared a longer than usual look with Maurice before glancing away.

Mattie and Mrs. Moon watched their every move.

That Sunday morning Bella was the last one to join the others on the veranda for church. When she walked out, everyone stared at her in silence.

"You look lovely," Mattie told Bella. "Come on, Gabby. Let's go take our seat in the car." She took Gabby's hand and walked off down the driveway.

"How you do feel, sweetheart?" Mrs. Moon was looking at Bella with concern. She had been there before Bella's introduction to Avon makeup. She remembered the young, abused girl who avoided eye contact, suffered from low self-esteem, and felt she was ugly. Bella only gained confidence after Sophia introduced her to makeup and she was able to hide behind the makeup mask that covered the birthmark she detested.

"Bella, you don't have to do this if you're not comfortable," Maurice finally spoke. "Don't get me wrong, I think you look stunning. But are you sure?"

Bella was wearing a closely fitted black and gold dress that stopped at her knees with black, high-heeled sling backs. Her hair was pulled back in a bun from her naked smooth face, except for the clear lip gloss on her lips. Glancing from Maurice to Mrs. Moon, she replied, "I'm sure. Don't get me wrong, I'm so nervous right now, it's not even funny. I haven't looked in the mirror since morning because I'm afraid of what I'll see. But everyone knows by now that I'm Gabby's real mother but they don't know what else we share."

Bella was tearing as she went on, "I continued to wear the makeup because I wasn't ready to expose myself to everyone. After all this time I still felt as if I would be judged and ridiculed. Isn't that funny? So today I'm doing this not just for me but for my daughter as well. I don't want her to grow up feeling like she has to hide behind makeup to be beautiful. She's perfect just the way God made her. As her mother, I don't just want to tell her. I want to show her too. Who knows? Maybe one day I'll also believe it for myself."

"You've grown up so much, my darling." Mrs. Moon drew her in for a hug. "You know I almost lost my mind when I found out what those people did to you. But now I'm beginning to understand that it was all a part of God's plan for you." She pulled back and stared in Bella's eyes. "Now I know you need Gabby just as much as she needs you. God never makes a mistake."

"No, He doesn't." Bella sniffed loudly. "It took a while, but I'm beginning to see that now myself."

"Me too." It was Maurice's turn to give Bella a big hug. The two stood that way for a while locked in their tight embrace. They didn't see Mrs. Moon as she walked away to the car.

Beep! Beeppppp! Gabby had reached over from the back seat and pounded her little hand on the car horn per Mattie's instruction.

Bella and Maurice jumped apart, while the occupants of the car chuckled at their expense. They were teased mercilessly by the two older women all the way to church.

Christian Deliverance Church of God was packed to capacity when they got there. The air was filled with anxiety and curiosity. Maurice had attended church services since the scandal, but he never preached. This was done by the associate pastors. Until today.

"Listen to all that whispering and bickering," Mrs. Moon said in Bella's ear. She was sitting in the front row with Bella, Gabby, Mattie, and Sophia. "You would think after all this time they would have gotten over everything and keep their mouths shut."

"They're probably staring at me." Bella touched her birthmark. "This is the first time I'm coming to church without my makeup." She consciously lowered her head toward the ground when she felt a tug on her hand. It was Gabby. That was what it took for Bella to raise her head and look toward the podium. *You're doing this for your daughter,* she reminded herself. With her arm around Gabby, they both began to sway as the praise and worship team took the church on a spiritual, musical high.

Then it was time for the word. The congregation was still standing when Maurice approached the podium, a Bible in the middle with a glass of water covered up beside it.

"Shall we praise the Lord!" Maurice waved his right hand in the air, his face turned up in the air. "If God has been good to you give Him some praise!"

And it was obvious that He had been because the church did so at the top of the voices.

"Thank you. You may be seated," Maurice told them moments later. As everyone took their seat, he glanced at the front row. Bella gave him a smile, Mattie gave him a thumbs-up, Mrs. Moon winked, Sophia pointed at him, as if to say, "You're the man," and Gabby blew him a kiss and waved enthusiastically.

"It has been a while since I've stood up here before you," Maurice began. "And I must start by thanking the Lord for keeping me through the toughest time of my life. The devil knocked me down, and I must confess I was down for a while. But as you all can see, I'm now standing!"

"Amen," "Thank you, Lord," and "Hallelujah" rang out.

"We all know the unfortunate incidents that occurred a year ago. For some it was like watching a soap opera or something, but for me and my loved ones," he looked at the front row where Bella and the others sat, "it was our lives being turned upside down. Especially for my daughter, her biological mother, and myself."

People were now craning their necks to stare at Bella and Gabby as if they were hearing something new. But Bella kept her arms wrapped around Gabby who was now sitting on her lap, her eyes fixed on Maurice.

"But today I'm not here to point fingers and lash out at anyone. Today is a day of restoration. Today I'm taking back my position as senior pastor of this church as I continue to do the work that the Lord wants me to do."

The associate pastors on the pulpit stood to their feet and began to clap. Mrs. Moon, Mattie, and Sophia did as well. Soon some church members were on their feet and before long most of the church were applauding with the exception of a few disgruntled ones.

Maurice continued, "Every one of us is trying to recover from something we didn't choose. I didn't get to choose if I wanted to go through what I did. It just happened to me. We were all born into something that we didn't choose."

"I know that's right, pastor," someone yelled from back.

"We didn't get to choose our mother or father, whether we wanted them to be good parents or to abuse us. We didn't choose when and where we were born. Whether we wanted to be rich or poor. We didn't get to choose. Even our physical appearance, we didn't choose how we wanted to look. Some of you may feel your nose is a little too big, for others it may be your mouth."

A few self-conscious members looked down at their laps.

"Some of you may be vertically challenged, meaning you're short," laughter rang out, "while some of you may say you're too tall. None of us choose to be black or white. No, we didn't get to choose our ethnicity. We were born in a pre-determined situation and we cannot change it. We didn't get to choose but we have to learn to deal with it by the grace of God. Amen?

"I'm here to share with you that God doesn't always explain what He's doing but you just have to get through it by faith. And after you get through that storm you'll realize that you feel lighter and better because you have lost some baggage that was weighing you down. The storm destroyed what was holding you back and had you captive. The storm rooted up the trees of abuse, poverty, low self-esteem, unforgiveness, bitterness, hatred, anger, and malice and blew them away."

"Hallelujah." A gentleman shouted as he stood to feet, his hands up in the air.

"Thank you for the storms, Lord," a sister yelled.

"Blow them away, Father Jesus," an elderly woman screamed.

Pastor continued, "But listen, you won't know that until you come out of it! You have to go through some things just to destroy what is haunting you. Glory be to God!"

People were now on their feet, tears were flowing, hands were clapping, and feet were stomping. The words of the Lord were finding their mark.

"So even though we didn't get to choose our situations or to pick our storms, we know who holds the future and we know He holds our hands. Am I talking to somebody?"

"You better talk to me, pastor," a lady close to Bella shouted, waking up Gabby who had dozed off in her mother's arms.

"If God bring you to it, He'll bring you through it! Is there any situation too hard for your God? No! So embrace who you are, accept your flaws and imperfections, and seize what you've been through because you're special, you're peculiar, you're you."

The tears seemed to have a mind of their own and trickled down Bella's face, and Gabby reached up and wiped them away with her fingers. Bella squeezed her even tighter.

"You, my brothers, and sisters, are children of the almighty God. So even though we didn't get to choose, we can rest assured that we were chosen. Hallelujah!"

The church was lit by the Holy Ghost fire. Through His servant, God had spoken, healing wounds, mending hearts, and rejuvenating spirits.

Chapter Thirty-one

"Hey! Slow down!" Bella's eyes were tightly closed, one hand biting into Maurice's muscled thigh and the other gripping the car seat.

"Come on that's not fast." But Maurice slowed down his new toy; a brand new Acura MDX SUV. "I'm just testing it out."

Bella opened her eyes and rolled them at him.

Maurice roared with laughter. "You know Gabby starts to roll her eyes too. I wonder who she gets that from." He glanced over at Bella before turning his eyes back on the road.

Bella smiled and said, "She's getting so big, right before my eyes."

"I'm glad you're a part of her life. And mine too."

Bella nodded, her heart now beating a little faster.

"Thank you for coming with me. I love your company," Maurice added.

"No problem." Bella stared out the window as they drove toward the hospital. "I'm not sure what I'll do when we get there, but I don't mind helping if I can."

"We're going to visit Sister Rosy and pray with her. As her pastor, I have to encourage her and my other members when they're sick. Some do get discouraged and need to be reminded that Dr. Jesus is still in the healing business."

"Encouragement goes a long way," Bella told him. "It changes lives, and I'm a living witness to that." She touched her face, which was void of makeup. Ever since she decided to bare her face at church a few months ago, Bella hasn't worn much makeup since, except for her lipstick or lip gloss and a little blush on occasions.

"There are times I'll start feeling like the freak, just like when I was growing up, or the gorilla that Papa said I was." Bella took a deep breath, and Maurice reached over and clasped her hand in his, the other maneuvering the moving car. "But then you would pay me a compliment, and that's when I have a choice to make. Do I believe the nasty words of my wicked dead father or the kind words of a compassionate man? I choose you because you're nothing like him. I thank God every day that you're Gabby's father and she'll never experience what I did."

Maurice's hand tightened around Bella's hand and his nostrils flared in anger. Hearing about Bella's father always had that effect on him. He said through his teeth, "I wish I was around to deal with Mr. Pig."

The laughter rolled up from Bella's tummy and came pouring out. "It's Pigmore." She laughed so hard that tears ran down her face.

Maurice joined in, looking back and forth from Bella's laughing face to the road. "I love to see you happy. And I'm going to make it my mission in life for you to stay this way."

Bella blushed as she wiped her wet face with her fingertips. "Thank you," she said in a meek voice. No wonder she had so much feeling for this man. It wasn't gratitude or even the fact that they shared a daughter. It was those tingling butterfly feelings she used to read about in the romance novels when she was a child. Back then she fantasized about a man like this, especially after her father kicked her behind, literally. Now here he was in person—a prince. But could he be hers? She certainly wasn't a princess.

"Here we are," Maurice announced as he pulled into the hospital's parking lot. "What do you say we have dinner after we're done here?"

"You and me?" Bella's eyes were large in her face.

"Yup. I'll call Mattie and let her know. In fact, I'll ask Gabby's permission." He winked at her.

Bella chuckled. "Okay. You have a deal."

After leaving the hospital Bella and Maurice went to a Maxine's Soul Food Restaurant for dinner. It was a beautiful Saturday evening and the place was jumping with patrons while the tantalizing smell of the well-seasoned and cooked Jamaican dishes teased everyone's nose.

Sister Maxine was a member of Christian Deliverance Church of God. So in no time her pastor and Bella were escorted to their table for two in a secluded corner of the restaurant.

"Hello, Pastor. Hi, Sister Bella." Sister Maxine came over after Maurice and Bella were seated. "I heard you two were here and just wanted to welcome you both." Her grin looked like a dog that was given a bone. "You also have a lot of privacy over here." She rubbed her hands together in glee. "I don't mean to overstep but—"

"But you're going to anyway." Maurice's eyes twinkled as he looked at the bubbly older woman. He had known Sister Maxine since he was a child.

"Well, you know me." The dimples in her chubby cheeks deepened. "I think this time you've found your helpmate, Pastor. I can feel it in my soul."

Bella's cheeks reddened, and she lowered her head toward her lap.

"Thank you, my sister. Now that you've embarrassed my date, please be prepared to answer to our daughter tomorrow."

Bella laughed with Maurice and Sister Maxine, grateful that he had taken them out of the hot seat. But it certainly felt good that a longstanding member of the church felt she was a good match for her pastor.

Sister Maxine took their orders and sashayed away as if she were proud of herself.

"Sorry about that," Maurice said to Bella. "She meant well."

"I know," Bella replied. "It's just a little weird. It's like we're on . . ."

"A date?" Maurice finished. "I would like to think so. It's been almost two years since Rachel died and almost took my trust in women. But thanks be to God I'm reclaiming my life. I like you a lot, Bella. Several months ago we decided to just focus on Gabby while we both continued to heal. Now I want to get to know you more. I mean we talk a lot and share so much with each other. Can we see where this goes?" His eyes pleaded with her.

"Huh?" Bella's eyes bugged. She locked eyes with him before glancing away. "You really want to . . . hmmm . . . to get to know me like that?"

"I really do. And I know the hell you've been through, even before you met my wife and brother. I can't change your past, but I'm committed to help you now, and if God's willing, in the future. Think about it and not just for Gabby's sake, but for us—you and me."

Bella bobbed her head. "Okay. I'm new to all this, and it's a little overwhelming . . . but God, right?"

"That's right, darling. He's the potter, and we're the clay. He'll mold us the way he wants us. So let's trust Him on this."

And that Bella did. There were many more secluded dinners between her and Maurice as their relationship grew. She accompanied him almost everywhere as her time allowed between work and school; to visit the sick and shut-in members, to rallies and conventions all across Jamaica, and to every event at church.

It wasn't long before some of the members were referring to her as 'First Lady, Bella.' And six months after they began dating Maurice decided to take things to a whole 'nother level.

Mrs. Moon and Sophia came to spend the weekend. Mattie went into full cooking mode, preparing every dish that she could think of. Gabby was happily wandering around the house with Tuff right on her heels. Maurice seemed to have a fixed grin on his face with mysteriousness flashing in his eyes.

Bella was happy. As she took a moment and sat in her bedroom, the chatter and laughter floated up from downstairs, cloaking around her. "Hi, Mama." Bella peered out through her open windows, the rays of the bright golden sun kissing her fresh face. "It has been a long time, but I still miss you so much. I wish you were here to see how happy I am now. Although I think somehow you know, don't you? This was what you always wanted for me, even when I failed to believe it myself."

She went on, "I had only known pain and heartache, except for those special moments we shared. When you died, I just about gave up. It has been a very long, winding, exhausting, and painful journey to get here, but you have an awesome granddaughter. I think she looks like you, especially when she smiles." Bella's wet eyes shone with glee. "And I'm also dating her father. Can you believe that, Mama? A man like him likes me for me, and he's nothing like Papa."

"God, I hope not."

Bella spun around to face Maurice as he entered the bedroom.

"Sorry if I'm interrupting." He walked over and sat down on the bed beside her, wrapping his arm around her waist, tugging her closer to his side. "The door was open."

Bella felt that intoxicating sensation she got when he was close. "It's all right. I was just talking to Mama. I know it may seem foolish, but it makes me feel close to her."

"It's not foolish at all. I do the same with my mother and father," Maurice told her. "I believe they are around us as our guardian angels. I wish I had met your mother."

Bella's face lit up. "She was so beautiful, even after losing a few teeth to my father's fists. To this day I wonder why she stayed with a man like that. But I'm not going to judge her. I'm sure she had her reasons."

"I'm sure." He kissed her on the cheek. "I was sent to get you for dinner. Mattie and Mrs. Moon cooked enough food to feed the entire community."

"Let's go and see how much damage we can do then." Bella stood to her feet and took a few steps before Maurice wrapped his arms around her from the back, his chin resting on her head.

"Are you sure you're okay?" he asked her. "Do you want to talk?"

"I'm okay. For the first time I can say that and mean it."

"Good. You know I'm always here, right?"

Bella nodded. "Thank you for everything. Come on."

Hand in hand they entered the dining room where everyone else was sitting. Tuff had already started and was slopping up whatever was in his bowl on the floor.

"I thought you two were lost," Sophia commented. "I almost fainted from hunger."

Dish after dish of white rice, stewed chicken, tripe and beans, and dumplings disappeared as everyone ate to their heart's content. Gabby was the first to rest back in her high chair, her little tummy shooting out.

"Looks like you're throwing in the towel, baby." Maurice tickled Gabby's tummy, and she dissolved into giggles.

After dinner everyone gathered in the living room. Mrs. Moon was telling embarrassing stories about Sophia when she was a child, everyone laughing while Sophia playfully groaned. Bella especially enjoyed listening to another child's happy upbringing with a devoted father. It was so unlike hers.

No one noticed when Maurice slipped out with Tuff. Moments later Tuff returned to the living room with a bell tingling on his collar. All eyes turned to look at the dog.

"Tuff, what do you have there?" Bella reached down and took off a little gold box that was attached to the bell.

"That is something for you," Maurice answered as he took Gabby out of her high chair and strolled over to where Bella sat on the couch. He placed Gabby on her feet before he lowered himself to his knees in front of Bella.

Everyone gasped in surprise.

"Gabby, come here, baby." Maurice held out a hand to Gabby, and she knelt down beside her father, her face lit up with excitement. "Please open it," he said to Bella.

Bella lifted the top off the box to reveal a huge, oval-shaped diamond and platinum engagement ring and exclaimed, "Wow."

"Wow. This is so awesome," Sophia yelled, bouncing up and down on the couch like a kid.

"Yes, Father Jesus." Mattie was advertising her dentures.

"Oh, dear Lord." Mrs. Moon's eyes were already wet.

Even Tuff was yapping and running around the room, as if he sensed the excitement of the moment.

"Bella," Maurice took her hand into his. "It took heartbreak for me to learn what love really is. But it took an even better woman to show me, and I just want to thank you for that. I love you very much and would be honored to have you as my wife. Will you marry me?"

Bella sat frozen. Her mouth was hanging open, and tears escaped her eyes and ran down her face. The room was arrested in silence as all eyes were locked on her.

"Bella?" Fear was etched across Maurice's face. He loudly swallowed against the lump that felt like a tennis ball in his throat.

"Ma?" Gabby got off her knees and rushed into her mother's arms. Her face made up like she too was about to cry.

Bella let go of Maurice's hand and held Gabby close. She looked down at her man still down on his knees. "I . . . hmmm." She cleared her throat and tried again. "I feel as if I'm having the most wonderful dream of my life and I'll wake up any minute. But it's not a dream, is it?"

"No," Maurice responded. "This is real, sweetheart."

"I never knew it would be possible for me to fall in love with a man or for him to love me." Bella's eyes met and held Maurice's. "But most importantly, for him to accept me—flaws and all. Until you."

Sophia reached over and took Gabby out of Bella's arms, handing over the ring to Maurice.

"I love you so much," Bella continued, and the tears started again.

Mrs. Moon, Mattie, and Sophia allowed their tears to freely flow, while Maurice bit his quivering lips, his eyes never leaving Bella's face.

"Once I would feel so undeserving of this but you've taught me to accept God's blessings and have helped me to love myself. I still have a little way to go but with you by my side I know I'll be all right. Yes, I'll be honored to marry you, Pastor!" Bella threw herself at Maurice, sending him back on the carpet, her landing on top of him.

The laughter and happy squeals ricocheted around the room, bouncing off every wall in the house, announcing the engagement of Bella and Maurice.

Chapter Thirty-two

Five months later Christian Deliverance Church of God was packed; joy, happiness, and anticipation permeated the air. Their pastor was marrying the woman they had come to love as their first lady, Bella Pigmore. This was unlike Maurice's first marriage to Rachel, where only a handful of people attended.

The church was beautifully decorated with bouquets of pink roses and white lilies tied to the pews, while the aisle was strewn with pink and white rose petals. There were four gigantic flower stands in each corner, with hundreds of colorful peonies that perfumed the atmosphere. Mounted high on top of the altar was a huge photograph of a smiling Bella, Maurice, and Gabby—the birthmarks now looking like beauty marks because they were lit up by the happiness shining in Bella and Gabby's eyes. The dozens of flickering candles in lanterns below created a romantic setting for the wedding.

Smart phones were clicking nonstop as folks took pictures, recording the beauty of the day. Selfies were being uploaded to Facebook, Instagram, and Twitter faster than the speed of an Usain Bolt 100m race. All this as the organist played soft, soothing music.

Just then Sister Althea, the wedding planner, ran to the front of the church in her ruffled pink and white dress, waving her hands for everyone to quiet down. Within seconds only the organist could be heard. Everyone watched as Maurice entered the church from the back in his black-and-white tux. He went over to kiss Mattie and Mrs. Moon, who were sitting on the front pew.

Beside them he also hugged Bella's Aunt Dorothy, who came up from Frankfield for the wedding. Her mother-in-law had passed away, but she was still living in Bella's house with her husband. And as she told Bella when she arrived yesterday, "I haven't seen or heard a peep from the rolling calf. He know he better stay put in hell." This was in reference to Bella's deceased father.

Maurice went and took his place at the front with Minister Sonny standing beside him as his best man.

All eyes then turned to the door where flower girl Gabby stood in her pretty, frilly white dress and matching shoes and socks. She had waterfall braids going back with curls and a white floral crown around her head. Gabby started slowly down the aisle, tossing white rose petals as she walked, smiling as big as her father.

"Isn't she adorable?" someone said, capturing Gabby on the cell phone as many others were doing.

Once she reached the front, Gabby went and stood at her father's side.

"Great job, my little princess," Maurice whispered in Gabby's ear, then kissed her on the cheek. He straightened up as the organist began to play "Here and Now" by Luther Vandross. This was one of Maurice's favorite songs that he had shared with Bella, and it had become one of hers. They decided that it would be their wedding song.

Bella was now standing at the entrance. Her hair was pulled back in a French twist with a white asymmetrical crystal-encrusted wedding veil hanging down her back. Her stunning face showed high rose blushed cheeks with matching full rose pink lips; the only products used from Avon.

"First Lady is really the bomb," a church sister whispered to the lady beside her.

"She's so gorgeous." An older woman wiped at her eyes with her handkerchief.

"Do you see the dress?" someone asked, snapping one picture after another. "Hello!"

Bella's floor-length, cap-sleeved, A-line white Chantilly lace dress patterned with flowers and ribbons, and fit her hourglass figure to perfection.

"Here and now, I promise to love faithfully," crooned Luther with his sexy voice. On that note Bella nervously traveled down the aisle to fulfill that promise, with Sophia, her maid of honor, carrying her long train. She smiled as dozens of pictures were being taken, her eyes fixed on the man she was about to marry.

Bella finally reached Maurice, and he took her hands into his. As they faced each other, she saw the tears welling up in his eyes that were filled with his love for her, mirroring her own.

"Dearly beloved," Elder Davis began loudly after the organist stopped playing. "We are here . . ."

Maurice, unable to resist, leaned over and gently kissed Bella on her lips.

"We haven't gotten to that part as yet, pastor," Elder Bloom remarked and the church erupted in laughter.

Bella threw her head back and laughed out loud. It was laughter laced with exhilaration and well deserved acceptance.

After their wedding, Pastor and First Lady Bella Osbourne went on a two-week honeymoon at Sandals Ochi. With unlimited superb dining, relaxing swimming, enjoyable scuba diving, exploring the exotic, private green tropical gardens and, of course, each other, the couple had the time of their lives.

Epilogue

"Mommy! Look at me." Gabby, five years old, twirled around in her pretty pink dress with white patent shoes and white socks. Her hair was parted into two side ponytails with big pink ribbons the same color as her dress.

"You look so pretty, baby." Bella beamed at her daughter, and Gabby ran and wrapped her little hands around her mother's legs.

"There are my girls." Maurice came out of the adjoining bathroom, adjusting his tie.

Gabby dashed over to him, and he picked her up in his arms. "Who's this little princess?"

"Princess Gabby!" Gabby laughed, twisting, and turning as her father tickled her tummy.

"Okay you two," Bella said. "We're going to be late for church."

Maurice lowered Gabby to the ground and walked over to Bella. "I guess we better get going, first lady." He wrapped his hands around his wife's waist, gave her a big kiss followed up by butterfly kisses all over her face.

Bella giggled.

Gabby peered up at them with a frown on her face and said, "Yuck." Then she ran from the room and down the corridor with Tuff following her.

"Grammy Mattie," the couple heard her shout. "Mommy and Daddy are kissing again."

"Come, baby. Those two have absolutely no shame," Mattie remarked loudly for her voice to travel into the master bedroom. "Gabby and I are waiting by the car."

In the bedroom Maurice and Bella chuckled.

Maurice fell to his knee in front of Bella and said, "And how are you, MJ?" He kissed Bella's swollen tummy, then gently rested his head against his unborn son. "Your daddy can't wait to see you."

"And your mommy too," Bella added.

"And your big sister." Maurice replaced his head with a hand. As if the baby had heard his father's voice, he kicked.

"Hey, little baby." Bella placed a hand over her husband's. "I think he heard us."

"Yes, he did," Maurice said as he stood to his feet in front of Bella. "He'll be here before we know it." His eyes sparkled with happiness, his big grin revealing his thirty-two pearly whites. "What did I do for God to be so good to me? Huh?"

Bella locked eyes with him, a testament of how far she had come over the last few months, and replied, "I think he's giving you double for your troubles. After everything we've been through, He brought us here together."

"Maybe you shouldn't come to church today, darling." Maurice peered intently at his wife's face. "We're expecting our son in less than two weeks and you know Dr. Morris said he could come earlier."

"I feel fine," Bella told him. "MJ is going to wait. Don't worry. Plus, Gabby is singing with the children's choir, and I want to see her."

Maurice hesitated for a few seconds, then bobbed his head. "Okay. I guess there are worse things than me delivering our son at church."

Bella playfully slapped his arm, picked up her handbag off the bed, and walked out of the bedroom, with him following behind her.

As they went down the stairs together, Bella felt a sharp pain in her stomach and took a deep breath.

"What's wrong?" Maurice asked.

"I felt a pain but it's . . . ahhh."" Bella bent over and groaned deep in her throat.

"You're having contractions." Maurice lifted Bella in his arms and took her to the bottom of the stairs and out to the veranda. "Stay right here while I run and get your bag. Mattie. Gabby. The baby is coming," he yelled to the occupants of the van in the driveway before dashing back inside the house.

Soon another bout of pain sliced through Bella's body. She felt liquid running down her legs and knew her water broke.

"Your water broke,' Mattie remarked as she hurried onto the veranda.

Gabby's eyes were large in her head.

Bella awkwardly leaned down and kissed Gabby on her forehead, one hand on her huge stomach. "Your brother doesn't . . . Lord, have mercy." She clenched her teeth as a wave of pain surfed through her stomach.

"Okay, we're ready to go." Maurice was breathing heavily when he came back. He saw the puddle on the floor and said, "Oh, your water broke. Come on, let's go." He scooped up Bella again in his arms. "Mattie, can you please bring the bag for me?"

He placed Bella on the back seat of the van, so she was almost lying down on her back, her feet dangling off. He closed the car door and took the bag from Mattie, placing it on the front passenger seat. "Mattie, please call the church and let them know what's going on. I'll call you as soon as I can. Gabby, come here, sweetie."

Gabby ran into her father's arms. "Mattie will bring you to see Mommy and your little brother later, okay?" He kissed her on the cheek before he hopped into the driver seat and quickly drove out of the driveway onto the street to the hospital.

At the hospital, Bella's coworkers gave them immediate and special attention. Bella was quickly rushed into a hospital room for examination, while her doctor was summoned.

"We have to see how far you've dilated, Mrs. Osbourne," the nurse told Bella as she helped her out of her dress into a hospital gown. "Dr. Morris will be here soon. Luckily, he's working today so he's already here."

"Are you okay, darling?" Maurice hovered over Bella, rocking back and forth on his heels like he was playing on the U.S. Open tennis court. "I think she needs something for the pain," he said to the nurse when Bella bit her lips to keep a scream inside.

Bella breathed deeply in and out through her mouth, her hand locked tight in her husband's, almost crushing it. But he seemed not to notice; breathing in and out with her as if he too were in labor.

Suddenly Bella began to laugh. Both Maurice and the nurse stared at her in surprise. Who laughed when giving birth?

"Darling, are you okay?" Maurice sat on the edge of the small bed and leaned closer to his wife.

Then Bella started to cry, deep, loud sobs.

"Where is Dr. Morris?" Maurice yelled. "I think she's having a breakdown too. My wife needs some attention in here."

"Pastor Osbourne, please calm down. She'll be fine," the nurse said to him. "I'll go and page Dr. Morris again."

"It's okay." Bella sniffed loudly. "These are good tears. Really."

"Are they?"

"Yes. My mind flashed back to when I was giving birth to Gabby. Both Rachel and Bobby were there, but I was so alone. You know?"

"I know." Maurice kissed her forehead. "They were just waiting for you to have the baby so they could take her and run."

"And now here I am about to have our son and you're here breathing with me." The tears ran freely. "Look at God, sweetheart." Bella's eyes met and held her husband's. "Look at the way he has turned my life a . . . Mercy!" Bella took quick, short breaths through her mouth to get through the contraction.

"Here I am." Dr. Morris rushed into the room with the nurse on his heels. "Pastor, I heard you were up here making a lot of noise instead of praying." He playfully slapped Maurice on the back.

"Man, shut up." Maurice's eyes twinkled with happiness. "Kindly get my wife out of this pain and deliver my son please. Thank you."

Dr. Morris chuckled as he pulled on two blue medical gloves. "Mrs. Osbourne, how are you?"

"I'll be better when this is over and my baby is okay," Bella told him, perspiration washing her makeup free face, the birthmark the least of her attention right then.

"I hear that. Well, let's see how far along we are," Dr. Morris responded and proceeded to examine Bella.

But it took another four hours for Bella to be fully dilated and ready to give birth.

By then Maurice's shirt was just as wet with perspiration as Bella's hospital gown. During the birth of his son he coached his wife through the pain, her hands locked in his, breathing in and out with her and wiping her wet face.

"You're doing well, Mrs. Osbourne. I'm seeing his head now," Dr. Morris said under the mask covering his nose and mouth. "Give me another big push. Come on, we're almost there."

"You can do it, baby," Maurice encouraged Bella. "After three, okay? One . . . two . . . three."

Bella screamed and pushed with all her might, her eyes closed and her hands crushing her husband's.

"Awww, here he comes." Dr. Morris had the baby in his hands. "Pastor, you want to do the honors?"

Maurice almost tripped over his feet to go and cut the umbilical cord. He cried with Bella when Dr. Morris slapped Maurice Osbourne III aka MJ, on his buttocks and the baby wailed, formally announcing his entry into the world.

After cleaning up the baby, the nurse handed him to his father before she and Dr. Morris left the room to give the couple a little privacy.

Maurice walked over to Bella. "Here is MJ, darling."

Bella sat up against the pillow and took her son into her arms. "He doesn't have it." She looked up at Maurice in astonishment. "I thought . . ." Her voice trailed off as she gazed down at the baby.

"No, he doesn't have a birthmark," Maurice said. "And it wouldn't matter if he did. My son would still be perfect. Just like my wife and my daughter."

Bella couldn't help the tears that quickly filled her eyes. She never knew she would ever be loved like this and capable of loving back in return. "I love you my dear husband." She gazed up at Maurice with adoration.

"I love you too, Mrs. Osbourne." Maurice's eyes reflected his love for Bella. He took his hand and gently ran it over the area where the birthmark was on Bella's face. "Psalm 139:14 says, 'I will praise thee; for I am fearfully and wonderfully made: marvelous are thy works; and that my soul knoweth right well.' We're perfect just the way we are." He bent down and kissed the birthmark on his wife's face that she had loathed for most of her life.

Pastor Maurice continued, "Each of us was marked at birth in our own special way."

Discussion Questions

1. Unfortunately, people like Bella who appears to be "different" physically are often ridiculed. Discuss how this affects their self esteem? How did this contribute to some of the decisions Bella made? Do you believe despite our physical differences we are all perfect in our own way?

2. Agatha Pigmore stayed with her husband despite years of physical and verbal abuse. Why do you think she did that? If it was you, would you stay? Why? Why not? Do you think Burchell had something to do with her death?

3. What's your opinion of Burchell Pigmore? Why do you think he behaved the way he did? Do you believe in karma? Do you think Burchell got what deserved?

4. What are your impressions of Mrs. Moon and Sophia? What impact did they have on Bella's life, if any?

5. Bobby Dawkins had a lot of anger and resentment toward his father and younger brother. Was he justified in his actions? Why? Why not? What do you think of his relationship with Rachel?

6. Rachel Osbourne was determined to get what she wanted at any cost. How do you feel about the things she did? What surprised you the most about her? In the end was it good over evil?

7. What do you think about little Gabby? Did you notice the contrast of her father's feelings and actions toward her versus her mother's father? Do you think what she shared with her mother was a coincidence? Why?

8. Do you think Paster Robert Jr. was naïve in his relationship with Bobby and Rachel? What do you think of him as a pastor? A husband? A father?

9. Describe Pastor Maurice Osbourne Jr. and Bella's relationship. Is there anything you would change about it? What? Why?

10. Do you believe we were all marked at birth by our uniqueness? Please explain.

Other Books by *Theresa A. Campbell*

Are You There, God?
(Book One)

God Has Spoken
(Book Two)

His Final Deal

Visit Theresa A. Campbell online at:
theresaacampbell.com